BURNING BLUE

BY PAUL GRIFFIN

Dial Books
an imprint of Penguin Group (USA) Inc.

DIAL BOOKS
An imprint of Penguin Group (USA) Inc.
Published by The Penguin Group
Penguin Group (USA) Inc., 375 Hudson Street, New York, NY 10014, U.S.A.
Penguin Group (Canada), 90 Eglinton Avenue East, Suite 700, Toronto,
Ontario, Canada M4P 2Y3 (a division of Pearson Penguin Canada Inc.)
Penguin Books Ltd, 80 Strand, London WC2R 0RL, England
Penguin Ireland, 25 St. Stephen's Green, Dublin 2, Ireland
(a division of Penguin Books Ltd)
Penguin Group (Australia), 250 Camberwell Road, Camberwell, Victoria 3124,
Australia (a division of Pearson Australia Group Pty Ltd)
Penguin Books India Pvt Ltd, 11 Community Centre,
Panchsheel Park, New Delhi – 110 017, India
Penguin Group (NZ), 67 Apollo Drive, Rosedale, Auckland 0632,
New Zealand (a division of Pearson New Zealand Ltd)
Penguin Books (South Africa) (Pty) Ltd, 24 Sturdee Avenue,
Rosebank, Johannesburg 2196, South Africa
Penguin Books Ltd, Registered Offices: 80 Strand, London WC2R 0RL, England

Designed by Jasmin Rubero
Text set in Warnock Pro with Neuteit Office
Printed in the U.S.A.

1 3 5 7 9 10 8 6 4 2

Library of Congress Cataloging-in-Publication Data
Griffin, Paul, date.
Burning blue / by Paul Griffin.
p.   cm.
Summary: When beautiful, smart Nicole, disfigured by acid thrown in her face, and computer hacker Jay meet in the school psychologist's office, they become friends and Jay resolves to find her attacker.
ISBN 978-0-8037-3815-7 (hardcover)
[1. Disfigured persons—Fiction. 2. Computer hackers—Fiction.
3. Beauty, Personal—Fiction. 4. Mystery and detective stories.] I. Title.
PZ7.G8813594Bu 2012
[Fic]—dc23
2012003578

*for Sheila Hennessey, guardian angel
and amazing friend*

Sent the night before the attack:

Subject: Why?
Date: Wednesday, September 08, 11:19 PM
To: Assistant Principal Nadine Marks
N.Marks@brandywine_hollows_hs.nj.edu
From: Arachnomorph@unknowable_origin.net

Because I'll never have it.
Because I'll never be it.
Because after a little test run, I find that I like the sound.
The hissing.
She will burn.

ONE

I was at the cemetery when it happened. I didn't even know Nicole at the time. Well, I knew *of* her. Everybody did. She'd won a high-profile beauty competition the year before, the under-sixteen division. She had been on the front page of a lot of newspapers. People in the pageant world were saying she was sure to win Miss New Jersey. I had seen her in the halls and hungered for her from afar like every other dude at the Hollows, but we hadn't talked. Not yet. Still, that afternoon, that moment, when that first molecule pierced her skin, was the beginning of our connection, one that led me into a darkness that was as twisted as it was sublime.

The water brought us together. The storm. The sky was horrific, a dark, dirty green. According to maps.google, Pinemont Cemetery and Brandywine Hollows High School are 4.11 miles apart, but Nicole and I were bound by the rain. It was something that day, so strange, too hard to be liquid, too cold for the second Thursday of September. It smashed my mother's gravestone, a nothing-special marker the size of a high-tops shoebox. The first burst of downpour ricocheted upward at my eyes and stung my face like a sucker punch. I'd cut my last two classes to clock an extra hour on my shift

1

card after my boss texted that a lot of people had called in sick. I often stopped by the cemetery on my way to work. I loved the quiet, but with that rain I didn't linger. I was chasing down the bus, dodging the spray the wheels drew from a lake-like puddle the exact moment Nicole was hit.

She was with Dave Bendix, our wrestling team captain and thought by many, me included, to be one of the nicest guys in school. He was definitely the most popular. This was just before last period. They were messing around in a cutout in the lockers past the C-wing water fountain, by the windows that overlooked the creek. They had been together maybe five months. Nicole would tell me later that up to this point Dave was a sweetheart and a total gent, but that afternoon he was jacked up on too many Red Bulls or whatever, desperate. He wouldn't let her go. He kept saying, "One last kiss." The first bell had rung, and the last few stragglers were moping toward their classes.

Dave was playing safecracker, circling Nicole's belly button with his fingertips. She had to get to AP chem. Mr. Sabbatini, chairman of our science program, was looking for a reason to ruin her. He'd dreamed of being the next big pharm sellout and ended up at the Hollows. The man reeked of bitterness and schnapps. He loved to knock down anybody who looked like she was going to one-up him. You're late to his class, you get docked in a very big way: thirty points off the midterm. Nicole had already been late once, thanks to another impromptu make-out session with Dave.

The second bell rang. The hallway was empty. Nicole wriggled out of Dave's hug and ran for the circle that connects A, B, and C wings.

Whatever your concept of gorgeous, Nicole Castro trumped it. Tall, thin but not too, round in all the right places, long chestnut hair. More than that?

Her face.

Her lips, full, pouty, except back then she was always smiling. High cheekbones. No need for makeup, not a blemish to cover. It was unassailable, her splendor. Almost unassailable.

She hooked left for B-wing. She turned back briefly to airmail a kiss off the tip of her index finger to Dave, but he wasn't there anymore. She sagged for a second and then spun away for Mr. Sabbatini's class. She was halfway into her turn when it happened. Life as she knew it: gone. Took maybe half a second.

The last thing she saw was the squirt bottle coming up toward her face. A squeeze machine wrapped in orange foam, the lightning bolt.

Sent moments after the attack:

Subject: The new Nicole
Date: Thursday, September 9, 2:13 PM
To: Assistant Principal Nadine Marks
N.Marks@brandywine_hollows_hs.nj.edu
From: Arachnomorph@unknowable_origin.net

Now she's beautiful.

The first person to hear her scream was Dave Bendix. Not that Nicole could see him with her eyes clamped shut. When one gets hit, the other reflexively closes down to protect what's left of your vision. Trying to wipe off the acid made the situation worse. She burned her hands. Interestingly, Dave had the presence of mind not to touch Nicole, even before she stopped screaming long enough to weep, "It burns!"

I don't know that I would have been that smart. I probably would have been like most everybody else in that situation. You find somebody writhing on the floor, covering her face and screaming, you instinctively try to peel her hands away to see what the problem is. Not Dave, though. He told Nicole to stop rubbing her eye, that she was only going to spread the burn.

From what I heard, the classrooms emptied into the halls. Everybody had to see what all the screaming was about. Nicole managed to get out that someone had squirted something into her face. Everybody was asking "Who?" Only Mr.

Sager, one of our custodians, realized that right now the primary question was "What? What did he squirt?"

Nicole didn't know, but whatever it was, it was still burning. She begged, "Please, get it off, I can't *see*."

Mr. Sager wrapped his hand in a rag towel and pried away Nicole's hands. He told a girl with a water bottle to douse the burn. Everybody with a water bottle did the same. Nicole couldn't breathe. The water filled her mouth and throat. She was choking on it when Mr. Sager told them to stop. In his statement to the police, Mr. Sager reported that Dave Bendix slid down the wall and said, "I'm sorry, Nic. I'm so sorry."

TWO

The following is from Nicole's journal:

The prep room is cold green curtains. A window tinted violet, the color of my eyes, what's left of them.

"Multiple grafts," the surgeon says. "A degree of paralysis is certain, Nicole. But you were fortunate."

"*Fortunate?*" Mom says.

"The rule of nines. We use it to describe burn coverage. The front of each leg is nine percent of your skin's total surface area. Same with the back. The front of your torso: eighteen percent, the back too. Each arm is nine percent. And then your head is nine percent. You've burned somewhere between a quarter and a third of the left side of your face."

Mom: "*She* didn't burn anything, Doctor."

Doc: "I'm just saying that if you break it down, the burn covers less than one percent of her body."

Mom: "It was her face. It was Nicole."

Doc: "It could have been much worse."

Mom: "Her face. Can you get her back to—"

Doc cuts her off: "No. You can't think that way. This is a life-altering event."

Me: "The other one percent?"

Doc: "Excuse me?"

Me: "The rule of nines. If you add up all those numbers, the body parts, you get ninety-nine percent. What's the other one percent?"

Doc: "That's what we use to describe the males' private parts."

Me: "One percent, huh? I'm sure they'd be thrilled."

Doc: "A sense of humor is important, Nicole. You're doing great."

Me: "The girls get nothing. The boys get the extra point. They're complete at one hundred percent. That's why women are stronger: We live with omission."

Mom (sobbing): "Can't you give her more morphine?"

Doc: "The left side of your face. I'm hopeful you'll still be able to blink. If you can't, we'll give you drops to keep your eye lubricated. If you can't cry, you'll go blind."

Me: "I'm sure I can cry, Doctor." I'm crying all right. "I can't see out of that eye anyway. I can't see. I can't *see.*" It's blinding my rage!

Mom: "Don't touch it, Nicole. Oh my god. Oh my baby."

Me: "What does it look like, Mom? How bad is it? Please. Tell me."

The doctor rolls me onto my side. With two tugs on the strings he unties my hospital gown to expose my left leg, and then he draws lines into the back of my hip with something.

Me: "Is that your fingernail? What are you doing?"

Doc: "I'm surveying the donor site, Nicole."

Me: "Please. No."

Doc: "I know this is horrible for you. Don't try to look, Nicole. If you have to, look at your mother. That's right, close your eye and hold Mom's hand. Hold it tight."

Close your *eye*, as in *one*.

"My other eye," I say. "Is it—"

Mom cuts me off: "Hush now, sweetie. It'll be all right."

Worst liar ever.

The surgeon's hands are cold and way too soft on my hip. I feel tapping and tugging and a vague sense my skin is being stretched beyond the limits of its elasticity. A minute later they're wheeling me down the hall for the surgery, the first of several, I'm told. The doors to the OR swing in. I see through a slit eyelid a nurse is checking the equipment. The scalpel flash reflects in the glass of one of the implement cabinets. Mom gasps. She nearly collapses as the OR doors swing shut on her.

Doc: "Do you like this music, Nicole?"

I didn't notice any music was playing. It's New Age, waves crashing, whale calls. "Got any Eminem?" I say.

Doc: "Atta girl."

My attempt to make the doctor laugh surprises me as much as it does him. Where is this bravery coming from? I feel bolder now that Mom isn't weeping over me. Or maybe I feel worse. The situation is absurd. Have I really burned my face?

Anesthesiologist: "We're ready to go."

Surgeon: "Beautiful."

That word.

My first memories, going back to when I was four years old, maybe even three.

Beautiful.

My identity.

Oh Nicole, you're simply beautiful.

Not the real me.

Sixth-grade yearbook: MOST BEAUTIFUL: NICOLE CASTRO.

The fake me.

Ridiculous, how beautiful you are—just beautiful.

Just? Nothing else?

Isn't she just the most beautiful thing?

A thing.

What will it be like, not being *the word* anymore?

The mask goes over my mouth. Dad, where are you? I'm afraid of the dark.

Anesthesiologist: "Count backward from one hundred, Nicole."

"One hundred, ninety-nuh . . ."

THREE

The police brought Dave Bendix in for questioning. His father was an engineer with claims to numerous patents, and he refused to let Dave be interviewed without lawyers present. They rolled up to the precinct in a chauffeured town car. The detectives didn't have any evidence, or any that pointed to Dave.

They found the squirt bottle in the stairwell with traces of latex glove dust, no fingerprints. The bottle was new technology, coated on the inside with a flexible glass weave that was resistant to extreme heat, cold and in this case battery acid. This sports drink company that was trying to compete with Gatorade had developed the bottle. Volta-Shock was their name. They made a big deal about the bottle back in my freshman year, giving one to every athlete in school. The top athletes got hoodies too, Day-Glo orange with double helix lightning bolts on the sleeves. Dave was given one of those.

The vast majority of Hollows students respected Dave Bendix not just because he was a remarkable competitor but also because he had founded an anti-bullying support group. A few cynics said Dave was doing ZERO TOLERANCE FOR DOMINANCE to look great to the Harvard admissions officers, but he was a shoo-in anyway. His father and grandfather were Crimson, and even if they hadn't gone there, Dave was top ten of our class academically. More than that, I had proof that he was sincere in his efforts to quash bullying.

I knew Dave from before I quit wrestling freshman year. I was definitely an outsider, not a geek but a loner by choice. When you're a freshman, it doesn't matter how you see yourself. The upperclassmen on the team are going to give you hell either way, especially when you beat one of them in a scrimmage the first day of practice. His name was Richard Kerns. He wore his hair in a Mohawk dyed bloodred. The way he was looking at me, licking his lips like I was puff pastry, I was pretty sure he was going to honor his word when he promised he was going to break both my arms. My fear must have provoked a serious self-defense adrenaline surge, because I ended up pinning him. Just headlocked him, flipped him pretty hard, knocked the wind out of him. After practice the guys stuffed up the sink and held my head under water, until Dave came in. He shoved everybody back, said anybody who touched me would have to deal with him.

Dave was All-State since freshman year, 195 lb. weight class, and he benched 385. Those same few who doubted his sincerity about his anti-bullying efforts said he was shooting anabolic steroids. Back two years ago, when I was still on the team, I was 152 lb. class and three inches taller than Dave. Figure if I was just over six one back then, that made Dave a five foot ten killing machine who was, if the rumors were true, willing to do anything to win, including possibly giving himself steroid-induced testicular cancer, while I was pretty much a tall skinny newbie who was only going all fours in the goofy suit because his old man forced him to do an after-school activity. Wrestling was what my dad had done, so you bet it was good enough for me too. Those mats stank of anger. A desperate fear of letting your parents down, of not getting recruited by some overpriced country club that passed for college, Dartmouth or wherever.

As grateful as I was for Dave's protection, he scared me. When he was wrestling, he had this look, the intense stare of somebody who wants to beat you, sure, but more than that he wants to eat you, caveman style.

The detectives interviewed him for half an hour, and then they let him go. Dave was a weak pick on motive. They were looking for somebody who hated Nicole, not somebody who was trying to bone her.

FOUR

While Nicole was in surgery and Dave Bendix at the police station, I was home in my dumpy little bedroom, doing my thing, remotely scanning cruel people's phones and computers, looking for nastiness to leak. I considered this my community service. And there must have been some other reason. Oh yeah, it was fun.

I had just hacked Chrissie Vratos's iPhone and landed on a trove of hate gossip, a long string of texts that began with *Is it just me or is diana a bitch?* and ended with *Somebody should blow her boyfriend and post the video on her fb.* I anonymously posted the plot not just on Diana's page but also her boyfriend's and then Chrissie's and her co-conspirators' too. For the kill shot, I posted it and Crew Chrissie with a blinking red alert on the Brandywine Hollows HS community page, which the teachers and administrators checked all the time. That was when I saw the news about Nicole Castro.

Someone had set up a well-wishers page. Not quite nine hours after the attack, the page was filled with more than a thousand comments, and not just from the BHHS community. Somebody posted a link to a news clip. I clicked to a video of Mr. and Mrs. Castro outside the hospital. Mr. Castro had to be president of some company or other, a young general in a Wall Street suit, conservative haircut, ramrod posture. He glared out at the gathering crowd with fierce blue eyes. Mrs. Castro I couldn't see so well. The reporters were sticking microphones in her face. Her head was down. Her shoulders shook. "If anybody has any information about this, please, please come forward. We're offering a fifty-thousand-dollar reward." When Mr. Castro tried to comfort her with an arm over her shoulder, she leaned away and wove through the crowd, back into the hospital.

Like I said, I was on my way to work when it happened. My boss made us leave our phones in the lockers, and this was the first I was hearing about the attack. I felt bad for Nicole, but not as terrible as I would have felt if it had happened to somebody nice or at least not a rich gorgeous snob. I was definitely freaked, though, that it happened to somebody I knew. Not knew. People like Nicole Castro didn't *know* loners like me. But somebody who went to my school. Somebody I had seen around. Would see around.

Except I didn't see her. She didn't come back to school, not at first, and not for classes. Her mother got clearance to home-school, something I knew a bit about. She hired a team of high-priced private tutors, something I did not. Not only was the one-time golden girl working with three PhD candidates, she was seeing two shrinks. The primary therapist had been hired by Nicole's mother and paid for by Nicole's father at nine hundred dollars an hour, which is what it costs to have a psychiatrist make house calls. Julian Nye was a strange dude. That was Nicole's perception. Mine too. While I never met him, I had the opportunity to see him in action—see him by proxy rather, but I'll get to that, to him, later.

The secondary therapist was the school psychologist, Mrs. Schmidt. She had been charged with ensuring Nicole Castro's eventual return to the Hollows and her transition back to normalcy—whatever that could be with half your face burned away—went smoothly. I was seeing Schmidt too, about this messed-up thing that happened not quite two years earlier.

My seizures have no pattern. Once I went two years without an attack. And then there was the time I had three in a week, and the third one almost killed me. Status epilepticus. The seizure won't stop until you're injected with benzodiazepines. I've gotten used to it, walking around as if I have a time bomb glued to my back, except the bomb maker forgot to tell me when the thing is supposed to go off. The vast majority of my attacks are called absence seizures. Everything fades. I'm sleeping with my eyes open. People tell me I look like I'm spacing out. Sometimes I twitch the slightest bit or shiver. Absence seizures are embarrassing when the teacher calls you to the board to do a trig proof, and you're just sitting there because you don't hear her saying "Jay? Jay? Jay, are you all right?" or your classmates' whispering, "Guess Sbarro's is closed." This is why I don't go out of my way to let anybody know my last name. People have a habit of getting goofy with me: "Nazzaro? As in rhymes with Sbarro?" "Exactly, as in that's about as funny as me kicking your ass."

Not that I would. I just act tough. You have to; otherwise you get your ass kicked. Anyway, the absence seizures aren't always noticeable. Then there's the other kind of seizure, the really bad one, where I fall down and convulse. They don't come along very often, but when they do, they wipe me out.

Maybe twenty seconds or so before the seizure I slip into this thing called an aura. Everything radiates a very peculiar light. It's either soft or smoldering, I'm never sure which. The world slows down and stretches out as if I'm looking through a fish-eye lens or sometimes a kaleidoscope, everything hyper-colorful. Lightning arcs. Sometimes it's scary, but other times it's intoxicating. I forget I'm about to crash until this dark hole appears and starts sucking everything into it, and then I'm into the nothingness, a painless mini-death.

I wake up not remembering how long I was gone or what happened while I was out, part of my life erased. Every once in a while, when I come back, I'm not where I was when the aura started. Back when I was twelve, I was in bed reading, and the lights flickered, except they didn't. Pink lightning wiggled across the ceiling, and everything faded. When I came back I was on the fire escape with a saltshaker in my hand. I might have tripled down on my meds that day. When I forget the last time I popped the tablet, everything gets messed up, which is why it's easier not to take the medication at all sometimes. My prescription is one of the newer anticonvulsants out there, still in the experimental stage—read: *free*, the only reason I'm on it. My father and I have the worst health insurance. The meds might have worked if I dosed them the way I was supposed to, but they made me feel like I was packed in cotton.

I get a little panicky when people are looking at me. Like in front of a crowd. At least that's what provoked the attack I was seeing Schmidt about. It happened December of freshman year, in the middle of a pep rally. We were going to the state championships, and the whole school was in the gym to cheer us on. The coach called us out to center court individually. This was my first year wrestling. I knew three moves and would have sucked except for the fact that I'm naturally wiry. My father was a strong dude before he decided to throw in the towel and become obese, three manicottis shy of a life-ending coronary. Basically my strategy was don't get my neck broken, don't try to kill anybody either. Just get by. About midway through my jog out to center court, lightning flashed. The rest is a blank, or would have been if not for the fact that everyone with an iPhone clipped me. I was a Hollows Facebook phenomenon for a week until Mrs. Marks, our assistant principal, said anybody caught circulating the video would be suspended.

I still have it on my laptop. I look like I'm doing the backstroke in the middle of the gym floor and a widening puddle of urine. I get really thirsty when I'm nervous, and I'd drunk the bulk of a two-liter Coke before the run-out. I hadn't been taking my meds, because as I said they just make me feel a little whack sometimes. More than that, when I go long stretches without a seizure, I get to thinking maybe I'm cured.

It flipped me out, knowing I lost control of myself with the entire school watching. Most people were cool about it, but more than a couple were not, and I begged my father to let me home-school for the rest of the year and then the year after. He relented on the condition I see the good Mrs. Schmidt once a week. She was free too, and the old man couldn't pass that up. And then this past summer, Schmidt decided— I'm sorry, *we* decided—it was time for me to go back to the Hollows for junior year, college prep, whatever. So the third Thursday of October, the 21st, six weeks after the acid attack on Nicole Castro, I was in the school psychologist's waiting room, a little early for my 3:30 with Schmidt, and in walked, yes, Nicole Castro.

FIVE

Nicole had always been talked about, but after the attack she was a rock star. And she was *here,* ten feet away from me.

She wore oversized sunglasses that blacked out her eyes and a fair portion of her cheekbones. Her hair hung long over her shoulder, swept to cover the left side of her face. Black turtleneck, black jacket with the collar flipped up. She could have been on the cover of a fashion magazine, except that parts of her fingers were bandaged.

She sat as far away from me as she could. I pretended to be lost in my grimy library copy paperback, *Maximum Ride,* I forget which number in the series. I love sci fi, Daniel X, anything by James Patterson, anything that lets me escape. I had my earbuds in too. I wore them pretty much every time I was outside my apartment. They didn't connect to anything. The wire just ran into my pocket. But people don't talk to you so much when you appear to be listening to music. In my peripheral vision, Nicole was faking too. She seemed to be into her phone, except her fingers weren't moving. Even if she was reading an ebook, she would've had to flip her thumb to turn the page. Nothing. And that's when I saw it, the tear hanging off her chin. She was afraid to let me see her wipe it away, because then I could only conclude she was crying. I went to the watercooler and kept my back to her as I sipped. I took my time drinking to give her what I hoped was enough time to get herself together. Sure enough, when I turned back to my seat, the tear was gone.

About a minute later, Dave Bendix came in. He did a double take on me and said, "Heya Jay, glad you're back, man." He grabbed my hand for a palm grip, pulled me up out of my chair and did the bud hug thing. "How come you never called me back? I must've reached out to you ten times."

"I know. I appreciated it."

"Jay, if you need anything, let me know. I'm serious."

"Thanks."

He spun back for Nicole. They whisper-fought for half a minute or so. Nicole kept saying, "I can't. I can't do that, David." Dave exploded with, "Well, that's just messed up, Nic. Seriously. You know what? Forget it." His lips were quivering, and his eyes were wet. "I can't believe you," he said, and then stormed out.

"So I'm taking the bus home, then?" Nicole said. "Dave, c'mon, it's pouring." But he was gone. Nicole dropped her head into her hands.

I didn't know what to do: Pretend not to see her crying? Get her a cup of water? She'd probably be like, what are you doing, I don't know you, get away from me.

Schmidt's door opened and slammed with this girl hustling out, Angela Sammick. She often wore her hair in cat's ears, lots of piercings, lips, nose, eyebrows, tongue, her speech thick. I knew her, sort of. I nodded hey.

She looked at me like she kind of remembered me, and then remembered *how* she remembered me, from this weird thing we got into together two years before, shortly before I started home-schooling. She hurried away. When she saw Nicole she stopped like she'd stumbled onto a rape in progress. She gulped and said, "Hey, Nicole."

"Hey," Nicole said, trying to cover a sob.

After maybe five seconds that felt like five minutes, Angela stopped gawking and headed out.

"Later," I said.

At the sound of my voice, she looked vaguely embarrassed. The history of our night together had come back to her full force, I'm guessing. "What'd you say?" she said, absently.

"Later. As in, good-bye?"

"Sorry about that, Spaceman," she said, "I was . . ." She turned for the door and said "Welcome back" as she slipped out.

Before I left the Hollows for home school, pretty much everybody called me Spaceman. I'd gotten used to it back then, like whatever. What freshman doesn't have a derogatory nickname pinned to him? But now that I was two years older, I don't know. It stung. I felt even more humiliated since Angela had alluded to my spacing out—my seizures—in front of Nicole Castro. I know that was dumb, the idea that Angela was revealing something new to Nicole, as if Nicole hadn't heard about my attack at the pep rally. But being trapped in that waiting room with her, and her being reminded that I was the Spaceman who'd pissed himself in front of three thousand people? Not cool.

I really wasn't ready for this, being back at school, starting over, pretending that everything was great, that I was this happy-go-lucky junior at one of the top five public high schools in the country, my ticket to an Ivy practically punched—until the next time I seized in front of everybody. I was meant to be a hermit. I was cool with this, a life of self-imposed isolation. I really was. I was deciding this was going to be my last day at school when she spoke to me. "Sad or mad?" Nicole whispered. Her hair was swept back a bit more now, and I saw the edge of what must have been a pretty big bandage covering her cheek.

"Huh?" I said. Brilliant comeback. I remembered to take my earbuds out. I put my hand in my jacket pocket and pretended to turn down my nonexistent iPod.

"That look in her eyes?" Nicole said, sniffling. "Was she mad, or sad? I'm gonna go with sad."

She had Angela Sammick figured out. Angela was definitely lost. Face jewelry looks very cool on some people, but Angela's piercings looked like they were meant to hurt. This scythe-like thing hooked one of her eyebrows. I don't know how she didn't cut her eyelid every time she blinked.

For those few months I was in school, back in freshman fall, Angela and I were in the same comp sci class. I was pretty sure she'd failed that one. She never took notes, never seemed to be listening to the teacher. She was forever biting her fingertips, chewing off bloody hangnails as she stared out the window. Meanwhile I'd be staring at her, as I had nothing else to do. I'd kind of found my calling at the age of ten with the hacking and had taught myself everything in the text-book years before. Some days Angela would come in dressed simply, khaki pants and a blouse, no jewelry. She was really pretty those days, when you could see her face. But most days she'd be in her getup, the lip metal, the jet-black hair, or sometimes it was green or red. She dyed her hair a different color every week. I had no problem with the coloring. I really wasn't judging her. I just felt bad that she felt the need to pull her hair down to cover her eyes. She was hiding, but at the same time she seemed to need attention. Her clothes were eye-catching. She was small boned to begin with but seemed to be starving herself, and she wanted everybody to know it with her skinny jeans and tight T-shirts. She struck me as the actress who's constantly trying out for very different parts, never sure of which role she's supposed to play. I figured she was like me, on meds, not exactly compliant. I'd actually kissed her once a few years earlier. Or she'd kissed me.

She was always hanging around practice, sucking a Blow Pop. The guys, of course, invited her to this party with—I found out at the party—the intention of having her pull the train. I saw it coming and snuck her outside with the intention of walking her home. She was smashed, tackled me onto the hood of this Mercedes sedan, rammed her tongue down my throat. Maybe three seconds later she started to heave, literally almost regurgitated into my mouth. She fell to all fours and barfed all over the lawn, and I was rubbing her back, telling her it's okay, get it out, whatever stupid stuff you say when somebody pukes, even though you feel like a total loser, because you were just kissing her before she puked, and you could only conclude that you were THE PUKE TRIGGER, the tag that would show up under your yearbook picture, right next to SPACEMAN. This other girl had seen the whole thing. She said she and Angela lived in the same neighborhood, and she would take her home.

We put Angela into the car, a junker that must have been getting into annual crashes since the 1970s. Angela said she loved me—"love you *so, so much*, Brett"—and kept saying it over and over, even after I told her my name was in fact *Jay*. They were halfway to the corner before I realized it might have been nice if the other girl had asked me if I needed a ride instead of stranding me at a party where all the guys hated me now because I had just screwed up their night, the purpose of which was to screw Angela Sammick. I still had the taste of metal in my mouth, Angela's tongue stud. Better than puke, though, I guess. Only girl I ever kissed. I mean, I'd gotten hand jobs before, from this chick in my building who was a year older than I was, but when you kiss a girl on the mouth, even if it's only for three seconds and she pukes after, that's kind of serious in my book. I know, I'm a loser.

I got back to my *Maximum Ride*, but I could hear Nicole every time she drew breath through her tears, this kind of *slee* sound. It was after 3:30 now, and the door to Schmidt's office couldn't open soon enough.

"Sorry about that," Nicole Castro said.

"About what?" I couldn't believe this girl was talking to me again. That she actually seemed to want to initiate a conversation.

"Fighting with David like that in front of you. Really rude. I hate when people do that. What's your name again?"

Again. Like she'd ever known it in the first place. Why do people act fake? Like I don't know you're lying? For some reason I said what was on my birth certificate, "Jameson." My mother was a *Masterpiece Theatre* junkie back in the day, total anglophile. Did I actually believe an aristocratic-sounding name would impress somebody who lived in a neighborhood where the power lines were underground? "Jay, I mean." I held back my last name, of course.

She didn't bother to say her name, first or last, because you would've had to be from another high school or maybe even from out of state not to know who she was. After that beauty pageant win and then the acid attack, her face had been all over the news. I was thinking, *What kind of girl does the beauty competition circuit?* It's not like she was poor, humiliating herself for a chance at college scholarship money like the rest of the girls strutting their bikinis past those ogling judges. She was from Brandywine Heights, the wealthiest part of a very wealthy school district. The real estate taxes her father was paying would have been double the amount of money required to ensconce her in the most expensive boarding school. He'd gone to St. Paul's and wanted Nicole to do the same, but Mrs. Castro insisted that Nicole stay home. Whatever, if a rich girl does the pageant circuit, she's doing it for attention. Pathetic. I had it in my mind that she'd grown up spending four hours a day in front of the mirror, narcissism to the point of solipsism. Then again, the mirror thing was kind of understandable. If I looked as good as she did—or as good as she looked before the attack anyway—I would've been staring at myself all the time too, not to mention playing with my perfect breasts.

On top of being a pageant princess, she was VP of the National Honor Society. The tools in NHS wanted her to run the show, but you weren't allowed to be the leader of more than two things, and she was already tennis captain and junior class president. All these wannabes killing themselves, running around hanging the lamest posters and FB-ing everybody with Like me requests, and Castro wins without even being on the ballot, as a write-in. She was the queen of the Hollows, and here she was deigning to waste a few of her precious words on me, a kid from Valedale?

Valedale was also known as The Pit. It was the one not fabulous section in Brandywine, a narrow valley of older apartment houses between the dumps and the highway that bordered the next school district. If I lived on the other side of my street, I would've gone to McKinley, average SAT score 1190, as opposed to the Hollows' 2030.

"You're a sophomore, right?" Nicole said.

"Junior," I said. "Sixteen, not fifteen."

"Or seventeen," she said.

"Right."

"Or eleven or nineteen or a hundred and forty-six." She nodded slowly and for a little too long. "Yeah, I know you."

The way she said it, I felt she really did. That she knew me better than I knew me. She was reeling me in, even back then. Behind those dark shades she had the lasers working, cutting through my front, that I was too cool to give a damn about anything. She was peeling back my skin and bones and looking into my heart, splitting it wide for me to see, and what I would soon find there terrified me.

The door opened. Schmidt leaned out. "Ready, Nicole?" Then to me, "My friend, sorry, I clearly forgot to tell you, I had to move you to four o'clock."

Nicole rushed into Schmidt's office with her face in her bandaged hands.

"Better make it more like four thirty, Jay," Schmidt said.

I should have figured it out right there. Nicole's secret. Looking back, maybe I knew. Maybe I just didn't want to believe it. That she could, that she would. That she did.

SIX

From Nicole's journal:

Thurs, 21 October—

This was my first face-to-face talk with Dr. Schmidt. She suggested I start logging my thoughts to chart the progress of my recovery, as if recovering from this is possible or even necessary.

Me: "You want me to *blog* about this?"

Dr. Schmidt: "No, a diary, just for you."

Me: "As in Anne Frank."

DS: "Exactly."

Me: "Or Sylvia Plath."

DS: "Let's shoot for a nicer ending."

Me: "Virginia Woolf."

DS: "Just think about it."

Still, I like Dr. Schmidt. Dr. Nye on the other hand scares me. He's motionless. That red microphone icon blinking on his iPhone. The angle of his head, looking over his rimless glasses at me. The top edges of the lenses cut his eyes in half, and they look like blue suns on a warped horizon. "Did your father ever hit you?" "Do you think you're still beautiful?" As if I ever thought I was in the first place. What kind of person asks that?

My face was on fire the whole day. My mind is on fire. My heart. The rage feels good. I only pretended to take my pain meds.

Mom: "You're sure you took them? Promise?"

Me: "Swear." Worse liar than she is, and she knows it. Magically the meds appear on the bathroom counter with a glass of cranberry juice. I wonder if she suspects I'm flushing more than pee. I'm sick of feeling numb. I want to be awake again. I was today, this afternoon, for about five minutes. In the waiting room, with Jay. The way he went to get a cup of water, pretending not to see the tear rolling down my cheek. He wanted nothing from me. He only wanted to give me the time I needed to wipe the tear away. To get myself together. He made me smile. It hurt more than crying, wrinkling my mouth up like that. But it was the good hurt, the one that makes me feel alive. Real. Remarkable, that his simple act of kindness triggered a relief from the numbness. It was a forgetting and an awakening at the same time, transitory but deep. Then there's David.

He keeps telling me this doesn't change anything, but how can it not? How can anybody look at me without pity, the last thing I need? He keeps saying it. The word. Rests his hand on my heart as he says it. "You're still beautiful." He knows he's lying. What must people see when they look at me? No symmetry. No balance. Only Emma sees the old me. She's incapable of lying, but for how long? Em, what will I do when you're gone?

I won't feel sorry for myself. I don't. I can keep pretending.

SEVEN

While Nicole was getting her brain tweaked by Schmidt, I was off to grab coffee. I dropped my long board and slalomed fast-forming puddles to the Starbucks next to the tire center. When the hydraulic lifts let the cars down, the air escaping from the pistons sounded like screams of people being crushed. This kept the Starbucks nice and empty. Sometimes I asked the girl behind the counter for help with my phone. I holstered what was to all appearances flip-style junk. In public, I pretended I didn't know how to use it. Nobody suspects you for a hacker when you can't figure out how to send a text from your eight-year-old Nokia. "How do I get to menu again?"

"Oh my god, if you weren't almost cute I would totally smack you." She grabbed my phone and started pressing buttons. "No rejoinder to my 'almost cute,' huh? You look like a vampire."

"Thanks, I guess."

"I like long hair on guys. What kind of product are you using?"

"Grease."

"Brand?"

"The kind that comes from washing your hair only every other shower."

"That's gross but also slightly hot." She was ready to key a message into my phone. "Who's the target?"

"Father. Message is whatever."

"Whatever comes to my mind?"

"Just 'whatever.'" He'd left me a voicemail to tell me he might not be home until late, unusually considerate of him.

The girl slid a black coffee to me. "You're coming here two years now, right?"

"I guess."

"And I slip you a free Grande whenever the manager isn't around."

"Are you telling me you want me to pay for all those coffees now?"

"I'm telling you that you never once thought to ask my *name*."

Actually, I'd thought about it since the first time I saw her. She was exceedingly cute. Sadly, she was too short. Not too short for most people but too short for a Lurch like me. I wasn't even sure I was done growing at six three, and given the way this girl's body was banged out double-D, she was likely done at five feet even. Plus we sort of looked the same, dark hair, eyes. We'd look goofy, like I was holding hands with my little cousin instead of my girlfriend or whatever. More than that, what if I had a seizure in front of her and wet myself? I didn't want to start something that was headed for disaster. "Can I borrow a to-go lid?"

"You mean can you *have* one." She slapped the lid on. "You probably should know my name if we're gonna go to the rave together."

"I thought raving was declared dorky before the end of last century."

"At my friend's house. Her parents are away this weekend. You can drive, okay? My car is literally falling apart."

"Duct tape holding up the bumpers?"

"What bumpers?"

"Civic, right?"

"How'd you know?"

Secondhand Civics were ubiquitous in New Jersey. You couldn't go two blocks without passing one sputtering along in the slow lane. "I don't have a car," I said.

"Fine, you, me, my half a Civic. If the car breaks down, *I'll* get out and push."

Last thing I needed was a retro rave, flashing lights, drunk Goths slamming into me, somebody slipping an e-ball into my Coke, setting off god knows what kind of chemical reaction in my already messed-up brain. And anyway this girl was no raver, hair pulled back into a simple ponytail, barely any makeup, certainly no piercings I could see. She had Catholic school written all over her. I couldn't imagine her in anything other than a Starbucks getup or a plaid skirt. "I'm not really into parties," I said.

"Ouch. Flat-out rejected by boy without a car."

"It's just not my thing, raving."

"I so believe you with your black army jacket, black jeans, black high-tops."

I started feeling bad for saying no. "Look, my name's Jay."

"I know," she said.

My slightly greasy, vampiric hair stood up a little.

"Hello, your phone?" she said. "The time you asked me to email a picture to your Hotmail? JayNaz666? Who even uses Hotmail anymore?" She put out her hand. "I'm officially introducing myself to you. Cherry DiBenneditto. For real is Cherisse. Which do you prefer?"

"Both."

"Okay, so forget the rave. How about a slasher flick?"

"Why after all this time are you asking me out?"

"You look really different today," she said.

This was a lie. I always looked exactly the same—same clothes, hair, expression, midway between bored and aggrieved. "In what way?"

"I don't know. You look lit up. You smell different too."

I'd run out of deodorant that morning and had to snake some of my dad's. He was into that all-natural, fruit-based crap, because the regular kind, with zinc or aluminum or whatever in it, gives you Alzheimer's, I forget why. The natural crap only makes you smell like you're cooking up a banana in your armpit. I thought it was rank, but apparently she was into that kind of thing. "Cherry?"

"*Jay?*"

"I can't."

"That'll be four ninety-five for the Grande. I'm kidding. Sort of. You may go now."

"Thank you." I backed out of Starbucks, nodding thanks, and I backed into this old dude. He rapped my shin with his four-pronged cane. I grabbed a newspaper from the garbage and read as I walked back to the Hollows, my board tucked into my backpack straps. Six weeks after it happened, the attack on Nicole Castro was still fresh news, at least locally. The headline story of the page five updates section of the Brandywine Vine said students were still being questioned, but no new leads. I couldn't get it out of my mind, what Nicole said to Dave Bendix in Schmidt's waiting room: "I can't do that." He wanted her to lie about something, I was pretty sure. And he was definitely desperate.

EIGHT

About twenty minutes into the half-hour session was when Schmidt always asked: "Are you taking your medication?"

"Mostly."

She nodded and frowned, a popular combination with her. "We know what happens, right, when we don't take it? Do we need help being reminded about this?"

We. "Nah, we, I can handle it. I'll put a beep into my phone."

"Which is exactly what we said last time."

"I couldn't figure out how to do it."

"Give me your phone," she said.

I did, and she put the beep in there for me.

"So *that's* how you . . . Cool, thanks, Mrs. Schmidt."

"It would be Ms. if it weren't *Doctor.*" She took a break from the nodding but kept on frowning. "Any thoughts about rejoining wrestling?"

"Yeah, no, I'm not. It's too much. PSATs coming up." Like I'd even cracked the book. That stupid vocabulary builder download? I need to know that *ramify* and *bifurcate* are synonyms, if they even are?

"How we doing on the college planning? Any schools jumping out at us?"

Accruing half a million dollars in high-interest loan debt for an engineering degree I can steal online? *No.* "Taking my time looking, enjoying the information-gathering process, you know."

"Jay, we need to develop *interests*."

"I know we do. And I appreciate the time you've taken to try to help us in that regard. I'm grateful. Really." Really I just didn't want my father to kick my ass for not showing up to therapy.

And then it came, the question that wasn't a *we* but a *you*: "What do you want to do? With your life, I mean."

"Dedicate myself to bringing the drinking age down to twelve."

"We're very distracted today. C'mon, Jay, what's up? And no BS, I'll be able to tell. You're a very bad liar."

Actually, I was a very good liar. But I was looking at Schmidt's hands, really wrinkled, chipped cheap nail polish. I felt sorry for her for a second, so sorry I felt compelled to tell her the truth. "What's on my mind, Doctor, is why haven't the cops caught the punk who messed up Nicole Castro?"

She nodded like a bobblehead doll. "I hear you, Jay. It's very difficult to figure out why someone would do such a horrible thing. It wasn't traumatizing to Nicole alone but to all of us. We have this burning desire to *know,* to *help.* At the same time, we need to leave the crime-solving to the detectives, don't we?"

"But what if they don't nab him before he gets her again?"

Schmidt leaned back in her chair. "Now, why would you say that, Jay? According to the investigators, it's highly unlikely the attacker will try for another strike, not with all the scrutiny. And even if that were to happen, we're nearly assured the perpetrator won't go after Nicole. The damage is done. The attacker's goal was met. The operating thesis is that this was a one-time event."

"The operating thesis. That's pretty funny."

"I don't know if I'd call it *funny*. Look, nearly all of the case studies show that acid throwers are not serial actors. They more often than not know their victims or imagine they have some sort of relationship with them. They feel the target has forsaken or wronged them in some way, and they're almost always motivated by revenge. Once they get their payback, they're done."

"Until the next time he remembers what made him mad in the first place."

"How do you know it's a man?"

"Excuse me?"

"Has it ever crossed your mind that maybe the attacker is a woman? For instance, somebody insanely jealous of Nicole?"

I'd never really looked into Schmidt's eyes before that. They were this stunning gray, so light the irises almost blended in with the sclera. My eyes went to the windowsill just behind her, one of those picture frame digital clocks. An old black-and-white snapshot, a baby in a swing, wide angle, nobody else in the picture. The readout went from 4:59 to 5:00. Without looking at the clock, never letting her eyes drift from mine, Schmidt said, "I guess that's all the time we have today."

Somebody jealous of Nicole, huh? Way to narrow it down, *Doctor*.

NINE

The rain was too heavy for me to skateboard. I waited under the side door awning for the storm to let up. Somebody called out, "Been looking for you, Spaceman."

I turned to find a huge dude rolling up to me fast and flexed. His orange Volta-Shock hoodie shadowed his face. "You don't remember me?" he said. "I'm hurt." He pulled back his hood. It was Kerns, the dude I'd pinned two years before. His hair wasn't dyed bloodred anymore but silver. He'd gone a little different with the Mohawk too, buzzing it close to his scalp and jagging it so it looked like a thunderbolt.

"You're taking this Volta-Shock promotion very seriously, Rick," I said. Everybody called him Dick behind his back, but maybe not so much lately. He'd logged much weight-banging time since I last saw him, that first semester of freshman year, when I got lucky and pasted him. No way that would happen now. He was well over two hundred pounds.

"Heard you were back," he said with a sly smile. I had been ducking him, and he knew it. He shook my hand way too hard. "You're still pretty tight. What are you, buck eighty? Eighty-five?"

I shrugged, wasn't into weighing myself every two min-utes. "Seventy-five or so."

"Rick, what's the holdup?" some other dude called from the locker room door. I recognized him as one of the meat-heads who held my head under the sink water before Dave Bendix stood up for me.

The hall monitor said, "Problem, gentlemen?"

"No problem here," Kerns said. "Right, Jay?" Kerns punched my shoulder somewhere between *See ya bud* and *I remember when you pinned me your first time on the mats and made me look like an idiot in front of my boys.* I'd have a bruise by tonight. "Good to have you back, Spaceman," he said as he jogged toward the entrance to the indoor track.

I pressed my face to the door glass and studied the sky. It was dark except for a fast-moving band of light gray that would be overhead in a few minutes. I checked my phone for the list I'd keyed into it on my way back from Starbucks:

Mr. Sabbatini—weak maybe, teaching science to snotty kids for 30+ yrs, would he risk his pension to burn student out of jealousy?

Jealous classmate(s)—which? Basically everybody

Mr. Sager—weak maybe, same as Sabbatini, mopping up after rich kids for too many years, pension for custodial services too good to lose.

Bendix—why, though? Why?

I added Schmidt's name. The way she leaned in close to me at the end of our session bothered me. That glimmer in her eyes as she said, "How do you know it's not a woman?"

Schmidt didn't wear a wedding band. And that fading snapshot on her sill, the kid in the swing, the clock in the frame ticking away. The girl didn't resemble Schmidt. Maybe a friend's kid? Childless, single, getting on in years? Her knowledge of psychology, of what people fear, losing their beauty? I had her down as a long shot.

I rounded the corner, toward the custodian's office. Mr. Sager's back was to me. He was at his computer.

"Sir?" I said.

He slapped down his laptop. "You don't have to call me sir. Mr. Sager will be just fine. You new here?"

I started to explain about home school, but then he remembered me. "The boy at the pep rally, sure. I didn't recognize you with that hair."

"I borrow some pliers?" I pulled my skateboard from my backpack straps and explained that my rear wheel truck was loose, a lie.

He drew a pair of pliers from his hip holster. He was in his fifties, lean, clean cut. I pegged him ex-military.

"Heard you were there when that thing went down with Nicole Castro," I said. "Heard you saved her life."

"I did no such thing."

"Telling everybody to pour water on her. What did it look—"

"It was a bad burn."

"Do you have an Allen wrench?"

"You don't need one for that wheel truck."

"The wheel itself. The spindle. I think it's a five-eighths fit."

41

He headed for the back. I flipped up his laptop screen. Somebody named Isabella1801 had emailed what she wanted to do with him that night. No whips or chains, but it was borderline hard-core. Sager was coming back. I closed the laptop and backed away from the desk into a bucket of water, accidentally kicking it. The bucket tipped but didn't turn over. Some of the water sloshed onto the floor. I grabbed a rag to wipe up the puddle.

"Stop," Mr. Sager said. "Leave it to me." He grabbed the rag and backed me away from the puddle. "Five-eighths," he said, holding out the Allen wrench.

"I'll fix it when I get home. Thanks." I headed out.

That was good of him, not letting me mop up the mess with bare hands. I hadn't spilled water. The label on the jug next to the bucket said MURIATIC ACID.

TEN

The rain was unrelenting. I headed for the bus stop a quarter mile up the road.

I'd buzzed through chemistry quickly in my home schooling, but I remembered muriatic acid. It was used in heavy industry to render other compounds like refined gasoline or polyvinyl chloride for plastic pipe production. Mostly it's a purifier, especially for water. You use muriatic acid to control PH, or the acid content of a compound. You might use it for cleaning, but only in extreme circumstances, like to strip rust from steel. For general cleaning, the kind a custodian would do in a high school, you'd go with a much gentler, cheaper agent, diluted bleach.

The rain fell harder. I jogged around the corner for the upscale strip mall just down the boulevard. I figured I'd wait out the storm under CVS's awning. Nicole'd had the same idea. She was huddled into herself, rubbing her shoulders. She looked down the boulevard. I thought she was looking at me, but when I waved she looked in the opposite direction. Why would she ignore me after reaching out to me in Schmidt's office? She simply hadn't seen me, I thought. How much of her vision had she lost in the attack? She hesitated at the CVS entrance and peeked through the glass, left, right, then she hurried in. I hurried in after her.

I grabbed from the top of the mix-and-match bin on my way into the store and ended up with a vent brush, a lame item for a guy to be carrying, especially when it's powder blue, but I didn't want Nicole to catch me empty-handed, checking up and down the aisles for her. I found her in a side aisle, her back to me.

This dude was following her. Okay, so I was following her too, but I was worried about her. The other dude was leering. He said to Nicole, "Last year's *Sports Illustrated*?"

"Excuse me?" Nicole said.

"The swimsuit issue? You're a model, right? If you aren't, you should be. I know some people in the industry." He'd approached her from her right side.

Nicole turned to show him the left side of her face. She pulled back her hair.

I was at the end of the aisle, pretending to look at bunion pads to hide myself behind the corner shelf unit, but I saw that the bandage on her cheek was not small. How bad was it under there? How deep was the burn?

"Sorry, I didn't hear you," Nicole said. "What did you say?"

The dude backed away with his hands up, staring at the bandage. Just before he stepped out of the aisle, he said, "I'm sorry."

By the time my line of sight was clear, Nicole had swept her hair to cover up the bandage. She headed for the exit, stopping briefly to check if the coast was clear. How do you live like that? Afraid to turn every corner?

I went to where she'd been in the aisle. Bandages. All different kinds, each promising it was the gentlest on your skin.

ELEVEN

By the time I was out on the street, Nicole was gone. I jogged to the bus stop. The rain hit me like thrown stones. I was trying to shake off the rainwater when somebody behind me grabbed my coat collar and spun me around. "You were following me," Nicole said.

"No I wasn't. I was pricing out, like, vent brushes. Seriously, I was."

She practically gasped, disgusted by the obviousness of my lie. She pointed to my earbuds. "Nice Skull Candy. I peg you the classic rock type. The Stones, Zeppelin, Hendrix, nothing after you were born."

"You got me."

"Then I know you have The Smiths all over your playlists, right?"

"In my top ten favorite bands, maybe even top five." I hadn't heard of them.

She pointed to my hip. The jack end of my headphone set had fallen out of my pocket. Clearly my Skull Candy knockoff wire led to no music player. "If you're going to pretend to be listening to music," she said, "you should also pretend not to hear what I'm saying." She hurried across the street to the east side waiting area. The eastbound riders had a well-lit modern glass awning that actually kept them dry. We westbound folk made do with poorly patched corrugated metal that leaked rainwater the color of old blood. The light in the ad box was dead, and the sun-faded poster was for a zombie show that had gone off the air three years before. Across the street, Nicole was leaning against an ad box that featured seasonal fare from Whole Foods, the prettiest pumpkins you've never seen in real life. We stayed like this for a while, each under our respective awnings, until the ridiculousness of the situation fully hit me. Why didn't I just tell her I was worried about her and apologize?

I jogged across the street. "I'm sorry," I said.

"For what? Stalking me, or lying about it?" She looked down the boulevard for signs of a bus, none coming. "Did you see it?" she said. "The bandage?"

"No."

"You're lying yet again."

"Not all of it."

"How much?"

"Only, like, the edge of it."

"Good."

I stood there for another half a minute or so, just nodding, waiting for an eastbound bus when she knew I was headed for the west side. "Take care," I said, flipping up my jacket collar in anticipation of the rain.

"The dude in CVS," she said.

"He was a douche," I said.

"He wasn't apologizing for being creepy, for hitting on me.

Did you see his eyes? They were filled with it. Pity. Genuine pity. He might as well have said 'I'm sorry your life is over.'" Her voice had softened, and I had a hard time hearing her. She was talking to herself. "Like at the hospital, with Emma."

"Emma?"

"The way everybody looks at her. The way I try not to." She seemed to remember I was there, turning to me. "My friend. She's sick."

I'd gathered that much. "Sorry."

"She doesn't let it get her down, though. She's amazing. Seriously, why did that dude have to look at me that way?"

Did she really expect me to have the answer? I regretted crossing the street. I should have just left her alone. "I'm running a little late," I said.

"Me too."

I caught myself before I said good luck. "Bye," I said, stepping off the curb.

"Work?" she said.

"Huh?"

"Running late for work?"

"Yeah. You?"

"No."

Course not, I'm thinking. *Why ever would you have to work?* Rich people's four-letter word. I wondered if I could make it across the street without being run down. The cars wouldn't stop coming.

"Your car in the shop?" she said.

"Not allowed to drive," I said.

"You're not sixteen after all?"

"No, I am. It's just, I have this condition. Long story."

"Sorry," she said.

"Not your fault."

"No, I know, I was just saying."

A thunder blast seemed to slant the rain for a second. She flinched, grabbed my sleeve, let go. I felt bad for wanting to leave her there. "I do, though," I said.

"Do?"

"Drive. Forklift."

"A *fork*lift."

"For work."

"Clearly."

Where not to work if you're a hacker who aspires to stay off government radar: the Apple Genius Bar. A better choice: a big box wholesale club, restock department.

"You don't need a license to drive a forklift?"

"The dude who's supposed to work the forks is always out sick. After a while I got tired of putting my life at risk to climb the racks to the fourth tier to pull down eight-packs of Similac for stroller mafia who don't know the words *thank you*." I stopped myself before I told her that whenever I worked the forklift, I always made sure I took my meds, usually.

"Costco?" she said.

"BJ's."

"Cool."

"Not really. How come you can't drive?" I said.

"Car's in the shop."

"Gotcha." I'd found myself hoping she had some kind of condition too. Not like she didn't have enough going on with her face. I'm an idiot.

She checked her phone for the time. "Yeah, I think I'm going to have to hoof it." She stepped out into the rain, east. "Good luck with the stroller mafia."

"You too," I said.

She turned back and looked at me like, *Wha?*

I wondered why, having been stranded by Dave, she didn't just call somebody else to pick her up. That's when it occurred to me that maybe she didn't have anybody to call. That maybe everybody thinks the pretty girl with the big brain has the world by the tail, that she wouldn't want to hang out with somebody average like you, so why bother trying to be friends with her. Or was it that she just didn't want to be around the people from her old life, their pity?

She walked fast up the avenue. Her backpack straps were uneven. She didn't have an umbrella. I pulled a busted one from the trash and splinted the broken spoke with a rolled magazine and a plastic bag ripped into strips. It held together perfectly for thirty seconds, the amount of time I needed to catch up to Nicole, and then it punked right in front of her. The one side of it was still okay. I handed her the umbrella. A truck flew through a pothole lake and threw a wave of muddy water onto us.

Nicole dropped to her knees in a silent scream. She covered her face as if to protect herself from a second splash. She was balled up on the side of the road. The gutter water tugged at the half umbrella. "It burns," she said. "Oh god. Please. It burns." I helped her up. She wouldn't let go of my arm. "Walk me? Please?"

The bandage tape was peeling off her cheek. She tilted her head so I couldn't see it. I'd always thought she was statuesque goddess height, at least five ten, but she was more like five five. In my mind she was all curves, but here, now, up close, my hands on her waist to hold her up, she was slight. She was just a girl, and she was shivering.

TWELVE

"As in rhymes with *Sbarro*?"

"Ex*act*ly, as in, exactly."

I found it hard to believe she didn't know my last name after I was the YouTube sensation of freshman year, spazzing out in the middle of the gym floor at the pep rally. Could she not have seen the video? Maybe she wasn't at the pep rally altogether?

"Nazzaro," she said. "I think I knew that. Wait, I've seen that name somewhere. Somewhere else, I mean."

"My father, maybe. It's a lame paper, but you ever read the *Clarion*? He's the art critic."

"Your father is Vincent Nazzaro?"

"Steven, but everybody always thinks his name is Vincent too. Not like I mean he has two names."

"I know what you mean."

"Thanks."

"For what?"

I shrugged.

She stumbled. I grabbed her arm. She regained her balance but kept her arm hooked through mine as we walked. "Was it as lame for you as it is for me, home school?" she said.

"My father just let me read whatever I wanted, as long as I passed those tests the state makes you take."

"I have to take them if I don't head back next quarter. How were they?"

"I took them all in the beginning of the year to get them over with. I home schooled online. This pilot program thing."

"And you passed everything, no tutors?" she said.

"Tests were designed to let a moron pull at least a B. You'll kill them. If you don't come back to the Hollows. Are you? Coming back, I mean?"

"I'm not sure. I'm being told I need to hunker down for a while, hang home with my mom. She's been awesome, total rock."

"Why didn't you call her? You know, to pick you up?"

"I can't have her dropping everything for me anymore. As it is, she's pretty much stopped her life to help me get through this. She needs to take a break from me every once in a while. From it."

I wondered how I'd react if I saw it. I'd read that burn wounds were the worst. Catastrophic disfigurement. Identities just erased.

We came to where the main road tied into a tunnel of very old, well-pruned elms, no cars at the curbs. A sign said: PRIVATE COMMUNITY, NO PARKING, VIOLATORS WILL BE TOWED. "I'm just down the street," she said.

I lived on a street. This was a drive with estates on either side. I had a cousin who lived in Englewood, plenty of money there but gaudy rich, lots of lawn statuary, half the saints in the Gregorian calendar sticking out of the *Ficus benjamina*. Nothing so cheesy as a prefabricated statue in this part of town, though. Just wide fields of flawless lawn. The mowing lines were invisible, as if the grass had been hand-combed.

"Your clothes are soaked," she said. "You can borrow some of my father's. We'll go visit my friend, and then I'll drive you home."

"Your car's in the shop," I said.

"Our housekeeper's. We have this old Subaru wagon for when she runs errands."

"Why didn't you call her for a ride?"

"She's in Florida for the week."

"Your friend," I said. "The one in the hospital?"

Nicole clicked her phone to play me a message. *"Nicole Castro, I wait for thee. Will I be eleven by the time you show up? This is my subtle reminder that E-Day is next week. I'm currently soliciting several presents, with a new OtterBox topping the list. Pink preferred, though lemon yellow is fine too, anything bright. Also, all forms of gift cards will be accepted, but I definitely wouldn't mind a Dolce and Gabbana certificate."*

Nicole laughed. "She'd so never wear Dolce, you know?"

I laughed and nodded, like of course I knew the wardrobe inclinations of this person I'd never met. We'd come to a guardhouse in the middle of the street. The attendant came out with an umbrella for us. "Nicole, let me call the car to take you to the house." His eyes ticked toward the main road. An older model Civic was parked off the shoulder, somewhat camouflaged by the woods. Somebody was leaning through the driver's-side window, aiming a telephoto lens at us. The guard frowned. He shined his flashlight toward the camera as he clicked his radio. "John, he's back again."

"I see him," came back through the radio.

A tug on my sleeve. Nicole pulled me behind the guard-house. "Rag mag reporter," she said. She peeked around the gatehouse.

Across the road, a security company SUV zipped up to the photographer's car, and the photographer sped out of there. I memorized the plate number, MBE-7921. "Let's go," Nicole said.

"Can't. I'm running seriously late for work."

"So that much was true."

The west side bus was coming. "See ya," I said. I started for the pickup spot.

Nicole hurried alongside to cover me with the umbrella. "Next week, right?"

"Next week?" I said.

The bus rolled in with foot-high waves. We backed up to keep the water from rolling over our ankles. "At Dr. Schmidt's," she said.

"Right. Take care, Nicole."

"I hate it," she said. "That they call you Spaceman. I'm sorry. That must have been awful for you. The thing at the pep rally."

I was seeing it all over again, and so was she, apparently. No hoping anymore. Nicole Castro had seen me wet my pants.

"On or off," the bus driver said.

I stuck my foot in the door to keep it open. "You must be

really into art to know my father. It's not like he works for the *Times*."

"My mother's an artist. She calls herself a hobbyist, but she's good. She's serious about it anyway, reads all the reviews. She likes your dad. Says he's one of the nice ones. You freaked me out, following me like that."

"I was just trying to—"

"I know why you did it. What's your number?"

I gave it to her. A second later my phone vibrated. "There's mine," she said. Nicole Castro had just given me her phone number. How was this possible?

"My friend," the driver said, "stay and play, or let's be on our way."

I hopped onto the bus. Nicole tossed me the umbrella the guard had given her.

"You keep it," I said.

"I have this one." She opened the crummy umbrella I'd put together for her. "Hey, Nazzaro? You're my hero." She saluted me with the messed-up umbrella.

The bus doors closed and I grabbed a seat with one last wave to Nicole.

"Excuse me, hero?" the bus driver said. "That's two seventy-five."

I dunked my card, a slug, but the machine showed *PAID $2.75* because I was palming my phone as I leaned onto the card reader. That junky little Nokia with the cat-scratched display could work some minor magic.

THIRTEEN

From the notes of Dr. Julian Nye, MD, PsyD:

Thurs, Oct 21, third session with Nicole Castro, begun at 8:30pm, at Castro residence. Patient initially appeared withdrawn and expressed that she was exhausted, complaining of a headache with pain 8 out of 10, but very quickly became agitated when I suggested I could write her a prescription for Relpax.

Per NC's mother, NC was AWOL after session with school psychologist Dr. Schmidt, for approx. one hour. I expressed concern that patient was walking around in the rain, alone. Patient said she wasn't alone. I asked who was with her. She frowned and said, "People. You know, just people on the street." Patient then asked what I thought about liars. I asked her to be more specific. She asked if I thought a liar could be a good person. "You know, if he or she is lying to do a good thing." When I asked for an example of a "good thing," patient stared out the dining room window and said, "I can't think clearly. I'm afraid to picture it. His face. If they ever find out who did it, I mean. I don't know whether I'd have a heart attack or claw his eyes out. We're doomed, the human race, when you have people like that walking around. Absolutely zero empathy. I want to live on the Moon."

I am beginning to suspect patient is holding back more than the name of the young man who, per security guard, walked NC home.

FOURTEEN

BJ's closed to the public at eight p.m., and I got to my restock work. At ten I grabbed my fifteen-minute break. I clicked one of the laptops to the local news links and found a short update on the Nicole Castro story, except it was hardly an update. That afternoon, some idiot had tackled some other idiot in Sports Authority after the dude tried to shoplift a Volta-Shock bottle. Other than that, there were no new leads in the case.

"Can you believe she actually got a boyfriend?" the woman who ran the electronics section said. She tapped the keyboard to a gossip site. The headline ran BURNED BEAUTY QUEEN BAGS NEW BEAU. I panicked, expecting to see a picture of Nicole's arm hooked through mine at the security gatehouse that blocked off her neighborhood. The follow-up would then be BENDIX VOWS TO BASH BEAU'S BRAINS IN, but the picture wasn't of Nicole and me. I wasn't the only one following Nicole in CVS. The picture showed Nicole with the guy who tried to pick her up, until he saw the bandage on her face. The headline and the camera angle were enough to suggest they were together. The photo credit was ©*Scorpion Imageworks*.

"What kind of guy would want to go out with her after that?" my coworker said.

"Dude must be desperate," I muttered, scanning the article.

"I bet you he's burned too. You know, like where you can't see?"

I got home from work at 11:00. We lived in one of those efficiency apartment complexes that are always full of bitterly divorced men and the odd widower with kids. The power lines sprayed from the phone pole and attacked the side of our building like blown snot. Dented, pigeon-crap-covered Dish Network discs tilted like begging hands. Even so, the rent wasn't cheap in this last outpost of the coveted Brandywine zip code.

My father was at the piano, this little electric job we picked up for his birthday at BJ's with my discount, low-end keys on ironing board stilts. I recognized the piece, Rachmaninoff, Vespers, some doleful notes to be sure. On the side table: bottle of red wine, the second one. The first, a dead soldier, was on the kitchen counter, next to picked-at Mexican takeout.

I would have asked him if he was okay, but he only would've told me to mind my own business. He'd catch an AA meeting the next morning on his way to work, and then he'd be good for a month or so before he fell off again. At least he wasn't drinking and driving anymore, or that's what he promised. But $4.99 a bottle? If you're going to be bad, at least drink something good.

You might think art critics make a lot of money. They're lucky if they make almost enough. They're really smart, and they dress like they're heading to a cocktail party at the Princeton Club, if you don't notice that their designer label clothes are irregulars pulled from the Marshalls clearance rack. They can carry on one heck of a conversation—charm you silly—but they're not to be confused with the millionaires they cover in their columns. Stevie Nazzaro from Hoboken did well enough to get into Columbia on a scholarship, art history of all the useless things, but he would have been better off if he stuck with the wrestling. Naz the Knuckler, WWE smackdown champ or some crap like that.

I think I was pretty close to getting him to give up on me, and then I could emancipate and be free of whatever it was I was living, just this day-to-day grayness. I'd move into the city and get by waiting tables or pushing flavored coffees at a godforsaken latte bar maybe. I could take subways instead of having to kick my skateboard everywhere. No more shoulder-less north Jersey roads without sidewalks, step-trucks and speeding Range Rovers sucking me into traffic. It would be better for my father too, having me out of the apartment. Couldn't be easy living with a son of minor ambition.

"You had therapy today, right?" he said. "You didn't ditch, did you?"

"I went."

"How was Mrs. Schmidt?"

"It's Doctor. Terrific."

"Any of that bullying crap going on again?" he said.

"Nope. Thought you were getting home late."

"I did. You were later. You have to get right in their faces and give it back to them, Jay. I told you how many times, you can't just roll over."

"It's fine, Dad."

"Sure it is."

"Okay, don't believe me."

"You're holding back. Something big too. Your breathing, it's solemn."

"How can breathing be solemn? It's just breathing."

"I need to be out of town for a week." He tapped the high end piano key. "This conference wants me to speak. The money is just north of lousy enough to turn down."

I checked the fridge for milk, nothing in there except duck sauce packets.

"You hear what I said?" he said.

"Yeah," I said.

"Then can you *acknowledge* you heard me?"

"I *heard* you, man. Have a great trip."

"Hey, Jay? When do I stop getting blamed?"

"Blamed for what?"

"Everything." He headed for his room with the wine. He halted at his bedroom door, as if he wanted to say something, but he didn't. He went in. The door puffed shut.

I grabbed what was left of the takeout and headed for my room, not much more than a closet with a bed that was too short for me, but it was on the back of the building and it was quiet, except for the old man's TV, muffled by the wall. I could barely make out he was watching the old movie channel again. I hated feeling sorry for my father. Writing him off as a jerk was a lot easier.

I remembered that I'd forgotten to take my meds. I swigged them down with this sports drink that looked like chalk dust suspended in antifreeze. I'd grabbed it at work, overstock they were looking to dump, and now I knew why: It was disgusting. I shoveled cold burritos into my mouth as I waited for my laptop to boot. Now that I'd spent an afternoon with Nicole, had seen her up close, helped her out of that puddle on the side of the road, touched her, I felt involved. Okay, maybe not involved, not yet, but scared for her. That she was being followed freaked me out. If a photographer could tail her so easily, without being caught, couldn't the psychopath who got away with throwing acid into Nicole Castro's face just as easily sneak right up on her again?

Maybe I thought about it for a minute before I did it. Maybe not that long. In less than twenty keystrokes, I hacked a line into the Department of Motor Vehicles. Plate number MBE-7921 ran back to one Shane Puglisi.

At this point I wasn't doing anything more than poking around. I had no inclination to do more than feel bad for Nicole and wonder whether or not she was going to call me before next Thursday, when I would see her in Schmidt's office. She wasn't particularly thrilled I'd followed her into CVS. Stalking her by way of my computer would win me a top spot on her hate list, if she found out about it. She might even be mad enough at that point to sic the cops onto me. I just wanted to be sure that Shane Puglisi wasn't a psycho. After I cleared him, I was going to delete my suspect list from my phone and mind my own business.

Turning Puglisi inside out was cake. Most of the actionable intelligence the National Security Agency and CIA scoop comes from open source information. Most of that comes from Facebook. Hackers don't have to hack so much anymore. Why would I take on the risk inherent in stealing information from you when you're willing to tell me everything about yourself for free? The challenge now is skimming and leaking without letting people know you're doing it. That's the real game: remaining anonymous. Not that I was planning on doing any leaking when it came to Nicole's case. Not yet anyway.

Shane Puglisi's LinkedIn profile said he was a freelance photojournalist. His Twitter profile picture was a shot of a rat sitting atop a cube of cheese, its legs crossed. I could have stopped there, reasonably sure that Puglisi, while a low-life sleaze, wasn't after Nicole Castro, not to throw acid at her anyway. But I didn't stop there. My fingers seemed to hammer the keyboard of their own will. I dipped into Puglisi's bank account.

He'd wired money to one Brian Meyers, whose Facebook profile picture was a direct match to the guy I'd seen hitting on Nicole in CVS. All of this made me feel, if not better, then somewhat relieved, at least about Puglisi and Meyers. They had run a scam to get a shot of Nicole and auction it off to the highest bidder, splitting the take, end of story. Then again, not quite. One of the wire transfers in Puglisi's account traced back to *The New Jersey Clarion*.

I found this more disturbing than surprising. Like every other newspaper desperate to stay in business, the *Clarion* had a "soft news" section, and Brandywine was almost exclusively the *Clarion*'s beat. But the paper paid my father's salary and our rent. We were getting by and in a sense getting over by taking money from a company that chased down people who were dealing with any number of miseries, including losing half your face to an acid attack. I can't say that it was this sense of guilt, though, that had my fingers itching to hammer my keyboard for some more digging—not exclusively.

How would my mother have reacted to my stepping away from this girl who was clearly in pain when I had a skill set that might be of help in catching the psychopath who had ruined her life? Would she think I was crazy for wanting to help Nicole, or would she be proud of me? What would Mom have done if I had been attacked instead of Nicole? That one was easy: exactly what Mrs. Castro was doing, putting her life on hold to help her child.

I'd lost her almost six years earlier. The loss was at times, particularly in reminiscences that for some reason came strongest at twilight, as stunning as it was the day she died. She was smiling at me by way of the visor shade mirror. She'd flipped it down to block out the high beams of the oncoming truck. The last thing she said to me was, "Jay-Jay, do you know what we're going to do tomorrow?" And that was it.

At the very least, she would want me to make sure the police were trying to catch Nicole's attacker. After that, I would stop my prying—I swore this to myself. I tapped into an e-string that linked Brandywine Hollows High School to the police. Sneaking into Mrs. Marks's computer was a joke. Her password was marksy123. Why bother? I found the two emails the acid thrower sent her, the first coming the night before the attack, the second moments after. Marks had forwarded the emails to the Division of Detectives, nobody specific, just info@. So now I knew where the emails ended up, but where had they come from?

I backtracked them to what we hacktivists call a zero-map, a changing series of relay servers that were part of the Conficker bot net. The emails had ricocheted off of a thousand drives before they landed in Marks's in-box. They were perfectly untraceable. I studied the first email: "after a little test run, I find that I like the sound."

Had the acid thrower burned an animal? I'd read that serial killers often started out with rodents, then cats, dogs, moving their way up to humans. Was there such a thing as a serial acid thrower? Schmidt said no, but I wasn't so sure. The bigger question for me at the moment was: Now that I have these emails, what should I do with them?

FIFTEEN

From Nicole's journal:

Thurs, 21 Oct—

Emma tried so hard to make me laugh when I visited her today, but underneath the cheerfulness she seemed so weary of it all, the pretending that everything is going to be all right. The bags under her eyes. The bruises on her arms from all the IVs. I don't know how she knows not to do it, but she never asks me who I think burned me.

After that little bit of peacefulness with Emma: another horrendous Nye session. I told him I didn't want to take the Xanax, that the stuff is too strong. He might as well have rolled his eyes as he said, "What do you think: Is it okay to be happy?"

He means numb. Dr. Schmidt tells me it's okay to feel the pain. To face it.

After Nye left, David came over.

We whisper-fought in the living room while Mom made hot chocolate for us.

David: "I was driving all over Brandywine looking for you."

Me: "You ditched me."

D: "I did not."

Me: "You said, 'Well, that's just messed up, Nic. Seriously. I can't believe you. You know what? Forget it.'"

D: "That doesn't mean I wasn't driving you home. How did you get home, by the way?"

Me: "Walked."

D: "Alone?"

Me: "Save it. Mom already gave me hell about it."

D: "Okay. Look, I'm sorry. I am." And then he asked me about it again.

I'm not lying for him.

I told him to leave. He tried to kiss me, and I gave him my cheek, the wrong one, by mistake. He went into the kitchen and said good-bye to Mom. He was teary as he left. I was too. Mom plunked next to me on the couch. We sipped hot chocolate, and then she held out her hand, the pills in her palm. I took the antibiotic but passed on the Xanax. I needed to be able to think clearly. Jay Nazzaro. What was it about him that made me act like a complete idiot, practically begging him to walk me home even after he lied about following me into CVS?

I headed upstairs to my bathroom.

They're all lined up so neatly on the bathroom counter: the vacuum-packed dressings coated with topical pain reliever, the latex-free surgical tape, the hydrogen peroxide, the prescription-grade antibiotic gel.

The bandage change. The horror movie I'm too terrified

to watch. The freak show I can't turn away from. *Who is that girl sitting in front of my bathroom mirror?* The FedEx delivery guy used to come right up to the door with that warm smile, and now he backs away. Not in his movement, not in his smile, but in his eyes. He's afraid to look at me. At the same time he's afraid *not* to look at me, and he just ignores the fact that half my face is bandaged and stares really, really hard into my good eye. Not asking what happened is conceding that what happened is cataclysmic.

How will I do college interviews now, job interviews? For the rest of my life, do I just not acknowledge what happened? They'll ask me to tell them about some of the formative experiences in my life. If I acknowledge It, will they think I'm asking for pity? If I don't acknowledge It, will they think I'm just not able to confront difficulty, challenge, hurdles, this absolute nightmare?

This is the worst part of the bandage change: too much time to think. No, it's the quiet. Nine months to the day after Dad left, and I still hear it. The yelling, the nastiness, the echoes trapped in the walls. Mom begs him to tell her how long it has been since he stopped loving her. The accusations. His denials. His growing exasperation with her cutting him off. Then, "To hell with it." The stairs groan as he stomps toward the master suite. The suitcase clumps to the floor. I'm listening to all this from the tub, the water hotter than I can stand it, to waylay the cramps snaking into my calves after two brutal tennis matches that day. I believed him. He's not the type to cheat. Too classy, too proper to have a girlfriend on the side. To betray his wife, his daughter. To lie.

The lie.

The stranger in the bathroom mirror.

Or is she the truth? The real me, hiding just beneath the gauze?

"Mom? Mom, please."

She appears at the bathroom door instantly, as if she's been waiting just outside, and she has, of course. She pulls the tape away quickly.

Six weeks after the burn, and I haven't yet dared touch it. I regard it as if it isn't part of me, an invading species that will never quite overtake me, or at least not the rest of my face. How do I live with this, being branded? My mind drifts back to my horse riding lessons. That sweet little red roan with the omega seared into her left shoulder. Riding her into the Meadowlands with Daddy on a clear Saturday morning, letting her graze the salt hay and cordgrass. She looks back over her shoulder to me, as if to ask if it's okay we've stopped.

"Is it okay?" Mom says, her eye on me, on It, what used to be my left eye. I clamp my good eye shut, but I easily picture what's happening. I feel the pressure stream. Mom pushes down on the hypodermic syringe full of saline to flush the wound. I keep seeing it, over and over. The bottle's nose. Coming up to my face. An explosion of liquid.

After the scrubbing comes the salve, a low-grade sting, then the dressing and the tape with its epoxy-like adhesive. Then comes the kiss to the top of my head, the hug that lasts a long time. She never says it'll be okay. I'm grateful.

"Mom, how can I ever ask anybody to be with me now? To put up with the way people look at me or see me or can't *see* me? The way *I* can't see me anymore? Where did I go?"

"Easy now, Nicole. Breathe. You're still here. You're with me, and I love you."

"This is crazy. I always saw myself loving somebody forever. Being there for him. Lifting him up when he was down. How do I do that now?"

"Honey, there are a lot of guys out there who . . . No, there aren't a lot."

"Exactly."

"But there are a few. The good ones. You'll see."

"I always saw myself with kids. How do I bring a child into my life now? Say I adopt as a single parent. How do I ask my kid to make eye contact with me? I read about it. It's all in the eyes, the facial expressions, the thousands of tiny movements in the muscles around your eyes, your lips. The child reads them without knowing it. How is she supposed to feel I'm her protector when she's reading a horror story? I mean, how are you doing this?"

"It makes me feel good to be able to do this for you."

I tap her heart. "How are you keeping it together?"

"You'll get past this. We'll get past it. Find the good in this, Nicole."

"The *good*?"

"You and me. Us. You were running here, there, and everywhere before. Now we have this time together. And when we're together, we're stronger. I really mean that. I feel it. I feel stronger, seeing you overcome this. Being with you. You're empowering me, giving me the courage to face it."

"I don't know how you can even look at It. You don't even flinch."

"I don't mean the burn. I mean face the . . ."

"What?"

She sees herself in the mirror. Suddenly she's exhausted. She strokes my hair. "You're allowed to cry for exactly three more minutes. By that time I want you in your Snuggie and in bed, and I'll scratch your back."

We hug and rock in front of the mirror for a while. My eyes are closed. When I open them, I catch Mom eyeing me in the mirror. She sees I've caught her and holds me a little closer, but she was staring at me for just a half second too long.

"What?" I say.

"Nothing," she says. She winks and I try to wink, but it hurts too much.

She holds out her hand, palm up. The little blue pill. "You just seem so agitated, Nicole. Please, sweetheart."

I pop it. For her, I swallow the Xanax dry. Anything to get out of this bathroom, to escape the sterile bandage smell, except it's always with me, the faint scent of bleach. Still, I have to get away from the mirror. From that girl. Me. It.

Mom tucks me into bed. She cuddles with me and combs my hair with her fingers. The Xanax is starting to work. I think I only blinked, but my eyes are closed for hours. When I open them, Mom's gone and the sun is strong. I haven't dreamt a thing. Time just stopped.

It hits me: that look I caught Mom giving me in the bathroom the night before. Was it suspicion? My second thought is that Jay Nazzaro hasn't called. I feel like an idiot all over again. I thought he felt it too, a connection, the possibility of deep friendship rooted in common experience: being afraid of the next attack, not knowing when it's coming. But can you build a real friendship on fear?

I'm groggy as I head downstairs. Mom is in her studio. She left me a breakfast plate on the counter, steak and eggs. I slide it into the microwave and stare through the window, watching the carousel turn as the food starts to smoke. Suddenly the rain is back . . . loud on the windows. I kept the umbrella Jay fixed for me. He knows what it's like, people trying not to stare at you. They smile sweetly, but really they're thinking, *Freak*. Maybe we could be alone together.

The microwave blips. I cut into the meat, overcooked, gray. The stringiness. The veins. I clench my jaw to keep myself from screaming. I try not to look at it as I cut it up and bag it for our neighbor Mrs. Gluck's cat. On impulse I grab my phone. To hell with it. I check my recent Calls Sent for Jay's number and tap it.

# SIXTEEN

She wanted to go riding, as in horseback. I'd been on one of those miniature ponies once, the kind out in front of old-school drugstores. Two quarters get you two minutes of slow-motion bobbing. Other than that, the closest I'd come to a horse was when I stepped in a pile of hay-threaded crap left in the middle of the trail at Ramapo Mountain State Park. "Look," I said, "you and Dave, I don't want to get in the middle of anything, you know?"

"That's a little presumptuous of you, don't you think? If you don't want to go—"

"No no, I want to."

"Do you ride?"

"Sure."

"The forklift."

"You can ride the horse, I'll chug alongside on my skateboard."

"Yeah, no, the horse won't like that. We'll see what we can do."

After school I met her at the stables. My horse was a big black Arabian with a half-moon shock of white for a bib. He ignored whatever I was trying to do with the reins and followed Nicole's horse into the trails. After a few minutes of smashing my nuts every time the horse trotted a step, I had to ask Nicole if we could take a break. She showed me how to absorb the shock with my knees. I was doing squats for half an hour straight. I had no alternative but to come to the conclusion that horse riding sucked. On the upside, Nicole was wearing riding pants. She had amazing legs.

We came to a clearing and stopped. Nicole popped a pill. "Allergies," she said. She dismounted and led the horses to a water trough. She whispered to them, and they bent their necks to nuzzle her. She laughed quietly into their ears as she fed them apple bits. I found this resilience almost disturbing. How does a girl who has just been burned in an acid attack find the will to smile? But when she got back onto her horse she grimaced. A very long hour later we were done. She led the horses to their stalls, and I went to the concession stand. We grabbed a picnic table at the edge of the eating area. Nicole squinted into the tree shade.

"Photographers?" I said.

"I left through the service gate. Didn't see anybody following me."

Two middle school buses were pulling into the parking lot. The kids were loud.

"Thought you were going to get some peace and quiet, did you?" I said.

"The trails were nice though, right?" she said.

The kids mobbed the concession stand. They were shrieking more than laughing. All the bouncing around on the horse had given me a headache. Nicole adjusted her sunglasses so they were closer to her eyes. She made sure her hair covered the left side of her face. "My second surgery is coming up," she said. "I can't believe I have to keep doing this. The anesthesia. Going dark like that, bam, you're dead, you know?"

"I do."

"The harvesting is the worst of it. The idea of it." She pushed her cheese fries away. "My mother begged me not to ride. She said I would open up the wound. I said, 'I'm not doing any headstands on the horse today, Mom,' and she said, 'No, I mean your hip. You'll split the stitches.' I had to sneak out of the house."

The kids threw ketchup-soaked fries at each other.

"Did you?" I said. "Split the stitches?"

"They were ready to come out anyway. The wounds stayed closed. I checked them in the bathroom." She winced. "Hurt more than my face right about now, though."

The kids' screaming was really getting to me. Underneath it was this crackling buzz. About twenty feet away, a dude was spot-welding a hinge onto the pasture gate. The stink of acetylene and burning metal cut into my nostrils and seeped like a nosebleed into the back of my throat. "What does he do, your dad?" I said.

"Finance. I better call my mom."

I gagged on the metal taste. The sun flickered. Nicole said from a great distance, even though her face was inches from mine, "Jay, are you all right?" as I fell backward.

SEVENTEEN

I came to on a cot in the stables office. The woman who ran the concession was taking my blood pressure. Nicole mopped my brow. I put my hand down to my crotch.

I was dry.

"How long was I out?" I said.

"Maybe two minutes," Nicole said.

"Was I—"

"You were shivering, sort of," Nicole said.

"I don't think you were all the way out," the woman said. "You stood up when I told you to and you let us walk you back here. Has this ever hap—"

"Yes," I said.

"Are you taking any medi—"

"Supposed to be."

"When was the last time you—"

"Yesterday." She had taken off my sneakers. I sat up and put them back on.

"Hold on a second there," the woman said. "The ambulance is on its way."

"I don't need an ambulance."

"Jay," Nicole said.

"My father's insurance doesn't cover ambulance rides."

"That's no reason not to get medical attention," Nicole said.

"It is for me." I was done pretending, acting as if I belonged here at a *riding* stable, of all the ridiculous places, one that catered to a bunch of spoiled rich kids.

"Let me call your mother, then," the woman who ran the concession said. "Just lie back there and breathe until she gets here."

"My name is Jay Nazzaro. I'm at Huntington Stables. Today is Friday, October twenty-second. I'm alert and oriented with no signs of physical trauma or amnesia. I was eating fries, and I had a seizure. I know the drill, okay? By law you have to let me go." I left.

Nicole followed. "Can I at least take you to the hospital? My father'll pay, Jay."

"No way. Can you pop the hatchback?" We were at her Subaru, or her *maid's.*

"You're not seriously thinking of skateboarding?"

"Could you just open the door, please?" I clicked the autolock dangling from her bandaged finger. The hatchback popped. I grabbed my backpack, dropped my board and kicked off on legs that would have been a lot wobblier if I weren't so mad at myself, at Nicole, for bringing me down here, into her pain, looking for a shoulder to cry on. Like I didn't have enough hassle in my life without pulling hers into it. She tried to follow me, but I rode into the shoulder of oncoming traffic and lost her in the side streets. My phone rang. I turned it off. I went to Barnes & Noble but was too mad to read. I wandered the mall, hitting the electronics spots, first Radio Shack, Best Buy, moving my way up to the Apple Store, coveting things I'd never be able to afford.

EIGHTEEN

From Nicole's journal:

Fri, 22 Oct—

I lost his friendship before I ever had it.

Mom's pissed I went riding, says she's thinking about not letting me leave the house until Nye clears me for "public interaction." Exact opposite of what Dr. Schmidt said, that I should be getting out there, getting back to normal, getting my life back.

David left me six apology messages today, extremely annoying, probably as annoying as the six I left Jay tonight. That forced look in David's eyes. I can't bear it again. Staring too hard at me, pretending he doesn't see the bandage when all he's thinking about is what's underneath it. I should show him. How would he look at me then? He wouldn't. He wouldn't be able to.

Emma's still sick.

Xanax time, two bullets tonight, with Mom's blessing.

I hate myself.

NINETEEN

My father was out when I got home, no message as to his whereabouts. He had probably covered an opening and was grabbing a late dinner with the gallery owners at some fancy place on their dime.

I forced myself to take my meds. I had grabbed a can of soup on my way home and a loaf advertised as "Health Bread" that was suspiciously spongy. After I got that stuff into me, I took a hot shower. I was still mad. I'd spent an hour with Nicole the day before, walking her home. I'd spent two hours with her this afternoon. In those three hours, she was happy to tell me her problems, but she hadn't asked me much about mine. Did it occur to her I might be as messed up as she was? Then again, I still had my face.

To torture myself, I logged into my YouTube channel, searched "epileptic seizure in public." Sure enough, somebody had clipped me at the stables. There I was, flailing in the dust. Just like before, most of the kids watching me seize were at least concerned, but others were out there with their phones. One girl was snickering. I was on my side, riding an invisible bicycle. Then there was Nicole.

She pushed them back. One kid stuffed a bunched lunch

bag into my mouth. Nicole pulled the paper out. The kid protested, "So he doesn't bite his tongue."

"No," Nicole said. She knew exactly what to do, the only thing you're supposed to do when somebody seizes: Just keep him clear of anything he might smash his hands, legs, head on and let him get through it. But Nicole Castro did more than that for me. She smacked the phones from the hands of the kids who were clipping me. "How dare you?" she kept saying. "How *dare* you? What's wrong with you? How can you do that to him?" She knelt over me and shielded me from the kids' phone cameras. When I had for the most part stopped shivering, she cradled my head and brushed the hair from my eyes and called my name.

I paused the video there and reached for my phone. I had to thank her, to apologize for being an idiot, jilting her at the stables. I hesitated. It was two in the morning. I had doubled down on my anticonvulsant meds. I had enough trouble not saying anything stupid when I wasn't looped. I put the phone down.

I didn't have to think about it for very long before I decided to commit to it, no matter what. I was going to catch the son of a bitch who burned Nicole Castro. I pulled up the two emails I'd ripped from Mrs. Marks's hard drive, the ones Arachnomorph sent her from an unknowable origin, and I got to work.

TWENTY

The next morning, Saturday, just before sunrise, I heard my father pull his suitcase from his closet. He was headed to Philadelphia for a fine arts conference. I had the place to myself for the weekend, right through to the next. I waited until he was gone before I got out of bed. I burned myself some toast and scanned the so-called news sites for bits about Nicole. The "New Beau" garbage was still out there, but it had fallen lower in the most-read story rankings. Why weren't the detectives all over this thing? A girl gets burned, and they're not worried the perp is going to attack again?

Before I left the apartment to log a double shift at BJ's I tapped out an email to Nicole: *Sorry I was an idiot. Hopefully I'll see you at Schmidt's.*

Perfect: non-stalkerish, leaves the door open for her to reply.

Work was busy with people lining up to save money on Halloween crap, five-pounder sacks of Three Musketeers, pumpkin lanterns big enough to pass for parade floats. I was too beat to skateboard home and grabbed the Access-A-Ride bus. Another rider gave me a dirty look. Nobody suspects you for an epileptic until you seize. I wondered if Nicole had been issued a bus pass.

When I got into the apartment, I took a few seconds to relish the fact that I wouldn't have to deal with my father for a whole week. I cranked up a playlist of alternative rock that was heavy on Pearl Jam. Nicole's suggestion of The Smiths had me digging through my father's CDs. His collection was vast: classical, jazz, a ton of rock, five albums that featured Tuvinian throat singers. I found a Smiths compilation disc and added it to my mix. They were good. "Please, Please, Please Let Me Get What I Want" ended too abruptly, though, or maybe that was the point. I cracked a Red Bull and then my backup laptop, which wasn't really a backup. From the outside it seemed to be an antiquated Dell, the same open-box special with the scratched screen my mother got for me when I was in fourth grade. But I had modified it. Actually, I'd gutted it. The transplants were Mac turbo. I built my computers piecemeal from parts picked up at swap meets and shady discount stores in the city. I always paid in cash, so my machine ID was as untraceable as my IP address, which was changing all the time. I never used Ethernet or any other type of cable-based communication, sponging off my neighbors' wireless instead. I had snaked fencing wire up and down the underside of the fire escape outside my window, hiding it in the wild ivy that covered the side of the building. This six-story antenna grabbed signals from three miles away. My computer had thousands of wireless networks to choose from. I'd programmed it to switch accounts every ninety seconds. Whether or not those networks were locked didn't matter. Cracking a laptop firewall is ridiculously easy, pure script kiddie stuff. I'd tell you how to do it to save you the trouble of downloading what you need from The Pirate Bay, but then you'd do it, and you shouldn't unless you have a good reason, and you don't. I did.

My main thing back then was outing the bullies at my school. Once in a while I'd leak stuff about phishing scams. Presently my focus was tracking down Arachnomorph before he struck again. I admit it: I was crushing on Nicole. Not that I expected she would like me back, not romantically anyway, but that was fine. Sometimes a crush is better when it's a one-way, as long as you keep quiet about it and don't freak the girl out with creepy leering or unsolicited corny texts or whatever.

I typed "www.njclarion.com." They were running what I had been leaking since the night before, the two emails Arachnomorph sent to Marks, the ones I had scooped from that poorly guarded brandywine_hollows_hs.nj.edu server. The link was near the bottom of the Local News section, the eighth click down, but I was on the boards.

The *Clarion* reported that the police were angry the emails had gotten out to the public, as this was an ongoing investigation. Whatever. Anybody who has seen two episodes of *The Shield* knows that if a perp isn't identified in the first forty-eight hours, the likelihood of nailing him is cut in half. After ninety-six hours, your chances drop to twenty-five percent, and so on. Six and a half weeks since Nicole was burned, and the police hadn't made a single arrest? That's not an ongoing investigation. The detective running this thing was a joke, whoever he was. They were holding that information back, for some reason. I'd invested most of the previous night's hours into hacking for a name, but I couldn't find anything. The police were working undercover.

I got a little more play with some of the other news sites, smaller local outfits. They were calling the attacker the Recluse, a spider that wasn't much in the size department, but it packed a sick bite. The fanging itself was so light as to be unnoticeable, but the venom was devastating. The necrosis was comparable to a third-degree burn in some cases. The recluse spider only attacked when provoked. Maybe Schmidt was right. Maybe the Recluse was a woman, jealous of Nicole, her perfection. How many women would be capable of that kind of envy? The answer to that was a question: How many women had seen Nicole's face?

The Recluse had to be keeping tabs on the press's coverage of the investigation. I scrolled through the readers' comments, mostly sympathy for Nicole, anger that the cops weren't doing enough. I searched for "bitch deserved it" and the like and of course came up empty.

I checked my suspect list: "jealous classmates" was too unfocused a target to dig into without a lot more information. I'd added Rick Kerns after he'd gone all Mr. Volta-Shock with the lightning bolt Mohawk, but I'd knocked him off the list almost immediately. The lightning bolt was too obvious if you really were the acid thrower, and I didn't see anything on Facebook that led me to believe he had a beef with Nicole. That left me with Schmidt, Mr. Sabbatini, Dave Bendix, and Mr. Sager.

Sager did have a military record, honorable discharge, literally a Boy Scout as a kid and now a troop leader. He had two kids he doted on, never missed his child support payments, worked a second job as night security to pay for his daughter's violin lessons. He met the woman he was seeing, Isabella1801, through a dating site for the divorced. She was a nurse, spotless record. Their credit card statements showed nothing suspicious. A night at a Catskills motel that billed itself as Lovers' Lane was as crazy as they got. I still couldn't imagine why he needed all that muriatic acid, but would he keep that much around if he really was the acid thrower? I kept him on the list as a weak maybe.

My eyes ticked to Dave Bendix's name. If I was going to invest precious hours into turning him inside out I would have to overcome the fact that I was—again—light on motive, seriously so. Dave was headed for big things. He was a great athlete, had perfect grades, came from money. Why would he risk all that to burn his girlfriend? On the other hand, even if he didn't throw the acid, he knew not to touch her. Biggest of all was the tiff in Schmidt's office. What did Dave Bendix ask Nicole Castro to lie about?

My phone vibrated with a text. It was in my backpack. I ripped the zipper so fast I broke it. Starbucks Cherry: **Heya, rave lame. Still wishing you were here though.**

My mind flickered to Nicole, drenched with rain, the bandage tape beginning to peel away from her cheekbone. Then back to Cherry. Raves we don't want to go to, movies we don't want to see, pushing her castaway car through the mall parking lot after we can't get it started, up to the gas station, begging the mechanic to give us a battery jump. *Bowling.* Those fungus-ridden rental shoes. Back to Nicole, the left side of her face. What was under the bandage? Or what wasn't? How much had she lost? How much was she still losing? Bursting into tears like that, on the side of the road? Where does that kind of fear drive you? She had made herself get out to the stables, to socialize, but she was constantly looking around, waiting for the next media hit, maybe even the next acid attack. How long can you keep living in fear of turning every corner, before you give up and hide out in your house for good? Back when I was doing home school, I had to force myself out of the apartment, food shopping, the Laundromat. Falling into that pit of self-imposed isolation didn't take long. I wasn't exactly out of it yet, either. Sometimes I went the whole day without speaking to anybody.

My cell vibrated again. I let it. Two calls from Starbucks Cherry two minutes apart? Now I knew how Nicole felt Thursday afternoon in CVS: like I was being stalked.

TWENTY-ONE

From Nicole's journal:

Saturday, 23 Oct—

AP chem tutor quit today. "You're not concentrating. You're wasting your father's money and my time. If you fail, I fail. That goes down as a stain on my reputation." A stained rep. Wow. How will you face the day, Lance? Possible real reason for Lance's leave-taking: The check Mom wrote him bounced—again. I checked the accounts. The one has plenty of money, the other twenty bucks, so Mom cuts Lance a check from the empty account? She's losing it. Has she slept a single night since this happened? She won't let me past the village gates. Feel like I'm six again. Have to get out of this house. I'm stir-crazy. Skype w Dad tomorrow. Possible ride with him, if Mom says cool to go out. They'll fight over it. Awesome. New painkiller hard on my stomach. Email from Jay: *Sorry I was an idiot. Hopefully I'll see you at Schmidt's.* A polite blow off. Totally sucks. Need a new plan. Emma still sick. Please don't let this be the end.

TWENTY-TWO

The rest of the weekend passed without any word back from Nicole. This didn't stop me from trying to catch her attacker. I may have been doing it as much for me as for Nicole. I couldn't accept that such a malevolent crime might go unpunished.

Mondays were slow at *The New Jersey Clarion*—I remembered that much. After my mother was killed, my father would pick me up after school and take me with him to his office. You don't get a lot of homework in fourth grade, and I didn't have anything to do except make mini snowmen with my earwax. This guy Pete Keller worked the local news desk back then. He was a good reporter, could have been better if he weren't such a boozehound. Uncle Pete, he wanted me to call him, and after a while I did. We played a lot of Nerf hoop. Every day at four o'clock Pete took me with him to the diner next door. The *Clarion* is across the street from the precinct, and Pete liked to buy the cops ending their eight-to-fours a pony beer or two. For the ones coming in for the four-to-midnight, he'd spring for takeout coffee. Sometimes the detectives dropped him a line on how an investigation was going. Uncle Pete was too old to be chasing NJPD through Newark alleys now. He'd moved into the obituary pit, my father told me, but I was betting he was still on the Friendlies list of a gold badge or two.

I stopped off at the bodega and grabbed a six of Becks. With my height and my absolutely unimpeachable fake ID I never got shut out. I didn't like to drink myself—not that I could, with my meds—but some of the computer shows required you to be twenty-one to get in. Uncle Pete was hung *over*. That didn't stop him from cracking a beer. "I'll give you twenty bucks, you go get a haircut," he said.

"Gimme twenty bucks then."

"If I had it. You keep looking at your phone."

"Three forty-five. Thought we could hit the diner."

"Little Jay-Jay Nazzaro, what happened to you? And what are you up to?"

"Who's on the Castro case?"

"The acid thing? PD doesn't want to let that information out just yet."

"So the paper says."

"They don't want the Recluse to see them coming."

"Of course not."

"Wouldn't you rather brick some Nerf?"

"I just want to find out where they are on catching this psycho."

"Yeah, huh? You stick with your geometry or wherever it is you're at in school. How damned old are you now?"

"Sixteen and calculus. Pete? Nicole Castro. She's my friend."

Not having heard from Nicole, I wasn't sure if I was telling the truth about that.

Pete sighed. "Jessica Barrone. Gold for ten years, at least. The best. If the Recluse is catchable, Barrone's the one to do it." He studied me with night-after-Heineken eyes. "You're your mother through-and-through."

"What's that supposed to mean?"

"I used to hook her up with freelance work now and then. Did you know that?"

"I don't think so." My mother had been a journalist before she had me. She and my dad were in the same grad program at Columbia.

"This was back when you were in diapers," Pete said. "A few dollars here and there to help with rent. You know, check out this guy's story, stuff she could do over the phone from home. But now and then she would come into the office for an editorial meeting. She was so damned nice to everybody. That lopsided smile, that ridiculously loud laugh. People were suspicious. 'What does she want from me?' Like that. I had known her for a while by then. 'Nothing,' I'd say. 'That's just how she is.' 'Nah, she's fake,' they'd say, but after a while people got it, that she was the real deal."

"And what was that?"

Pete shrugged. "She was just an other-centered person. C'mon, kid. Buy your old uncle Pete a cup of coffee."

"Think she'll tell us anything, Detective Barrone?"

"I'll tell her you're an aspiring reporter."

"As in I'm your intern. Smart."

"Son, you don't get to be fifty-six-looking-sixty-six, twice divorced, forty pounds overweight, and alcoholic by being an idiot."

"The truth is, the majority of cold cases go unsolved," Detective Barrone said. "Most perps if they're going to be caught are picked up in the first forty-eight hours. After that, the likelihood of an arrest is halved. After a week, you have a ten percent chance of closing the case."

"Wow, I had no idea," I said. "That sucks."

Barrone nodded, sipped her coffee. She was ridiculously pretty. I imagined perps would come to her on their knees to confess if only to be eye level with what I dreamed was her very tanned, inny navel. "I know your dad," she said.

"Wouldn't imagine cops are into fluffy stuff like art."

"You'd be surprised, but that's not how I know him. My daughter is at Pratt."

"The art college in Manhattan?"

"Brooklyn."

"You don't look old enough to have a daughter that old," I said.

Barrone nodded to Uncle Pete. "How old's this kid?"

"Sixteen."

"Kid," Barrone said, "never try to charm a cop."

"My apologies."

"And never apologize."

"Sorry."

"My daughter had to do a paper, some art history thing.

She was using one of your father's books. I recognized the name, told her I'd bump into your old man here at the diner every once in a while. She asked me to set up an interview. He was very helpful, she said. Very nice guy."

"Oh, he's the best all right. What if it's a serial?"

"How's that?"

"The Castro case. If it gets hot again. Say just for example the Recluse tried to attack Nicole a second time, the other side of her face. You know, finish what he started. Or if he decided to go after somebody else."

"Like whom?" she said.

"I don't know. Anybody. You, me—"

"Why would she go after you?"

"No, I'm just saying," I said. "Why do you think he's a she?"

"Who says I do?"

"You did."

"I'm using 'she' as a global pronoun."

"I suck at grammar."

"Tough luck for you if you want to be a journalist, worse for Pete if you're his intern."

"A second attack," I said. "Catching *her* after that. Do the odds swing back in the police's favor?"

"Yes and no. The new evidence is a warm lead, obviously, but serials are tricky. They live for the cat-and-mouse, and they think twenty steps ahead."

"Do you think you'll catch him, her, *whom*ever?"

"Not my case."

"Whose is it?"

"Can't say." Her phone beeped. She checked it and put it back down on the table. "How *is* your dad?" she said.

I shrugged. "Fine."

She nodded as she stared at me just a hair too long. Suddenly the diner was way too hot. Barrone sipped her coffee. "Drop a hello on the old man for me."

"Definitely." I pretended my phone beeped, checked it, put it on the table. The lights flickered, except they didn't. I was dizzy. "I have to pee," I said.

She smiled. "You're not under arrest . . . yet."

We all laughed. Yeah, so funny. I went to the bathroom and shut myself in. The zigzag lightning. The aura. Everything going fish-eye. I sat on the floor in case I seized. The aura didn't always mean an attack was coming. Most times it just came on its own.

It passed.

I splashed my face with water I wished were colder and hung out in there for about as long I would have needed if I really had to pee bad. When I came out, Barrone was looking at my hair. I realized only then I'd run my wet hands over it. I wondered if this was some kind of tell, a show of my guilt. Was she onto my hacking?

Pete was standing now. "Thanks for your time, Detective," he said.

"Yeah," I said. "Thank you very much."

"Pete said if I give you twenty bucks you'll get a haircut."

"Might just blow it on meth too."

"Trying to build a sheet, huh?"

"It's tough, but I'll get there."

She winked. "What'd I tell you about not trying to charm a cop?" Then to Pete: "I like this kid." Back to me: "Don't forget your phone."

"I'm an idiot."

"And don't forget to tell your old man Jessica Barrone said what's up."

I nodded and hoped my smile didn't look as fake as it felt. She was really hammering this say hi to Pop thing.

When we were outside, Pete said, "Come on back to the office. I have those Velcro tennis paddles."

"I gotta go."

"Don't be such a stranger. I mean it. You look good in a newsroom."

"Threatening to make me your intern for real?"

"Make my coffee light and sweet, shine my shoes, pick up my dry cleaning, all for not a single penny: What else could you want?"

"Plus I'd get to be around *Daddy* more."

"Hell, that mop. You really are a punk."

"Pete, do me a favor, don't tell Pop I stopped by?"

"What's up, kid?"

"Maybe I really will take you up on the internship thing."

"Your old man would love that. Only natural for a father to want his son to walk his walk. He always said he thought you'd be great at the paper business."

97

"Seriously?"

"'Jay has a special sensitivity,' he said. 'That and his natural inquisitiveness, he'd win a Pulitzer.'"

Took me a second to absorb that, a compliment from my father, albeit indirect. "Then let's let the internship be a surprise."

"Whenever you want to start, let me know. Another Nazzaro at the *Clarion*. I wonder if the paper can survive it." He slapped my back.

I dropped my board and kicked away from the diner as fast as I could. I forced myself not to look over my shoulder, but I felt them on me, Detective Barrone's eyes.

I docked my phone to my laptop and downloaded everything I'd stolen from Barrone when I put my Nokia on the diner table next to her BlackBerry and let it sip her drive. I almost puked when I saw it in her Calls Made list: my father's cell number. Call duration: twenty seconds. Long enough to leave a message, maybe something like, "Call me back. I'd like to talk with you about your son." Then again, she'd called him the previous Saturday, two days *before* she and I met. Whatever Barrone's reason for reaching out to my father, he didn't call her back.

He was horrible with messages, rarely checked his voicemail or texts. And when he was on the road he kept his phone off to save the battery, too lazy to bring his charger, which was tangled up in knots with the rest of the wires strangling his desk. Sometimes he'd forget the phone with the charger and wouldn't notice it was missing until he got home. Art critics get e-vited to shows, go, have a couple of drinks, write their bit and post it, done, no need to talk to a soul, which got me thinking that maybe being an art critic wasn't such a loser thing to do after all. He was due back from Philadelphia Saturday, and he'd get the message by then, if not before. I had at most five days to figure out why Jessica Barrone was calling my father. Did she know I had leaked those two emails the Recluse sent to Mrs. Marks?

It didn't seem possible. I had safeguard after redundant safeguard in place to prevent detection. I'd cracked an FBI server once, as a test, and gotten away with it. If the NJ police were onto me, they would have hit me right after my first hack into that server, in the middle of the night, and seized my computer—and me. I was gaining an appreciation for how Nicole felt now: hunted. I called her. She picked up with, *"Jay Nazzaro, I was just thinking about you."*

"Is that good or bad?"

"Could be either, depending on whether or not you know how to play tennis."

"As in Wii?" I said.

"As in meet me at the East Gate Tennis Club in half an hour. And Jay? Tell me you don't have Wii."

"PS3, thank you very much."

"Thank you very much, nobody plays Wii tennis anymore, or at least they don't admit to it. Not unless they're six years old and wear pigtails. Actually, you would look cute in pigtails."

TWENTY-THREE

"I want to see if I can still see the ball." She was wearing this knockout tennis suit, and here I was in my black jeans and army jacket. I was getting nasty eyes from many elderly, almost uniformly svelte model types who had gotten lost on their way to the L.L.Bean catalog shoot.

"Feed me," Nicole said.

I eyed her hands. She was wearing golf gloves. "You sure?"

"You ever swung a racquet?"

The lady at the counter had given me one that had never been picked up from lost and found. I hadn't held one since before my mother died. Mom was terrible at tennis, but she liked to take me up to the public courts and swing and miss and laugh at herself. We'd end up playing stickball. I pitched the ball to Nicole instead.

Her forehand was off. She kept grounding the ball into the net. She didn't get down on herself. She made adjustments until the ball cleared the tape. She kept checking her long bill cap, pulling it low to hide as much of the bandage as she could. Her backhand was better than her forehand. A couple of times she really drove the ball. I threw it right to her, so she wouldn't have to run to get to it, but she didn't last long anyway. She took a break every three hits or so, then every two, then after every ball.

"Your hands?" I said.

"My wind." She peeled off her gloves. Her hands weren't nearly as bad as I thought they'd be, four or five blisters on her left, a couple on her right. All had healed or were close to skinning over. We went to get a drink from the vending machines. She was pale. "Amazing how much you lose in a month. Can't wait to get back to running. Not as dizzy today, though. Skipped my meds."

"Not good," I said.

"You take yours?"

"Course not."

She put up her fist for a pound. We bumped knuckles. Her phone buzzed. It had been buzzing every few minutes. She checked it and frowned.

"Dave?" I said.

"No," she said. "You can take a deep breath now."

"Dave benches three hundred eighty-five pounds. Would you like to be caught sneaking around with his girlfriend, even if you and I are just friends, if we are in fact."

"You doubt that?"

"Maybe you just needed somebody to throw you a few balls."

"Right, because they don't have machines for that, ones that can't judge me as I'm making an idiot of myself, trying to play tennis with one eye open."

"I'm not judging you. I think you're awesome."

"Shut up. Anyway, I'm not sneaking around. I have nothing to—" Her phone buzzed again. "I'm AWOL. She won't stop calling till I pick up."

"Then pick up."

She turned off her phone and tucked it into her little tennis skirt.

"Did the doctor clear you?" I said. "Like for strenuous physical activity?"

"He said as soon as I felt up to it, I should get moving."

"*Moving* isn't *tennis*."

"Would be pretty boring if it weren't."

"But what if the ball hit you?" I said.

"So? It happens."

"In the face, I meant."

"What am I supposed to do, be a statue for the rest of my life? Never sweat again? Hungry?"

I grunted.

"This means 'Man want food,' one grunt yes, two grunt no?"

"You speak Cro-Magnon?" I said.

"To imply the Cro-Magnon were lug heads is wrong. They exhibited a cranial capacity approximately sixteen hundred cubic centimeters larger than modern-day humans."

"So I'm not a Cro-Magnon, you're saying, but merely a lug head."

"Grunt once for Taco Bell, twice for Domino's."

"At least you didn't say Sbarro's."

"Crap."

"Tell me about it."

"No, I mean Monday is roadwork," Nicole said, going tip-toe to look over my shoulder. "They weren't supposed to be here."

"Nic!" This girl from the tennis team, Samantha Rees, practically tackled Nicole into the Coke machine. "Did you get the Care Bears package?"

"Thank you, Sam. It was adorable. I meant to text you back."

"But you never do. How are we supposed to get in touch with you?"

"I know. I'm sorry. I'll try to be better."

"The gate guard wouldn't let us visit you the other day. Seriously nasty dude."

"It wasn't him. I think my mom was trying to keep the house quiet."

"Nic, we love you. We want to be here for you. When are you coming back?"

"This is Jay," Nicole said.

"Oh yeah," Sam said. "I remember you." She shook my hand a little too eagerly, and I knew that she was replaying it: my pep rally swim. "I mean, from the other day," she said. "The caf? I was at the table two behind you and one to the right?"

"Oh right," I said, pretending I remembered the exact location of all five hundred students in the cafeteria.

"He was eating alone," she said to Nicole. "For the record? I totally respect that."

More of the team rolled up in their running gear, a fog of wet red rain suits. They were all over Nicole with hugs. Nicole put up a happy front for a second or so, until her hand went to her hip to grab her phone. "Mom, can you hang on a sec?" She apologized that she had to take the call. The other girls headed off to the locker room with promises they would keep calling her until she called them back. "Welcome back, Jay," that girl Sam said. "Eat with us next time."

"Definitely," I said, knowing I never would.

This one girl, Marisol Wood, a sophomore who was by Facebook consensus the prettiest girl in her class, hung back. She was trying not to cry. "Nic, when you're done with the phone, could I talk to you for a sec?"

Seeing the girl was upset, Nicole became upset. She led the girl to the far side of the vending machines. Without bothering to tell her mother she would call her back, Nicole handed me her phone. She'd done it absentmindedly, her focus on Marisol.

I already knew her phone was off. She hadn't turned it back on after shutting it down a few minutes earlier. Nicole Castro had faked an incoming call to ditch the girls that were crowding around her. I never would have pegged her the type to be sneaky like that. She hugged Marisol, rubbing her back, smiling as she whispered into Marisol's ear. Marisol went from sobbing to laughing.

I went to the pro shop and marveled at how much money a person could blow on tennis crap. This was a long way from the hand-me-down Slazenger and a dented three-can of half-bald Penns. A limited edition faux snakeskin racquet cover for $600? Really? And why does sticking an alligator on a shirt raise the price eighty-five bucks? Tennis and reptiles: I see the connection. Nicole found me pricing out energy bars. "What exactly is partially hydrolyzed caseinate, and why would you put it in food?" I said.

"I actually know what that is, for some ridiculous reason," she said.

"The reason is you have a ridiculously high IQ. What world-ending problem did our friend back there drop on you? Her date to the dance stood her up?"

"Her parents are splitting up. They'd been trying to reconcile, but her dad left for good the other day, she's pretty sure. She wanted some advice."

"On what?"

"How not to hate her father." Then Nicole told me about *her* parents' nasty breakup. "I'm not taking sides. My father and I are staying close. Trying to. He lives downtown now, a block from his office. He wants to be around for me, but Mom gets weird when he's in the house, just really sad for the old days, I think, so we try to minimize when he comes over and meet elsewhere instead. Mostly we Skype, two sometimes three hours a week."

"Way more face time than most parents give their kids," I said. "At least that's how it shakes out in my house."

"You can tell me, you know? Your story. I can keep a secret better than anybody," she said.

"Not sure I can trust you."

"*Really* now?"

"Pretty sly there, pretending your mother called to avoid Sam and them."

"You should talk, with your iPod earbuds that lead to nowhere." She looked back over her shoulder, to where Marisol was punching a text into her phone. "We're all acting, right? Faking our way through." Her mood darkened, and suddenly. "Part of me wanted to shake her, hard, and say, 'Hey, I know things suck for you right now, but can you find somebody else's shoulder to cry on? My plate is kind of full at the moment,' as in, 'Do you not see this bandage on my face?'" Her face flushed, and then she gulped, and the red faded from her skin. Now she seemed exhausted. "I'm sorry," she said.

"No, I get it," I said.

"Do you really, though?"

"Yeah. I do. Really." I was actually relieved to see her angry. Before that, her seeming acceptance of her fate wasn't natural.

We were rounding a corner toward the parking lot when Chrissie Vratos bounced up to Nicole with a bump that was almost hard enough to be a shove. "You think it's funny, Nic?"

"What is your problem?"

"Like you didn't sic them on me?"

"Who?"

"Give me a break. The detectives? Yeah, they called me in for questioning. They told me they asked you who you thought might have done it, and that you gave them a list, and I was right there, on top."

"I didn't even mention you. I never even gave them a list."

"Right. They had that video, you and me scrimmaging, when you made that ridiculously shallow lob and I caught you at the net."

"You mean the one where you drove the ball at my head?" Nicole said.

"You told them about that thing with the squirt bottle. How could you do this to me? I was just joking around."

"I have no idea what you're talking about. What squirt bottle?"

Sam pushed between Chrissie and Nicole. Sam said, "The time Diana Poisson beat her and she squirted her water bottle into Diana's face." She grabbed Chrissie's sweatshirt hood and tugged her toward the locker room. "Nic wasn't even there that day, idiot," Sam said to Chrissie. Marisol and some of the other girls pushed Chrissie toward the door.

"I told the detectives I had a hunch about who might have burned you," Chrissie said. "I told them I thought you might have done it to yourself."

I said what I'm sure everybody was thinking: "Why would she ruin herself?"

Chrissie smiled. "Because, Spaceman, as you'll soon find out, chica is a psycho."

Sam jerked on Chrissie's hood and practically dragged her down the hall.

Nicole called out, "What did the detectives say when you said that I, you know."

"Burned yourself?" Chrissie said. "Nothing. They didn't look surprised at all. As if they'd been thinking it all along."

By the time we got out of the club it was almost 6:30, an hour past sunset, not that you could have seen it that day with the rain. The sky was gunmetal gray and swirling.

"I think Sam was crushing on you," Nicole said.

"Sure she was."

"You could have your pick of those girls."

"Do you think Chrissie could have done it? Attacked you, I mean. Maybe she was just sick and tired of being number two to you all the time?"

"No," Nicole said. "It wasn't Chrissie. I'm sure."

"How?" I said.

Her phone buzzed. She checked it. "David."

Something flashed from the corner of the parking lot, then another flash, stinging white light. I recognized the car: Shane Puglisi's battered old Honda. I headed for it, but he peeled out before I even got close.

No way I wasn't in that shot. Dave Bendix was about to see me hanging with Nicole. Puglisi would make me seem to be doing more than walking Nicole to her car.

Nicole was sullen. "I wasn't followed. I'm positive. How do they find me?"

"Seriously, you're good with secrets?"

"Promise."

I grabbed her phone and popped the back off of it with my Swiss Army knife.

"Okay, what are you doing?" she said.

"Tweaking your bandwidth, governor."

"You're *clipping* him."

"Now I'm disabling your GPS."

"I have it turned off."

"You *think* you have it turned off. It's only off when the phone is off, and even then the CIA is rumored to have a satellite that scans quiet drives for machine numbers. I don't think this will keep the tabloids off you entirely, but it'll be harder for them. Now you're like me: invisible."

"I wish. The boy reconfigures my phone in a parking lot. Scary."

"That was messed up, what Chrissie said."

"I'm letting it in one ear and out the other."

A black Mercedes pulled up. Nicole relaxed when she saw who was inside, a dour-looking woman in her fifties. "Thought you were Mom for a sec," Nicole said.

"She called the club," the woman said. "They said you were here. Let's go, Nicoletta. You follow me. Or better yet, I'll follow you."

"I have to drive Jay home. Jay, sorry, this is Sylvia. Sylvia, Jay."

The woman gave me mean eyes and half a grunt. Then, to Nicole: "*Now*, Nicole. Dinner is on the table, and then you have to talk to the doctor."

"I'll grab the bus," I said. "Have to go to the Apple Store anyway." I walked her to her car.

"My turn to come clean," she said. "Back inside, when you said to Chrissie, 'Why would she ruin herself?' The word *ruin*? It hurt."

"I didn't mean it that way. I meant like ruin your life. I'm making this worse."

"I know what you meant." She gave me a quick hug and got into her car and drove away. Sylvia gave me a glare before following after Nicole. I wondered if Nicole was even allowed to drive now that one of her eyes was ruined—*compromised*, rather.

I felt somewhere between uneasy and frightened. That Nicole had ruled out Chrissie so easily was, frankly, odd. In fact, she seemed not to be interested at all in talking about who the attacker might have been. Was this her way of coping, total denial? Was she afraid to find out who had burned her? A chilling thought flashed my mind and took root before I could suppress it: Did she know who the attacker was, and she was protecting him?

By the time I got home, Shane Puglisi's shot was on the 'net with more of that Burned Beauty's Beau garbage for a headline. Somebody's headlights had saved me, casting me in silhouette. Not that this mattered. The minute Sam and the rest of the team rolled into the East Side Tennis Club, Dave Bendix was sure to have gotten word I was hanging courtside with his girlfriend. If he confronted me, I'd simply tell him the truth: Nothing was going on. Nicole and I were friends, like she said, end of story. She had my back, I had hers. I revved up my laptops and started digging, not even close to knowing just how deep into darkness I would have to go to find out who burned Nicole Castro.

TWENTY-FOUR

From Nicole's journal:

Tuesday, 26 October—

Nye: "How do you feel about what Chrissie said?"

Me: "How would you feel if somebody accused you of burning yourself?"

Nye: "Have you ever wanted to hurt yourself?"

Me: "Have I ever wanted to hurt myself? No. Never. What possible motivation would I have? Do you really think I did this to myself?"

Nye sits there, reptilian in his stillness and as barren of warmth as the surface of the Moon, staring at me.

Nye: "You're under a remarkable amount of pressure. You're the go-to person for your peers. You're deeply empathic. You assume a great deal of others' pain and, by your own admission, internalize it. It would be understandable if you were feeling a need to let that pain bubble to the surface. Add to that your parents' separation—"

Me: "Dr. *Nye.* I. Did not. Burn myself."

Nye: "I believe you. My question was merely in regard

to any inclination you might or might not have to injure yourself. If you ever do feel such an impulse—"

Me: "I don't."

He blinks. I think this is the first time I've ever seen him blink. I excuse myself to the bathroom to catch my breath.

Skype session w Dad weird. He keeps asking me about David. I can't bring myself to tell him about David's asking me to lie for him. Three times now, he has asked. Begged. I wanted to scream, "Nobody thinks you did it, Dave. You're being paranoid. You have no motive. Relax."

Lying on my bed, picking at a scab. I'm a drone, painkiller makes the blankets feel too heavy, except I'm not under the blankets. How many days of rain have we had? Everything is slowing down. Out the bay window the wind bends the trees down, down, the branches creaking without relief, a deepening growl in the air. The rain isn't falling. It's floating, but not in a benign way. I see individual drops. They're bigger than I'd imagined, rounder, fine-milled buckshot.

All I used to think about was the future. It was bright, shiny. But after the burn, thinking about the future feels wrong in some way, an abstract sin. Is it bad to dream of myself as I was before? To dream I'm hanging with Jay and Emma and maybe Marisol and Sam, before I was The Girl Who Had Acid Thrown in Her Face; we're all at the beach, playing volleyball, glittering waves, the faint taste of salt and smiling and no sunburn, no bandages, no being stuck for the rest of my life in my room, my bathroom, staring at It?

Staring at the donor site this past Saturday as the surgeon removes the stitches. Me: "Why are they purple?"

Doc shrugs as he tugs the stitches from my hip: "Why not?"

Mom glares at him.

Doc: "How's the case going? Police any closer to finding out who did it to her?"

Mom slaps the examination table. "Could you not be so cavalier? You're not rehashing the latest *CSI* episode at the watercooler. She's right here in front of you. She's right *here.* You will acknowledge my daughter's presence, Doctor. Or else we'll just have to get another surgeon. There are plenty of you out there, but there's only one Nicole. And you will respect her. Are you clear on that?"

He takes a moment to let Mom's words bleed into him. He studies me, then he really looks at me. "Nicole, I'm honored to be working on you. Your bravery inspires me. It truly does. I'm sorry, I meant I'm grateful to be working *with* you."

Mom nods and wipes a tear from her cheek and tries to say thank you but the words are deep in her throat and come in a weak whisper.

The doctor doesn't need to be grateful. How could one be grateful for having to deal with the Thing that lives on the left side of my face? All of the pretending. It's dissolving me. Relying on her feels too easy but so good. Dead without her. Deadened without her smile. *I'm so grateful.* She winks at me. I try to wink back. She nods and mouths "I love you."

Emma on the mend. Nothing else matters.

TWENTY-FIVE

From the notes of Dr. Julian Nye, Tues 10-26:

Nancy, please transcribe and email the following to Jane Schmidt, Brandywine Hollows High School. Dear Dr. Schmidt, in my session with Nicole Castro tonight, I learned that you are concerned she is overly reliant on her mother. You and I spoke about this prior to your coming on in Nicole's treatment. As lead therapist in Ms. Castro's rehabilitation, I ask that you refrain from sabotaging my therapy plan. Your job is a simple one: apprise Nicole's teachers of her special needs. Sincerely, Julian Nye, MD, PsyD

Dr. Nye, Nicole needs to be getting out and about, not *hiding* out in her house. In my one conversation with her father, he seemed to be of the same mind. You're doing the Castros a disservice, particularly Mrs. Castro, who is worrying after her daughter 24-7, in prescribing this under siege, batten down the hatches mentality.

Dr. Schmidt, I am convinced that the patient exhibits a latent interest in self-harm, even if she herself is unaware of her inclination at this time. Until we figure out what this is and how it might manifest, if it hasn't already, I do think it's appropriate that the Castros "batten down the hatches," as you so delicately put it. God help you if, while she's following your "get out and about" admonition, that girl is attacked again.

TWENTY-SIX

Tuesday night I set out to eliminate the weak maybes from my suspect list, beginning with Mr. Sabbatini, except I couldn't eliminate him. He went from weak maybe to what's going on here after I cracked his Gmail Sent folder.

> JS contacted me. I have located what you need.
> Pick it up Wednesday during my office hours,
> between 3 and 4pm. Be discreet. If anyone finds
> out about this, considerable trouble will follow
> for BOTH of us, I am sure I do not have to tell you.
> Please do not be late, as I must leave promptly at
> 4. By the way, I am not pleased about this. I think
> it puts you at an unfair advantage.

JS was Jane Schmidt. The intended message recipient was Nicole.

I triple-checked my online anonymity and took a shot at worming my way into Detective Jessica Barrone's laptop. I had to see where she was on Sabbatini, if anywhere. At this point I was back to feeling fairly certain Barrone wasn't onto my hacking. Again, she would have shown up at the apartment door by now with a search warrant if she knew about it. I was less convinced that she didn't have a car of plainclothes officers tailing Nicole. Maybe they caught me following her into CVS? Why else would she have called my father? While I was poking at Barrone's drive, her firewall was re-upping with new patches, and I had to get out of there.

I had to overcome my want to trust Nicole blindly. I texted her, **Want to hang tomorrow?**

Nicole got back to me with, **Sounds cool. When where?**

4pm BHHS?

4 @ BHHS out front. Jay?

Yes?

'night.

Wednesday afternoon I was in the media center, reading my favorite book, *The Invisible Man,* or pretending to. Really I was looking out the window. I'd positioned myself in the front west corner, where I had a view of the parking lot. The buses and most of the cars were gone by 3:15. Nicole pulled into the lot at 3:38, when everybody was at practice or in chess club or whatever and she would have the lowest chance of running into anybody. She pulled right up to the front entrance and did her usual 360-degree scan for that idiot photographer Puglisi, or maybe she was looking out for the Recluse. Except that if Sabbatini or Schmidt was the Recluse, and Nicole knew this, then she was faking fear. Was she just acting scared, putting on a show in case Detective Barrone had eyes on her? Was I any better, spying on her from the library window?

I checked the lot for a tail. A couple of cars could have been unmarked police vehicles, a Ford sedan, a Chevy cruiser, but they were empty. I checked the woods for telephoto lens flare and didn't see any.

Nicole was wearing a ball cap with the bill pulled low. She adjusted her sunglasses, flipped up her collar, put her head down and marched into the building.

I hustled out of the media center and put myself out in front of the main entrance doors to sneak a peek down the corridor. Sabbatini's office was at the end of the very long hall, but this vantage point was better than none. I didn't want to get caught just hanging out in front of the building, staring through the door glass, so I pulled out my skateboard and knife pliers and pretended to tighten my wheel truck.

"Thought you would've had that fixed by now," Mr. Sager said, leaning out from behind the school's welcome sign. He had steel wool in his heavily gloved hand. He dipped it into that same bucket I'd kicked a few days earlier. He scrubbed a graffiti tag somebody had scribbled onto the sign with indelible marker. "I saw you," he said. "In the library window. Scanning the lot. Do you really think he's that stupid to attack her again, what with everybody on guard?" He slopped the acid onto the graffiti. The marker faded as Sager scrubbed it. The paint was coming off the sign too.

"Nail polish remover," I said.

"Say again?" Sager said.

"The indelible marker. It takes it right off, no scrubbing, just a wipe, without messing up the paint underneath. In other words, you don't need the muriatic acid."

Sager stopped scrubbing. He stared at me. "Except I'd need a whole lot of nail polish remover now, wouldn't I?" He gestured to the side of the building with his chin. I leaned around the corner to see it. The entire three-story brick wall was bombed with graffiti, taunts from our rivals, the Blue Devils.

I felt like a jerk, but at least I could cross Mr. Sager off my suspect list. He would need every can of muriatic acid he had in his shop to scrub that paint out of the brick. He shook his head and then got back to work.

A jacked-up Highlander rolled down the entrance ramp. One of the dudes leaning out the windows was John Kerns, kid brother of Rick, the Volta-Shock billboard I flipped freshman year. John's locker was a few down from mine. He wasn't pumped up like his brother. He was actually kind of wimpy. But he was happy to bully you verbally. "Need a little help with your ride there, Spaceman?"

"Now, now, let's be nice," this other dude said. "His name's *Sbarro*."

"Tell your mommy I'll have my eggs over easy tomorrow morning," I said.

"Dude, you're like a veritable king of comedy, you know that? Hey, do you wear diapers?" The doors opened, and they started to get out of the car.

"I was having a conversation with my friend here," Mr. Sager said, stepping toward the Highlander. "And you all interrupted."

That got an eye roll from Kerns's little brother. The Highlander peeled out with one of the kids throwing half a donut at my skateboard and "Sweet wheels, Spaceman." Sager waited till they were gone. He headed into the school without looking at me.

"Sir?" I said. "Thanks."

"What'd I tell you about calling me sir?" The rain was coming down harder. "Watch yourself, Nazzaro. You really want to find what you're looking for?"

A few minutes later Nicole left Sabbatini's office with a bulky plastic bag tucked under her arm. I stepped back from the glass door, hopped my skateboard and rode a curb rail in the vicinity of her car. "Hey."

"Hey. Waiting long?" she said.

"Nah." I kicked my board into a spin like the dude in Tony Hawk: Shred. I would have looked super-slick if I'd caught it with my hand instead of my chin. "So, that hurt."

"Ooh. Icepack?" Nicole opened the car door and held up a stuffed CVS bag.

The Highlander was ripping up the road again, coming from the opposite direction. John Kerns and his crew slowed to a roll when they saw me talking with Nicole. Kerns had his phone out, clip in progress.

"Get in," Nicole said, getting behind the wheel.

I'd checked the schedule, and the wrestling team was away on a meet two towns over, where Dave Bendix was likely grinding somebody through the mats into the floorboards. The meet would end in less than an hour. Dave would check his phone and find the link to the video mini-Kerns was recording. "Yeah, I better not," I said, indicating the High-lander with a nod. "I don't want Dave to get the wrong idea."

"Right, so you don't need to worry about that. David and I are over."

"Sorry to hear that."

"I promised my mother I'd be gone for forty minutes max, and if I'm late, she'll freak and call the cops and put out an APB for me."

I got into Nicole Castro's car, eyeing the Highlander. It sped out of the lot.

"Mind holding this?" She handed me the Sabbatini pack-age. Shaped like an Amazon box a foot wide and half as thick, it weighed about as much as a gallon of battery acid packed in on all sides by bricks of C-4 explosive. "When?" I said, my eyes on the package.

"When what?"

"When did you break up with Dave?"

"He broke up with me."

"Are you serious? Why?"

"I saw you, Jay." She geared the car. "At the media center window before. Watching me as I drove in."

"So?"

"You wanted to meet at four."

"Right."

"Why not right when school ended?"

"Nicole, relax, I wanted to bang out my homework before we hung out." This was true, too. I honestly spent about ten minutes on my calculus work sheet.

She looked at me over her glasses. "I have to ask you something."

"This is going to hurt, isn't it?"

"Are you a truthful person?"

I frowned. "Mostly."

"Okay, that's the right answer."

"Stop."

"Hitting too close to the bone, am I?"

"No, I mean *stop*." I reached between the seats and jerked up the handbrake, but it only slowed the car when we needed to have stopped dead fifty feet back.

"Oh my god—" Nicole hit the brakes and the car fishtailed as a deer flew across the road. Another half second, and we would have clipped it. It was a doe, so no antlers, but she was big, and she would have totaled the car, rolling right up the windshield and into us. Nicole pulled over. "How'd you see that?" she said.

"In my peripheral . . . Yeah."

"It's not true, you know? What they say about the eyes. You lose one, the vision migrates to the other? At least it hasn't happened yet."

The sunglasses weren't helping her either. Sky darkened by thunderclouds, hundred-foot pines close to the road, heavy evergreen. Driving in the near dark with one eye? That sucks, if it's even legal. "I meant to ask you if you were allowed to drive."

"I had to take a vision test. I now have *special accommo-*

dations." She showed me her temporary license. In big black letters it said VISION IMPAIRED. "The real card is supposed to come in two weeks. The woman said it's bright green with a red stripe."

"Christmas all year round," I said. Total idiot.

"Of course I'm not supposed to be driving unsupervised anyway."

I knew that much. You had to be seventeen to drive without an adult in the car, but nobody followed that rule. You couldn't. In Brandywine, if you didn't drive, you were stuck with me, on the bus. "I'd offer to drive, but my only experience is Grand Theft: San Andreas."

"And the forklift."

"Tops out at five miles an hour. It's a good ride, though. Come on down to work one day, we'll take her out for a spin in the appliances aisle, blades high, ram a few refrigerators, get the adrenaline going before start of shift."

She scanned the woods. "The doe."

I checked the woods, following Nicole's line of sight. The doe was grazing with her fawn. "She's fine," I said. "Not even close."

Nicole broke down. She grabbed my hand. We sat there like that. A truck whipped past. The Subaru shook. She took her hand back. "Sorry." She put the car into drive.

The package had been thrown to the floor when she stopped short. I picked it up, pretending to accidentally spill it. No wonder I'd thought it was shaped like an Amazon box:

It was an Amazon box. It definitely weighed between twenty-five and thirty pounds.

"Death by chemistry," Nicole said. "Check it out."

I opened the box—slowly. *Advanced Placement Chemistry, a Teacher's Guide*, last year's.

I could scratch Sabbatini and Schmidt off my list. Add them to the Sager scratch-out and I'd knocked off three suspects in one day. Not bad. I was feeling relieved until I remembered I still had no idea who was after Nicole. The only specific people left on my list were Kerns and Dave, and both continued to be nowhere in terms of motive.

Nicole tapped the teacher's guide. "How do you print a book twenty-eight hundred pages long? Murderers. How many trees did it take to make that?"

"Um, like, not even one. Just a guess."

"At least break it up into chunks. No book should be longer than two hundred and fifty pages, ever. I'm supposed to lug that thing around?"

"Beats going to the gym," I said. "They tell you to wipe the sweat off the machines with your towel, but all that does is spread the bacteria around. Even those sani-wipe things are only marginally effective. And then if you forget your flip-flops, you have to wear plastic bags on your feet. You have no idea what I'm talking about."

"I can only assume you mean for the showers."

"You assume correctly."

"Do we have a little OCD working there?"

"A tinge." I checked out the book. The student version had

the answers in the back, but this one had them written out step-by-step. "Firing your chem tutor?"

"Total perv. Dude was always looking down my shirt. Besides, he quit."

"You bummed him out because you're smarter than he is. Hate when that happens."

"He's post-doc at Columbia. Nobody's smarter than he is. I used to like chemistry. This is good, being in the car with you. Moving. Windows down. I don't even mind the rain. I can breathe. Before, in the hall, I was heading for the doors, somebody taps my shoulder, and I did a face plant with my backpack covering my head."

"Why do people find that shit funny?"

"No, she just wanted to tell me she was sorry about what happened. That girl in Dr. Schmidt's the other day, with the cat's ears hairdo? I forget her name."

"Angela Sammick."

"She wanted to apologize. For staring at me, you know?"

"More like gawking."

"She wasn't the first, believe me."

"Hey, you and Dave, what were you guys fighting about that day?"

She frowned.

My phone vibrated. Starbucks Cherry, text: **Congratulations, you've won our deal of the week. Just for YOU, Jay Nazzaro, we're holding a leftover day-old pistachio muffin. Please stop by to claim your prize.**

Now I frowned.

"Girlfriend trouble?" Nicole said.

"Just plain old trouble trouble. Where are we headed, by the way?"

"To awesomeness. Trust me. She'll knock you out."

"Emma?" I said.

"Emma."

TWENTY-SEVEN

The elevator doors opened. She flinched and checked to be sure the car was empty. We got in. "This was the best thing to come out of the pageant deal," she said. "Getting hooked up with volunteering here. My mom came with me that first day, just to check it out, and now she's here every afternoon. She comes to laugh."

"*Laugh?*" I could think of few things sadder than kids with cancer.

"You'll see."

The elevator made a bouncy stop on the second floor. The doors opened. Nicole held her breath. Nobody got on the elevator. The doors closed. The elevator rumbled upward.

"Hey, the pageant thing?" I said. "I don't know. You don't seem the type."

"My mother asked me to try out. She was freaked that Dad would play hardball in the divorce settlement. She had me apply for every scholarship out there. My grandmother made my mom do it, and that was the way she got the money to go to Sarah Lawrence. Everybody loves to hate the girls because they're pretty, but they're also really smart and motivated to

129

do great things, teach, go into politics, philanthropy. They're big-hearted. We were sisters."

"He's being a dick about money, your father?"

She shook her head. "He's the best. He never said anything about the pageant stuff, but I could tell he was bummed about it. He's the quiet type. Low-key, conservative, don't draw attention to yourself. He definitely has an eye for the ladies, though. Wait'll you meet my mom."

"Seriously?"

"Calm down, boy."

"I saw her on the 'net, but only partially. That news clip. The reward money offer."

We stopped at the sixth floor. The doors opened. A tall dude in a mechanic's jumper was fixing a light. He did a double take on Nicole. She tensed and turned to hide her face. The doors closed. "Bet your dad has an eye for the ladies too," she said.

Six years after my mother's death, and my father was nowhere near getting over her. "Why do you say that?"

"Because you're gorgeous. Therefore your mother must be gorgeous."

"You're insane."

"You don't like to talk about them, your parents. No response?"

I shrugged. "How many more floors?" I said.

"This one." The elevator doors opened, and Nicole was a new person, totally relaxed. She knew all the nurses' names as she led me down the hall. Anthropomorphized animals danced on the walls. A party clown with a therapy dog headed into a room. A boy, maybe six, hugged Nicole. His head was bandaged. "Mom was worried," he said. "She kept saying she hoped you weren't in a car accident."

"We hit a little traffic," Nicole said.

"And you couldn't call to tell her that?"

"You sound like Mom."

The kid grabbed my hands and used me as a swing. "We all call Nic's mom Mom," he said. Then, "Dude, wait!" He ditched us for the therapy dog. His sneakers lit up each time his heels hit the floor.

We turned into a room where a woman was sitting with a bunch of kids around a short table, teaching them to finger paint. Nicole would look almost exactly like her in twenty-five years. "I thought you were in an accident," she said.

"Traffic."

"And you couldn't call to tell me that?" Nicole wasn't kidding. Mrs. Castro may even have been as pretty as her daughter, but not as beautiful. She smiled warmly. "So *this* is Jay, bearer of broken umbrellas." She balled her hands so she wouldn't get paint on my back as she hugged me tightly. I was a little startled. She said to Nicole, "She's waiting for you."

Emma was in bed, asleep. She was maybe ten or so. A vaporizer puffed white smoke.

"Em?" Nicole tickled the girl's foot.

An oxygen cannula tied into her nose. She was pale with

dark circles under her eyes. I didn't see any signs that she was breathing.

"Oh my god," Nicole said. She shook the girl. "Em? Em!"

The girl grabbed Nicole and tickled her.

"*Not* funny, miss," Nicole said. "This is my friend Jay. Jay, this is my totally obnoxious friend Emma."

"Yo," Emma said. She gave me a high pound with a shaky fist. Then to Nicole: "He *is* a hottie." Back to me: "So how does that make you feel, that my ridiculously beautiful girl here thinks you're hot?"

"My experience is that girls often confuse hot with tall."

Emma grabbed my hand. Hers was tiny in mine and trembling and a little blue. "I like him, Nic. Like the vampire in the movie, the good one. I love vampires."

"We all do," I said.

"I like to scare myself stupid."

"Me too."

"Mom's gonna use the umbrella in one of her sculptures." She winked at me.

"How old are you?" I said.

She made her voice deep with a British accent: "Veddy, veddy *old*."

"Stop flirting for five seconds and tell us what trouble you were up to today," Nicole said.

"Wrote a poem for you. The assignment was: Find a small treasure and offer a gratitude for living in a free country. I wrote it this morning, before the rain." Emma flipped up her laptop screen. "'I look out my perfectly crooked window blinds and see freedom of an immaculate sort. The tops of the pines tickle into a wilderness of blue and white, and all I need now is red. And what do you know, I have it here, this heart-shaped Valentine's box Kevin Connelly gave me but last year. Sweet candy is this America.'"

Nicole kissed the girl's forehead and turned to me. "See?" she said. Then to Emma: "You were eating raspberry sherbet."

"That mind-reading thing? Annoying."

"It's all over your face." Nicole took Emma to the bathroom.

"I have your father's book," Mrs. Castro said.

"You and like three other people," I said.

"It was a best seller, at least in art history circles."

"Must've been before I was born."

"It was, actually. It's a definitive text, you know? I met him once."

"Seriously?"

"Briefly. At a show he was covering. We didn't get a chance to speak. My husband saw to that." Her eyes were glazing over. "He and your father had words."

"My father hit on you?"

"No, no, of course not. They were arguing about one of the paintings. Rafael can be a bit insecure, and maybe your dad had a little too much wine, and . . . You know what, Jay? It was a long, long time ago. I shouldn't have brought it up. Really, sweetheart, it was nothing more than a little tiff. Don't mention this to Nicole, all right? She gets mad at me when I talk about her father behind his back, and she's right to do so. Secret kept?"

"I'll let my father know you liked the book."

She smiled, but sadly. She nodded toward the bathroom. Nicole had left the door open. She and Emma were in a tickle fight at the sink. Nicole had an amazingly cool laugh, loud, nothing fake about it.

"Isn't it just awful?" Mrs. Castro said. "She was so beautiful."

TWENTY-EIGHT

"Because I don't want you driving at this hour," Mrs. Castro said. We were crossing the atrium that led to the parking lot. "It's not you, Nicole—"

"It's the other people on the road, I know, I know."

"With the glare?" Mrs. Castro said. "It's impossible for *anybody* to see."

"Then maybe you shouldn't drive either," Nicole said.

"You're not supposed to be driving without an adult in the car anyway, especially after dark."

"Everybody—"

"You're not everybody. Are we really fighting about this?"

"What about the car?" Nicole said.

"I'll come back later with Sylvia. Jay, we'll drive you home."

"That's okay, it's the exact opposite direction."

"What's with you two? Here's how it works: Mom says, you do, everybody's life is so much easier, see? We'll grab a bite at the diner on the way." She stroked my hair. "I love his hair," she said to Nicole. "So soft."

"I know. I hate him. He doesn't even put anything in it."

"I want to braid it."

"Just one long one, though," Nicole said. "Right down the back."

"Yes, Snoop braids would be too much."

"Listen to you, getting all Snoop," Nicole said.

"Hello, Snoop is my age. Drop it like it's *hawt,* drop it like it like it's *hawt.*"

"Oh my god, Mom, stop!"

I was trying to remember when Nicole had touched my hair. Must have been while I was recovering from the seizure at the stables.

"Call your mother, Jay," Mrs. Castro said. "Let her know you're eating with us."

I didn't want to get into the whole thing about my mom or the fact that my dad was gone for the week. I pulled my phone and texted **Grabbing dinner w a friend** and sent it to my Gmail. I smiled at Mrs. Castro. She put her arm around me and said, "Thanks." She was walking between Nicole and me, her arms over our backs. "Put your arm over my shoulder," she said. "Now shorten your stride."

"Just do it," Nicole said. "Now look." She nodded at our feet. The three of us were walking in step.

"I don't get it," I said, but they both laughed. And then they stopped laughing when we came to the exit. They scanned the parking lot, and then we hurried to Mrs. Castro's Mercedes.

Mrs. Castro paid the check, and then she and Nicole headed for the bathroom. Just as I was about to step outside, I saw

Shane Puglisi's battered old Honda in the back of the parking lot. The car was empty. I scanned the lot for Puglisi but didn't see him. I doubled back through the diner to the fire exit and crossed the alarm wires to fry the circuit. I'd forgotten my pocketknife, but out back I found an old-fashioned glass soda bottle in a recycle rack. I wrapped it in wet cardboard I pulled from the Dumpster. I cracked the bottle until the neck was a short sharp point. I tucked it point up under the right front wheel of Puglisi's Honda with the point between the tire seams. If I'd had more time, I would have just let the air out of the tire. On the way back in, I told a waitress the fire alarm door was broken. "How do you know?" she said.

"I went through it, and the alarm didn't go off."

Mrs. Castro and Nicole were waiting for me by the register. They were laughing and talking in low voices until they saw me, and then they stopped talking but kept laughing.

"He's outside," I said. "The photographer dude."

Now they stopped laughing. They followed me out the back way. Two waitresses were checking out the door. The one I'd talked to said to the other, "See?"

Puglisi was out front, his eyes on the entrance. He didn't see us coming around the side of the building as we headed for Mrs. Castro's Mercedes.

"Nicole!" somebody behind us said. We spun into the camera flash. It was Puglisi's partner Meyers, the dude who acted like he was trying to pick up Nicole in CVS. We hurried for the car, bunching around Nicole.

"Show it to us, Nicole," a third dude yelled from Nicole's

blind side, jumping up from between two parked cars with another camera flash.

Puglisi was in on it now too. The three of them circled us and clicked away. Mrs. Castro reached into her bag and pulled what appeared to be a foot-long club. She swung it, and it extended into a reflective silver umbrella. We clustered behind it as we pushed forward for the Mercedes.

"How bad is the burn, Nicole?"

"What about the eye? Did they have to take it out?"

They were right on top of us but careful not to touch us, because, I would find out later, any physical contact was considered assault.

Puglisi's telephoto lens was in Nicole's face as Mrs. Castro opened the car door and pushed Nicole into the back. "What's your boyfriend's name?" Puglisi said.

"I'm not her boyfriend, *Shane*. I'm her bodyguard."

The three of them laughed at that.

"How are things down at 14-98 34th Avenue?" I said. That was Puglisi's address.

"Things at 14-98 are fabulous." He kept right on clicking away.

I grabbed his camera and smashed it on the pavement.

"Seriously, dude?" Puglisi said. "Fuck you." He pulled another camera from his pocket. The flashes were messing with me. I was dizzy.

"Get into the car, Jay," Mrs. Castro said.

"Jay, is it?" Puglisi said. One of his crew, the CVS dude, ran for Puglisi's Honda.

We were pulling out of the lot when Mrs. Castro said, "Call the police, Jay. Tell them we're being followed."

"I don't think we have to worry about that." I looked back toward the diner. The three of them were around the car, in the middle of the lot, checking out the flat tire. Puglisi laughed and waved to me, his hand going from five fingers to one.

I turned to Nicole with a smile. She was shaking.

"You can just drop me here," I said.

"Absolutely not," Mrs. Castro said. "What's the address?"

I didn't want them seeing where I lived. Once in a while people hung out in the lot and smoked weed and drank and yelled and fought. It wasn't that bad really, but coming from Brandywine Heights, they would have thought it was pretty low-life. "I have to get milk anyway." We'd come to a red light. I opened the door and got out.

"Call me," Nicole said.

"Jay?" her mom said. "Thank you."

Somebody honked. The light had turned green. I nodded bye and headed into the 7-Eleven. My phone buzzed with a text. The caller ID stopped me mid-stride: Angela Sammick. The text said: **We need to talk.**

TWENTY-NINE

I called her. "How'd you get my number?"

"*Are you serious?*" Angela said.

"Amazing. I truly believed you were a newb in comp sci."

"*I didn't believe you for a second with that corny, 'Duh, how do you send a text message?'*"

"What's up?"

"*Not over the phone.*"

"Where are you right now?"

"*Home, but we can't meet here. My father's an idiot. We'll meet in the middle.*"

"Where's home?"

"*Classon and Route 22.*"

"Okay, I'm like a mile away—"

"*I know where you live. Meet me at the McDonald's on 22. You know what this is about, right?*"

"Nicole, obviously."

"*Obviously.*" Click.

On the way there, I ran a search on her address. It checked out: Michael Sammick, 1714 Classon Boulevard, not a great area.

She was waiting for me at the order counter. "You have any money?" she said.

"Yeah."

She said to the woman behind the counter, "Two vanilla shakes, two fries." She turned to me. "What are you getting?"

We grabbed a booth in the back. Angela drew her phone and clicked up an email from Arachnomorph: I know you're looking for me. It's over on my end, unless you start me up again. If you keep stirring the nest, I'll bite you too.

"Untraceable?" I said.

"Would I be here if it was traceable?" She was slamming the fries and shake. For somebody who couldn't have weighed ninety pounds, she could put it down.

"Why are you doing this?" I said. "Trying to help Nicole. What's in it for you?"

"Hello, moron, the reward money? That and she was nice to me."

"Nice doesn't mean you risk your life for her."

"She was *very* nice, okay? Last year, while you were gone. Things sucked and I'd had a few too many drinks." She saw I wasn't too surprised. "In *school*, Spaceman. I went to the bathroom to throw up. I'd been suspended once already for cutting too many classes. One more suspension, and I was done for the semester. I purged and was feeling better, or at least well enough to fake my way through the rest of the day. I'm walking out of the bathroom, feeling like I just might get away with it when I run into Nicole in the hall. She pushes me back inside the bathroom. At first I'm like, are you seriously

141

looking for me to dig your eyes out of your head with my thumbnails? But then she pointed to my pants. I had missed the bowl and splattered vomit all over my jeans. Lucky me, I happened to be wearing white that day. Nicole gave me hers."

"Her pants? And she wore yours?"

"Dude, I'm like size zero. You think Nicole Castro would fit into my jeans? She told me to wait in the stall, and then she went to the music room and came back with band pants and we made the switch."

"*Band* pants? Those goofy things that go up to your chest?"

"Baggy as eighties disco, exactly. She wore those and gave me her jeans."

"Why didn't she just stay in her jeans and give you the, like—"

"Band pants? I wondered the same thing. She said she didn't want me to risk drawing attention to myself."

"So then *she's* walking around like the goof, and everybody's looking at her?"

"Everybody was looking at her anyway, and *she* wasn't drunk. Look," she said between long pulls on her milkshake, "I don't know why people do these things, screwing themselves for other people, but they do. It's annoyingly inexplicable. They're just freaks, what can I tell you? Are you gonna eat those fries?"

I pushed them her way. My stomach was weak. I was suddenly panicked. If Angela had traced the leaking of the Arachnomorph emails back to me, then Detective Barrone and the NJPD cyber crime team easily could have too. "How'd you know I leaked the emails?"

"I didn't, till now. Not for sure, anyway. I mean, I suspected it, of course. Jay, c'mon, the way you were looking at Nicole in Schmidt's office? In love with her even after the burn, huh? I don't know if that's super-sweet or super-weird."

"I'm not in love with—"

"Right, okay, whatever, here's my proposal: We team up and split the reward."

"I'm not doing this for the money."

She rolled her eyes. "Okay, fine, more for me. Look, *whatever* your reasoning, you know by now this is too big a job for one person. Even if the Recluse is somebody from school, if you include staff, that's almost thirty-eight hundred suspects to check out. Then you throw in people outside of school who could be jealous of her, and you're dealing with like half the population of New Jersey. What are you riding for taps?"

"Conficker88."

"Please tell me you're not serious."

"What?"

"Freeware punched holes in that thing ages ago."

"You're kidding."

"*You're* kidding. Riding 88 and expecting to stay anonymous? Maybe teaming up with you is a bad idea."

"When was it blown?"

"At least yesterday. Maybe even the day before."

Somebody who could talk my language. Very cool. "What's your horse?"

"The Sleeze321 worm."

"Charming."

143

"At least she can keep a secret."

"Infect me."

"Thought you'd never ask." She zipped it to my phone with a patch that I opened first to prevent the worm from vaporizing my hard drive. We compared notes. We had the exact same suspect list. I told her I had ruled out Sabbatini, Schmidt and Mr. Sager.

"Let's get back to Bendix," she said. "What's your take on him?"

"Long shot."

"Right," she said. "No motivation. You're sure he asked her to lie about something?"

"What else could he have been doing?"

"We better check him out, then. I'll run strings on him."

"I already did," I said.

"And?"

"Nothing."

She popped a fistful of fries. "Look, that thing that happened back at that house party freshman year: Obviously I was bombed."

"I'm surprised you remember it."

"Caitlin told me what you did for me." She frowned. "Thanks."

"No problem."

"You can relax, though. I'm not into you that way. You're a little too clean for my taste, no offense."

"Absolutely none taken."

"Good."

"Hey, this is crazy, but do you think she could have done it to herself?"

"Why would Nicole Castro burn herself?"

"Right." I sipped my shake, studying Angela as she looked at her phone and Nicole's Facebook page. I was getting into business with a girl who drank in school, but did I have any choice? Angela was right: I needed a hand. She was going to hack at this thing anyway, until she got her reward money. She would be happy to do the one thing I couldn't: hack Nicole. I didn't want to violate whatever was going on between us, friendship or certainly the beginnings of it. Also, I was afraid of what I might find in her files. If nothing was there, Angela wouldn't bother to tell me about them. She didn't strike me as the type to waste time on gossip. If she did find something scary, she would tell me. I was okay with that. My ears were open to any information that would help Nicole, or help her help herself, if she did in fact burn herself. Whether Angela was an alcoholic or not, I had to work with her. That didn't mean I had to trust her, yet.

THIRTY

A little after one in the morning the phone rang. My father. I was sure he'd talked with Detective Barrone. He said, *"You couldn't call me to check in?"*

"You couldn't call *me*?"

"You sound weird. I don't know, afraid or something."

"You're leaving me alone since I'm thirteen. I'm just mainlining a little heroin."

"Jay? I'm sorry, okay?"

Now I knew he was drinking. I'd been about to ask him what went down between Mr. Castro and him all those years ago, but no way I was going to get anything substantive out of him when he was smashed.

"Jay?"

"I heard you. Look, just go to bed."

"I didn't mean it, Jay."

"I know. I gotta go."

"Okay. Okay. Jay?"

"Yes, *Dad*?" Rolling my eyes.

"I'll see you Saturday. Maybe we'll go to the driving range."

"Or we could just smash our hands with sledgehammers and guzzle Drano."

"Why do you have to . . . Look, just stay out of trouble."
Click.

"Right," I said to the dial tone. "'Night." I tapped into his phone account and scanned his Calls Made list. He still hadn't returned Detective Barrone's call.

Around two a.m., Angela sent me a link that had helped her worm her way through the NJPD firewall. She'd planted an evercookie when somebody somewhere in the NJPD clicked a link that promised three more inches. The girl was *good.* More than that, sharing information like this, she was beginning to win my trust. She'd only gotten to the gate, though. It was up to me kick it down. I used the code that listed Detective Barrone's call to my father to wiggle into the Division of Detectives mainframe. I probably had two minutes before the I.T. guys would notice the breach.

Folder: RECLUSE

Folder: DAVID BENDIX

Folder: VIDEO INT. 09 Sept.

I ripped it and got out of there. I played the video through the TV to get a better look at the faces, the eyes. They had Dave in a conference room. An older dude in a tailored suit sat with him. Dave was pale. Barrone was off-screen, pacing. Dave tracked her with glossy eyes.

Barrone: "Again, David, where were you?"

Bendix: "Ma'am, I *told* you."

Barrone: "And I told *you,* she said you weren't in the cut-out."

Bendix: "I *was.*"

Barrone: "I don't buy it. Here's my thing: It would be odd that you were just hanging out in the hall when the second bell had rung and you were late for class."

Bendix: "It was English. Mrs. Nally never cares if you're late. Seriously, ask her. We were doing the metaphysical poets. Would you be in a rush to get yourself some pastoral elegy of John Donne?"

Barrone: "You mean Edmund Spenser."

Bendix: "Him too."

Barrone: "This is what happens when you cut class. Why hang in the cutout, with nothing to do? Why not the cafeteria?"

Bendix: "Why not the *cafeteria*?"

Barrone: "I asked you first."

Bendix (exasperated): "I don't know what to say."

Barrone: "I know you don't. Okay, if you were at the water fountain, who threw the acid?"

Dave: "I told you, it happened out of my line of sight, just past the corner where the hallway splits."

Barrone: "No, David. No. I checked the acid marks on the floor. I stood where Nicole was standing when she was hit, and I could see the water fountain fine."

Bendix: "My head was down. I was drinking from the water fountain. I, was, *there*. She, Nicole couldn't see me. Maybe the glare in the windows—"

Barrone: "Nuh-uh. Nope. No glare that day. *Rainy* that day. Torrential. Besides, the sun never falls on that side of the building. Where were you, Dave?"

Bendix: "You keep asking me the same question, Detective."

Barrone: "And I'll keep asking until I get the right answer. Look at me. What are you hiding? I said look at me. Breathe. Listen. I don't have you pegged as the thrower. I don't. But you're lying to me. I can tell. I'm doing this a good while now. You know what? I'm going to do you a favor. I'm gonna tip you off to the two things a liar does when he's stringing one. Here they are, for the next time a cop taps you for questioning."

Bendix: "The *next* time?"

Barrone: "How do you *really* feel about Nicole?"

Bendix: "How do I feel about Nicole?"

Barrone: "See, right there. That's the first tell. I ask a question, you repeat it. You need time to think, and you try to fill the silence by repeating the question. Here's the second tell: A liar looks right. What's your name?"

Bendix: "Da-David Bend—"

Barrone: "You're looking me in the eye. You're telling me the truth. If I replay this video for you, you'll see that every time you tell the truth, you're either looking at me or to the left. When you lie, your eyes tick right. I ask where you live, you tell me Haasbruck Estates: eyes left. DOB, parents' names for the record, kid brother's grade in school: eyes left. But when I ask you about Nicole? Eyes right, every time."

Dave folded his arms on the tabletop and dropped his head into them. "I'm telling you the truth. I swear."

Barrone: "I get that a lot. Where, David? Where were you when Nicole was hit?"

Bendix's lawyer: "That's more than enough, Detective."

Dave Bendix wiped his eyes and looked directly into Jessica Barrone's. "Nicole either didn't see me, or for some unimaginable reason she's lying to you, Detective. I don't know why. I really don't. I was there. I was in the cutout, at the water fountain."

Barrone squinted as she studied Bendix. She shook her head and muttered, "Shit."

I watched the interview again, and then again.

Dave Bendix came into Schmidt's office that day to beg Nicole Castro to testify that she saw him in the cutout. But she wouldn't, because she hadn't. So then where was Dave when Nicole was hit?

Coach used to make us do sidestep drills to keep us light on our feet, light enough to tail somebody in silence. When Nicole turned to blow Dave a kiss, he could have sidestepped around her. When she spun back for B-wing, he could have been there with the squirt bottle. This was if Dave was lying. What if he was telling the truth? I replayed the end of the interview. He seemed absolutely sincere.

Maybe Nicole really didn't see him. The alternative was horrifying, especially after spending time with her that afternoon, seeing how awesome she was with the kids in the hospital: Nicole was lying.

I dug through my closet for my own Volta-Shock bottle. I was going to fill it with water to see if I could accurately squirt just one part of my face. Then I remembered I'd put it with my wrestling crap into the Goodwill bag my father was getting together.

I was checking out the Volta-Shock site to see if I could order the exact same bottle online when my email popped a notification that I had a new message. The sender line was **N CSATRO** with a Brandywine Hollows High School domain, and the subject line was **SOMEBODY HAS A CRUSH ON ME**. I realized too late something was very wrong, clicking as I reread the sender line. No way the real Nicole would misspell her own name. There wasn't any attachment, but just clicking the email was enough. A video overtook my screen, piercing strobe lights. My Nokia buzzed, caller ID "Angela Sammick." My brain couldn't coordinate my hands to pick up the phone. I just stared at it as it buzzed away, the strobe flashes popping at me from my computer screen. Angela tried a text, too late: **DID YOU GET CRUSH EMAIL? DO NOT OPEN!** Lightning flashed inside my bedroom. Everything went fish-eye.

I woke an hour later in the hallway, on the floor. My sweatpants were wet. I lay there for a long time, gasping, and then I sat up. I stayed like that for a while longer, trying to figure out who hated me enough to send me that seizure trigger. I was almost hoping it was one of the Kerns brothers or some other bully from school, knowing it wasn't. Eventually I was able to stagger to my laptop and the phone. I called Angela. She picked up with, *"Tell me you got my messages."*

"Yup."

"Glad I caught you in time."

"You didn't, but thanks for having my back."

"Sorry, Jay. Was it bad?"

"Nah. Did you get a backtrack on the source?"

"He scrubbed the machine ID when he ran the email through the school server, but I got the address, for what it's worth." She emailed it to me. I stared at it:

swdidpibwdipvbigoigiwubpi@brandywine_hollows_hs.edu.

"What's it mean?"

"Randomly tickle the keyboard, and you'll get the same sort of mess. Not that we needed any more proof of this, but this dude's a dick. He's just having a ball with himself. What'd you turn up last night?"

I gave her everything I had and instructions on what to do with it, then I headed for the shower, lay down in the tub and let the water burn me.

THIRTY-ONE

From Nicole's journal:

What day is it? What night? I'm burning, burning, burning blue.

THIRTY-TWO

Thursday morning I woke late. No way I'd make it to second period on time. I forged myself a note from my father and headed off for school, stopping in at the *Clarion* on the way. "Do I look as bad as you do?" Pete said.

"Do you feel as crappy as I do?" I said. I asked him if he could talk to his boss about killing the Burned Beauty's Beau storyline. He said he knew nothing about it. I flipped the paper to the gossip page.

"You think I read this rag?" he said. "I just work here."

"Can you get Puglisi to back off Nicole?"

"He's not one of ours. We don't have the budget anymore to do stakeouts."

"He's on your payroll."

Pete frowned. "Now Jay, I'm not going to ask how you know that. Anyway, if we are cutting him checks, it's on a freelance basis. I'm sure we pick up his pictures from the syndication pool. And even if he was in-house, the chances of my being able to freeze this story are zero." He circled the cap line over the picture: BURNED BEAUTY BEHIND THE UMBRELLA. "This kind of trash is the only thing selling papers these days. Her best bet is to stop running. The story dies when the mark comes forward and sits for an interview."

"The mark?"

"The object of attention. Nicole. Gossip junkies love the chase. End that, you end the story."

"She'll never sit for an interview. The only alternative is to nab him."

"Say again?"

"The perp. Catching him would kill the story."

Pete shook no way. "That's when it begins. They'll be running columns and talking-head interviews with so-called experts until the trial ends and they march the unrepentant nutcase to the psych ward. Your friend is going to be living with this for a long time, and the more she hides, the worse it'll be." Pete studied the picture of Nicole, her mother and me in the diner parking lot, doing our best to hide behind Mrs. Castro's umbrella and only half succeeding. "My advice?" he said. "Stay the hell away from her."

My phone had been buzzing with a text. Starbucks Cherry: **Hey, have you been getting my texts? Swing in for a free coffee sometime. Don't. Be. Scared. I don't bite, promise. I merely gnaw.**

THIRTY-THREE

The seizure the night before left me feeling punked. I felt a lot better after two cups of cafeteria coffee. Toward the end of the school day, I got a text from Nicole: **Need help please call soon as you can.**

I called her after sixth period, from a stairwell. Schmidt had emailed her to tell her that due to an emergency faculty meeting, she couldn't do her 3:30 session. The only slot she had open was two p.m. This meant Nicole would have to enter Brandywine Hollows High School during school hours.

"Skip it," I said.

"That's what Mom said too, but Dr. Schmidt said it'll be good for me," Nicole said. *"Being in the building when other students are around. You know, a first step toward coming back to school. Do you have class seventh?"*

"Free." I'd petitioned the registrar to have seventh and eighth periods open in case BJ's had extra hours available.

"Can you walk me?"

I'd skipped lunch, and I was starting to crash. No food, no sleep, no meds: Perfect recipe for a seizure. I headed to the cafeteria for a Coke. On my way out of the vending machine alcove, this dude *accidentally* bumped into me. One of Rick

Kerns's crew. As he drove his shoulder into mine, he whispered, "You're gonna burn."

Nicole parked right up front, in the handicap spot. A blue tag hung from her rearview. She wasn't in the Subaru but a black Saab.

"Yours?" I said.

"I know, I'm spoiled."

The bell had rung a few minutes earlier, but a straggler clipped us. The phone double-flashed hot pink light. The girl might as well have punched a nail into my visual cortex. The picture was MMS'd by the time we were halfway to Schmidt's office. People leaned out of classroom doors. Nicole smiled, waved once to the hall monitor, but mostly she kept her head down.

"Yo, Spaceman." Rick Kerns was up in my face before I'd turned all the way around. "Are you insane?"

"And are you serious, Rick?" Nicole said. "You need to chill."

He ignored her. "Sneaking around out and about is one thing, but parading through school like this, disrespecting Dave?"

"You need to back up, Rick," Nicole said.

"You need to *shut* up, Nicole."

She hit his chest with the heel of her hand. It did nothing to push him back, and she hurt her wrist. She winced as she rubbed it, but she stood her ground between Kerns and me. I kept trying to step between them, but she wouldn't let me. "Look, you don't speak for David, okay? We're cool, he and I. David knows about Jay and me."

"No shit. You guys are flaunting it everywhere."

"That we're *friends,* idiot."

"Not what I hear," Kerns said.

"You know what, I really don't care what you hear," Nicole said. She hooked my arm and marched us toward Schmidt's.

Kerns called out, "Faithless bitch."

"Dick," Nicole muttered.

We were at Schmidt's office twenty minutes before Nicole's appointment. We sat. Her new sunglasses were the kind that lightened indoors. She looked out the window, to the empty soccer field. The grass needed cutting. Schmidt's waiting room was stifling. I was taking off my jacket when the alarm went off. Nicole jumped.

"It's just a fire drill," I said, but I knew that somebody pulled the alarm to flush Nicole outside and get a look at her.

"Let's stay here," she said.

Or did he want to keep her inside while everybody else was outside?

Schmidt's door opened. She was on her cell with a headset. "Right, yes, but do we really want to do that?" She motioned for us to follow her into the hall. As we went through the doors, most people were nice, smiling, saying hi. Then somebody in the murmuring crowd said, "Did you see her? Dude, she's right *there.*"

Outside, a teacher did a double take on her and came over to give her a hug. "We need you, Nicole," the teacher said. "When are you coming back?"

"Soon."

They both pretended she was telling the truth.

Nicole put on a brave face, but I could see she was halfway to freaked, too many people coming up to her at once. They all said the same thing: "You look *great*." They too wanted to know when she was coming back. Didn't she know the tennis team sucked this year without her? That the student council was in open revolt against Mr. Davies, the moderator, without Nicole around. Nicole smiled and laughed and took them all in, until she couldn't anymore. Her hands shook as she pulled her phone. She checked the screen and said, "Guys, I'm sorry, I have to take this." She hooked her arm through mine, and we rounded the corner to the back parking lot and hunkered behind a Dumpster.

"Nice fake," I said.

"I wasn't faking." She handed me her phone. The text said: **Enjoying all the attention?** Caller ID: **UNKNOWN.**

I forwarded the text to my phone and worked it up for a trace.

"Just how much of a hacker are you?"

"You should know I rarely do this in front of people. This is akin to show me yours, and I'll show you mine."

"And what exactly are you expecting me to show you?"

"You've already shown it. Your vulnerability."

Another siren. A police car flew into the parking lot to meet the security guards escorting this idiot from my year, Dennis Biers. I remembered him from freshman fall, class clown wannabe, emphasis on wannabe. He was exactly the type to pull the alarm.

My phone pinged with a hit on the number trace. "You know Brittany Keyes?"

"She's on the tennis team," Nicole said.

"She's the one who sent you the text."

"No, it was Chrissie."

"Vratos?"

"She used Brit's phone. When we were at matches, we watched each other's racquet bags. You'd come back to check your phone and find a WTF text from somebody. You'd check your Sent folder and see you'd just zipped the dude an invitation to give him a blow job. Then you'd hear Chrissie cracking up." Nicole scanned the yard. The teachers were waving everybody back inside. "There." Nicole pointed to the B-wing entrance. Chrissie was waving to us.

Schmidt's door opened. "Wait, Jay, we're not on today. Did you get my email?"

"Just keeping my friend here company."

"We're quite the gentleman, aren't we?"

"We try," I said.

"I'll see you after, okay?" Nicole said as she went in.

I texted Angela to see where she was on our suspect list, particularly Chrissie Vratos. Angela had stayed home sick, apparently something she did at least five days a month, the maximum number of days you can be out before they make you repeat the semester. She got back to me with: **Chrissie V very dirty girl.**

Dirty hands? I texted back.

Dirty mind. No connection to Recluse. Yet. Will keep digging.

I headed off to grab a candy bar from my locker, a bottom row job. The thickening puddle at the foot of it suggested at least five guys had urinated into it. A mosquito circled. Somebody had stuck gum in my padlock keyhole.

"Tough luck, Spaceman," Kerns's little brother said. He took a break from stuffing books into his own locker to take a picture of me. "I guess that's why they tell us to use a *combo* lock, d'oh."

"Except people keep the combo in their phones," I said. "Phones get hacked. Can you imagine if somebody knew your combo was 36-24-36?"

"Spaceman?"

"Douche bag?"

"You have no idea what's coming." He slammed his locker and stormed off.

I hadn't actually hacked his phone. The genius had written the numbers on a piece of tape and hung it in plain view— where else—inside his locker.

I went to the office and asked the secretary for a paper clip.

"Gummed again?" she said, handing it to me.

I stopped off in the bathroom, slicked the clip with soap, headed back to my locker and dug at the gum. Somebody tapped my shoulder and said, "You bone her yet?"

I turned around, into the nozzle of a Volta-Shock bottle pointed at my eyes.

THIRTY-FOUR

I fell to the floor and clawed my eyes. "Please," I said. "No more."

"It's water, idiot," Rick Kerns said. He sucked the squirt bottle and spit the water at me. "That's for snaking Dave's girl, bitch. What's it like, getting blown by Half Face?"

I drove him into a wall of lockers. I headlocked him and didn't let go. I picked him up and swung him feet-over-head, over my shoulder, and I body slammed him to the polished stone floor, and even then I didn't let him out of the head-lock. He tried to poke my eyes, but I had seen him do that in matches back in freshman year, and I grabbed his hand and bent it back. I heard a pop and a crack. He would have screamed, except he had no air in him. All he could do was grunt. He clawed my arm, gasping. His head was bright red. His boys drop-kicked me. "Dude, let *go*, man!"

"You're crushing his throat, Jay! *Stop!*"

A voice cut through all the screaming. She didn't even yell. "Mr. Nazzaro," Mrs. Marks said. "Let go."

I got in one last shot, a right cross to Rick Kerns's thick-boned head.

"Brush your hair back," Marks said. "So I can see your eyes."

"He squirted—"

"I know what he did." She looked to the cop texting in the corner of her office. Back to me: "I called your father. He's not picking up, work, cell, home—"

"He's traveling."

"What's your mother's—"

"She's *really* traveling, if you recall."

Marks squinted and checked my file. She was midway into realizing my mother was dead when the cop said, "Okay, so I just heard from Kerns's mother. They're at the ER, waiting to see what they say about the hand. The family elects not to press charges at this time. You're still good, Nazzaro? You don't want to file an assault complaint?"

"No."

"You sure you don't need medical attention, Jay?" Mrs. Marks said.

My hand was stiff from cracking Kerns's skull, but I'd made my fist really tight, so I knew I didn't break anything. The kicks to my back didn't break any ribs, I was positive. I'd broken one before, when I fell off my skateboard a few years before, and that felt like somebody had a blowtorch to my gut. But here in Marks's office, I was more than fine, still throbbing with adrenaline. "Actually, Mrs. Marks, I feel great."

"That's terrific, Jay. Enjoy your suspension."

My locker had been cleaned up, the outside at least. I didn't have much in there anyway, textbooks I had PDFs of, a sweatshirt, half a box of Clif Bars. I tossed it all and went into the bathroom to wash my hands. The door banged open. By the time I turned, Dave Bendix was up in my face. He was furious, flexed in his wrestling singlet, that dark glint in his eyes. "I'm gonna kill him, Jay. Please, you have to believe me, I didn't put him up to that. I heard they were going to hit you, but I didn't know when or where. I was down in Coach's office, telling him about the rumor, when they got you."

"Not your fault," I said.

"Feels like it is. Are you okay? Did they—"

"I'm fine. Seriously."

"Look, I know about you and Nicole."

"Dave, nothing happened, I swear."

"Jay, calm down, okay? Even if something did happen—"

"It didn't. Whatever Rick said is a lie, flat out."

"You think I listen to him? Nic told me. She thinks you're awesome. Look, I know you guys are just friends, okay? Relax. I'm happy you're keeping an eye on her while she and I are . . . whatever we are, taking a break, I guess. You're like the one dude I can actually trust." He leaned back against the sink, rubbing his eyes. He looked pretty wrecked. "This whole thing is so messed up. How is it that one minute everything is perfect, and the next it's just *not*. Like, flat gone. I can't sleep, you know? Trying to figure out who would do this to her. Why? You know?"

We locked bagged eyes for a second. I didn't have any answers for him. His eyes ticked to the wall clock. "I gotta get back to practice. This scout dude from Harvard came down from Cambridge, unannounced, to watch me work out. My father's out there too. I feel like I'm gonna crack, man. If I don't get in there, my life is over."

"You're gonna get in."

"Jay, I'm not kidding. It has to be Harvard. My father'll disown me otherwise. He's told me I'm on my own if I don't get in. At the same time, it's like he wants me to fail, the way he cranks up the pressure. He knew the Harvard dude was coming, and he didn't even tell me. He—" Dave Bendix burst into tears, just for the length of a breath. "Shit." He took a second to get himself together. He sighed and forced a smile. "I hear you met Emma. Doesn't she just kill you?" He gently clapped my shoulder. "You coming back? To the team, I mean. We need you. I hear you rocked Rick pretty good."

"Nah, I think I'm done."

"I have your back either way. I already put the word out that anybody who steps to you is stepping to me, but if the guys start screwing with you, let me know, all right? Just like the old days. You're a good dude, and I won't stand for seeing you get hurt."

"I don't get it, Dave. Her face gets wrecked, and you dump her?"

"What? Jay, *she* broke up with *me*."

When I got outside, Nicole was talking with Mr. Sager as he lined a window with weather stripping. He largely ignored her until she tried to give him a brick-size box wrapped in brown paper. He held up his hand and said, "I can't." I tried to thank him for cleaning up my locker, but he cut me off. "She did it. I tried to make her stop, but she insisted." He gathered his tools and left.

I was beginning to feel sore from my fight with Kerns as I crouched to get into the shotgun seat of Nicole's Saab. "How was your Schmidt?" I said.

"Jay, thank you," she said.

"For?"

"Hello, you defended my honor. You did. And if you ever do it again, I'll have to crush you. Are you crazy?"

I eyed the box she tried to give to Mr. Sager. "This mysterious box thing: It's got to stop."

"Perugina."

"That's like chocolate, right?"

"It *is* chocolate." She opened the box.

"Hershey's is chocolate. Perugina is something you save in a drawer because it's too expensive to eat, and then you re-gift it at Christmas."

"I'm more of a Snickers girl myself." She snickered as she peeled me a Baci. "You hungry?" she said.

"Pretty much always. That was funny, the Snickers thing."

"The boy likes my lame jokes. Nice. Best pizza place you know of?"

"Ray-Ray and Eddie's. They only do takeout, though. It's just a window."

"Pick someplace cool to eat it."

I'd already let my guard down when I futzed with her phone and then again when I hacked in front of her, tracing that text during the fire alarm back to Chrissie. I was scared, letting Nicole Castro in on my secrets, but at the same time the vulnerability felt good, and I wanted to let her in a little more. "You want to meet my mom?"

She tilted her head to look at me over her sunglasses. "Definitely."

"The whole going AWOL thing: Isn't your mom going to flip out?"

"She says as long as I'm with you, she's not so worried."

"But not worry-free," I said.

"She'll never be worry-free." She started the car. "I'm not even sure I want her to be. Selfish as it is to say that." She rolled down the windows. The wind blew back her hair. When she turned to talk to me, I could see the bandage where the sunglasses didn't cover it. It spread from the bottom of her jaw up to her temple, from her eye to over her ear.

I put a slice in front of my mother's headstone.

"Jay," Nicole said.

"I do it all the time," I said. "Pizza was her favorite, except she liked everything on it."

"But the raccoons or whatever'll eat it."

"Exactly. What? They have to eat too. This one time, we were stuck at the train station."

"You and the raccoons?" she said.

"Mom and me. We'd gone to the Ziegfeld to see a movie on the huge screen, I forget which flick."

"Doesn't matter. Any movie rocks on that screen. Love that place."

"Yeah, and when we got back to Jersey, the snow was falling hard, and we couldn't get a cab. My father was away for a lecture or whatever. The train platform was cold, crazy wind, you know? I'm shivering, and Mom says, 'I got it,' like *eureka*, right? She grabs my hand and we skip across the street to Ray-Ray and Eddie's, and she orders a pie for delivery to our house, and we caught a ride home with the delivery dude."

"*No.*"

"Seriously."

"Genius."

"Tell me about it."

We sat back against the side of a crumbling mausoleum and ate our slices. "Did you ever do that bio lab, with the starfish?" she said.

"I said I did for the state test, but really I just read it."

"I hated that lab."

"I hated the idea of it."

"Right? Cutting off the poor thing's arm?" She pulled bits from the pizza crust and chucked them to the birds. "Everybody told me not to feel bad, because the arm grows back, right? But that's a myth. It doesn't. Not all the way. I saw pictures in the books. While I was talking to Mrs. Cletus about getting out of the lab, you know, like requesting a substitute lab, where I wouldn't have to maim anything, my lab partner cut off the arm. I screamed when I saw it. I took it back to the ocean."

"The starfish?"

"After the lab. I tried to put her back in the water, but she wouldn't go. You know Shale Beach, where it's all smooth stones they brought in from wherever? I put her at the shoreline to let the waves take her out gently, but she dug into the rocks. I was crying as I threw her back in, because maybe she would drown."

"Nah, starfish can't drown. You saved her. She would have ended up drying to death and then getting chucked into the trash with the rest of the starfish that never made it out of the lab."

"But maybe she just didn't want to fight anymore, missing an arm like that, you know? Even if it grew back, she'd never feel like it had. She'd always feel like part of her was missing. Maybe she just sank." She sipped from her Coke straw. "Question."

"Okay, and then I have one for you."

"Deal. What happened? Your mom, I mean."

Word had gotten out about the pizza crust, and the sparrows were hopping up to us. One perched on the toe of my worn thin Chuck T. I tried to feed it from my hand, but it looked doubtful. When another bird helped itself to my palm, the first bird got over not trusting me and got in there too. "You want to know about my mom?"

"Please."

"She came to all my baseball games. She never missed. She wore this bright pink Windbreaker no matter the weather. I mean, this thing was blinding."

"Fluorescent, you're saying."

"Plugged into some serious wattage, yes. She called it her cheering jacket, had a hat to match too. This, like, crazy winter cap. You ever see those hats with the ears, like this cat or monkey or whatever is clinging to your head, the arms are way too long and hang down, you knot them under your chin to keep the hat on, they sell them in the city by Rockefeller Center from the tourist trap tables at Christmas?"

"I have one, Tony the Tiger."

"Exactly. My mother's was the Pink Panther. Imagine her wearing that to every one of my summer league games. She looked like a lunatic. Here's the thing: No matter who was up to bat, me, one of my teammates, one of the kids from the *other* team, she screamed for him, like 'You can do it, Johnny-boy!' Or 'Great swing, Pablito!' even if the kid sucked and missed by a mile. She knew every kid's name." I nodded. "That's it," I said. "End of story."

"That's it?" Nicole said. "Are you kidding? That's everything. First the pizza cab and now the Pink Panther. That's so fricking awesome." She nodded with me. "Your turn. What'd you want to ask me?"

"Nah. I'll ask you some other time."

"Nope, now or never. Anything. Go ahead."

I hesitated. I couldn't look at her as I asked. "Who do you think did it?"

"Everybody always asks me that. That's *all* they ask me.

"Don't you ever wonder, though?"

"All. The. *Time*. Jay? I. Don't. *Know*. Okay? I can't think about it anymore. The idea that somebody out there despises me enough to do this? It's . . ." She shivered, and then she cried. "This is so crazy. I don't want to know, you know? I don't want to know who did it. How could I ever face him, you know? In court, I mean. They would make me testify, and he would be sitting there, staring at me. I almost hope they don't catch him. That he just fades away. He . . . I can't talk about this."

"Nicole, I'm sorry."

She stopped crying, almost too quickly, I thought, wiped her eyes and steeled herself.

"I'm sorry."

She kissed my cheek, just a quick peck, and then she stood up. "Seriously, let's go. Someplace where we can laugh."

"You golf?"

"Never."

"Then it's Hackers, Hitters and Hoops. I'll laugh anyway."

"Your house."

I hedged.

"What?" she said.

"No, nothing. Let's go, I guess."

Somebody left half-eaten takeout just outside the lobby. The rats were congregating. They didn't move, either, when we walked by. Waddling up to the party, one of them looked more like a possum. He eyed me like, *No, you move.* "I'm sorry," I said.

"About what?" Nicole said. "We had a mouse once. He was cute."

"Stuart Little versus Bubonic Plague."

We played Skyrim, and then she went to the piano. She

was great, of course, even with Band-Aids on two of her fingertips.

"You know that song 'How Soon Is Now?'" I said.

She played it. "Sit with me," she said. She showed me the very simple top part of a four hands version of the song. "The squeeze bottle," she said. "When it came up to your face. What were you thinking when the splash hit you?"

"It happened too fast. Start to finish in less than a second. I was like, okay, this psycho just squirted acid in my face. It was weird. I wasn't thinking about me. I was thinking about him. How screwed up he must be to do that. Even after he told me it was water."

She stopped playing. She looked at me.

I wanted to brush the hair away from the left side of her face. I didn't. Instead I did something I didn't want to do. Something I had to do. I said, "Dave."

"What about him?"

"He said you broke up with him."

She looked away, tapped the low end key. "I did."

"You told me he broke it off."

"I said the words, after he gave me an ultimatum."

"As in?" I said.

She squinted at me, and I realized I was squinting at her. It hit me: She didn't trust me either. Not fully. Not yet. She turned back to the keys, tapped out a very sad, slow version of "How Soon Is Now?" "He made Emma a bouquet once," she said.

"What, he bought her mixed deli flowers or whatever?"

"No, he *made* them. From paper."

"Like origami?"

"Exactly origami. He Kindled a how-to book. She loves sweetheart roses, the tiny ones, but they die after a day. He wanted to give her something that would last. Paper fades too, though. It curls in the sun. I wonder if she knows she has six months to live." She leaned her head on my shoulder. I put my arm around her. I was supposed to kiss her now, and I wanted to, but I didn't, I'm not sure why. So we just stayed like that for a while, until it was clear I'd let the moment go, and she got up to get her coat.

"Stay," I said. "PS3. Bootleg tennis. I'll let you kick my ass."

"Gotta get home. My dad. We have a Skype thing scheduled."

I walked her to her car. She checked the backseat before she opened the door.

"Look," I said, "I—"

She cut me off with a hug that was as tight as it was short. She slipped into her Saab and drove out of there a little too fast.

I watched her car disappear into the sharp red sunset. As I was heading back into the building, an engine revved, and a battered old-model Civic, black, eased out of the lot and swerved into the empty avenue. I was about to call Nicole to warn her, but the car turned west, away from where Nicole's Saab had gone. I grabbed the tag off the rear bumper with my phone camera. Pete had advised me to take pictures every time Puglisi or one of his guys showed up. That maybe the police would get on him for stalking if we gathered enough evidence. I realized that the tag numbers weren't Puglisi's. And the car's color was different. I remembered Puglisi's Honda as less black, more gray. The windows were up, but I could make out that the driver was a woman, short with long hair. She was wearing dark sunglasses, almost as if she were copying Nicole.

Battered Civic, short girl with long hair: Starbucks Cherry?

I scrolled to the last text she sent and replied: **We need to talk.**

It didn't take long for her to get back, of course, fifteen seconds, about as much time as she would need to pull over and grab her phone. **We most definitely do. When?**

Now.

Come to my house.

Someplace pubic. My JKL key was lame half the time. I'd already hit SEND.

Took her a while to reply to that one. **Mall?**

Apple pkng lot 20 min

Glad you figured out how to text. :o)

I called Angela.

"What's up?" She sounded a little out of it.

"You drinking?"

"Just straight vodka."

"You at your computer?"

"Where else would I be?"

"Need you to run some plates."

"You can't tap the lousy DMV yourself?"

174

"I have to check on something else right now."

"As in?"

"Why after two years of knowing me a certain girl is all of a sudden crushing on me."

THIRTY-FIVE

Took me fifteen minutes to skateboard to the mall. I scanned the parking lot entrances for Cherry's Civic. Somebody tapped my shoulder. I spun with my hand up to cover my face. I almost didn't recognize her out of her Starbucks getup. She wore a tight pink hoodie, tight jeans. Her hair was lighter than I remembered. She always had it in a ponytail, and I'd never seen it loose. She'd gone heavy with the lip gloss. "Hey," she said, big smile.

"Why are you stalking me?" I said.

"Okay, wait, *stalking*? I texted you like three times. You didn't get back to me, so I let it go."

"Cherry, coming to my building? C'mon."

"Dude, I don't even know where you live."

"I saw you, okay? You almost got T-boned, swerving out of the lot."

She put up her hands like I had a knife out. "This is messed up. I have no idea what you're talking about." She backed away toward a row of parked cars.

"Unless you come clean, right now, I'm calling the cops. I'm serious."

"I know you are. I'm definitely sensing seriousness." She

backpedaled to the driver's-side door of a Honda Civic that was at least ten years older than the one that had pulled out of the lot in front of my building, not to mention that this one wasn't black but *yellow*. "Take it easy, Jay. I don't know what I did, but I'm leaving now, okay? I don't want to hurt you." She opened the door and barked, "Step *away* from the *vehicle*," as if she'd Hulu'd one too many episodes of *The Shield*.

I was standing in front of the car, penning her in. "Maybe this isn't your car."

She turned over the ignition.

"Okay, so it is your car," I said. Which meant that Cherry DiBenneditto was not the Recluse. This also meant maybe the driver of the black Civic was. Were Detective Barrone and Schmidt right? Was the acid thrower a woman after all? Any male on my suspect list—Kerns, Dave Bendix—was if not absolutely safe, then safer. Or maybe the woman in the car really was working for Shane Puglisi or another gossip rag, stalking Nicole for a picture. Or maybe she wasn't connected to Nicole at all. She hadn't followed Nicole out of the lot. She'd gone the opposite direction. Then again, if I didn't check her out, and she was the Recluse, I would have to hold myself responsible for anything that might happen to Nicole.

A flicker zigzagged in my peripheral vision. I sat on the hood of Cherry's Civic to catch my breath. She came out brandishing the Club, but when she saw I was kind of out of it, she lowered her weapon. "Jay?"

"Cherry, I'm sorry. I had you mixed up with the spider."

"Happens all the time. The spider. Sure. What are you on?"

"Can I buy you a cup of coffee?"

"Are you *trying* to be a jerk?"

"What'd I say?"

"Hel*lo,* you know where I work?" Her eyes softened. "You can buy me a slice."

"Pizza's great," I said, even though my stomach was twisting to accommodate the ever-expanding, four-pound-ball of cheese there after my pizza slam with Nicole.

"Sbarro?" she said.

"Hardy har."

She had no idea what I was talking about. "Dude, what is your *prob*lem?"

"Where do you want me to start?"

I ended up forgetting my wallet, and she had to pay. Not that I touched my slice. I told her why I hadn't texted her back, that I was crushing on Nicole.

"I figured," she said. "What's she like?"

I told her.

She'd heard about the attack. She rolled her eyes. "You know, of course, that this only makes me like you more. Crushing on a disfigured girl? That's like an OWN movie waiting to happen. You really think somebody's spying on you guys?"

"I'm somewhere between possibly and probably. Her engine coughed before it rolled over. Means it was cold. Means she was sitting there for a while, watching."

"Or talking on the phone. Or taking a nap because she'd

worked a double and started to fall asleep at the wheel on her way home. Or you're *totally paranoid*. I actually do need coffee now. You?"

"Definitely."

She headed for the counter. I pulled my Nokia to see if Angela had run down the license plate, but my battery was dead. Cherry had left her phone on the table. I messed with it to make it untraceable. She'd notice next month when her data bill was zero.

"Jay?" Cherry was looking over my shoulder.

"What the hell are you doing, sneaking up on me like that?" I said.

"Getting my wallet, which, as you can see, I left next to my brand-new phone that cost me thirty hours worth of slinging lattes. What the hell are *you* doing? My poor Droid. What'd you do to her?"

My head was pounding. "You'll get much better reception now."

"You're the dude who asked me for help texting Dad, right? Wait, you're a *hacker*."

"You say it like it's a bad thing."

"It *is* bad!"

I needed sleep. I was really losing it. I had willingly let Nicole know I was a hacker, and Angela had found me out on her own, but getting caught by Cherry was just sloppy. Too late now. "I have to use your phone."

"I don't have a ton of minutes."

"You won't have to worry about that anymore."

"How did you get into the DMV? You know that says Restricted Access, right?"

"I'm a member."

"Of what?"

I ran the plates I'd seen on the black Civic. Sure enough, they tracked back to a red RAV4 that reported its plates stolen that afternoon. "She boosted somebody's tags," I said. "She tacks them onto her car when she wants to be anonymous. She can't be driving around in her real plates in case a street camera picks her up doing the loitering thing. If the cops pull her over for speeding or whatever with the bad plates, she plays dumb. 'What? Those aren't my license plates.'"

"I think I might have seen something like this on—"

"*The Shield*?"

"Except on *The Shield*, they need court orders to do what you're doing."

"I know, so lame. Want to know how many older model black Civics there are in the tri-state area?"

"I think I may just need to kill myself if I don't have that information. This is crazy, that you can get into government institutions like this. Imagine if you could hack into the Department of Defense?"

"Imagine." I ran the search command into the DMV database.

"I had you pegged for stoner sexy, but you're actually geeky sexy. Um, why is my phone flashing red?"

"Eight thousand, two hundred and twenty-two 1990s model Civics, black, are puttering around New Jersey. That's too big a list for me to go through on my own. You'd need industrial computing power to work up owner profiles, and then you'd have to cross-reference the potentials with information only the investigating officers have. Cherry, I was right. Somebody's stalking her."

"Or you."

"This was so much easier when I thought you were stalking me."

"I'll stalk you, if you want."

"I don't know how I'm going to catch this freak."

"You're not," she said. "You have to call the cops."

"I can't do that."

"Because?"

"They'd want to know how we got our information about the bad plates."

"How *you* got the information. I just watched you break my phone." She frowned. "I could do it. Let the cops know, I mean."

"No, I don't want to get you involved."

"Not me. My father. He knows a lot of detectives. He could drop a tip about the Civic, and if he asked them to keep it anonymous, they would."

"Okay, you couldn't tell me your dad's a cop before I hacked the DMV in front of you?"

"He's an undertaker, but the funeral home has a contract with the state, special discounts for civil servants, their families. They do a ton of business with the police. What do you want me to tell him to do?"

"Ask him to give the cops the plate number and tell them that the driver of this vehicle, a black Civic, was acting suspiciously in the environs of Valedale Boulevard."

"Acting suspiciously how?"

"Driving around parking lots, checking out parked cars or something. The anonymous witness said the driver was probably a woman. Have your dad say she was particularly interested in cars with baby seats. Actually, that's pretty good. The kidnapping thing always gets the cops hopping. They'll check all the local security cameras, maybe get a picture of the woman's face, run it against the mug-shot database with face recognition software. You never know, we might get lucky."

"You don't have a better description than 'a woman'?"

"She was in silhouette with the sun behind her, but she had nice hair. You know, long, a little wavy. Pretty, like yours."

"Like mine. Great."

THIRTY-SIX

Cherry dropped me off at the gate to Nicole's community, or "the village," as she liked to say. "I'll call you when my dad gets that info," she said.

"I don't know how to thank you."

"I do." She waved as she left. I wasn't exactly sure how, but she reminded me of me. In spite of that, I liked her.

The gate guard phoned the Castros, and another guard drove me to the house. Nicole's neighborhood was too quiet. The house was big and old. Placard out front: "Historical Landmark, Est. 1844." The doorknocker was this huge Siberian tiger head, something out of *Anna Karenina,* a book I never read but told everybody I did to sound smart. I felt like I should have been wearing a top hat and cape as I rang the bell.

Mrs. Castro was happy to see me. She said Nicole was out with her dad, but she was supposed to be back soon. "I just made pizza, super-healthy, whole wheat crust, no cheese, just vegetables."

"Sounds amazing." *Blehk.*

She led me through this enormous house toward the

kitchen. The rug tassels had been combed. Even the fire burned neatly, three perfect plumes. "That real?"

"Of course not."

They needed a golden retriever, and they would have nailed the center spread in *Better Homes and Gardens.* "No dog?"

She made a face and tapped her nose. "Nicole's allergies."

She served me this huge slice of vegetable pizza. Alfalfa sprouts on pizza should be a capital crime. "Best I ever had," I said.

"Do you think you could get your father to sign my copy of his book?"

"No problem."

She scanned a bookshelf built into the kitchen wall, all art books. She hit the intercom. "Sylvia?"

"What?" Definitely not pleased. Brief snippet of talent show TV in the background, the final round, crowd roaring.

"Did you see my book, the old one, Steven Nazzaro, *After Beauty*?"

"It's in your studio, on that small table by the easel." She huffed, *"I'll get it."*

"No, darling, I'll get it."

"I'll get it, I said."

Mrs. Castro slumped back in her chair and closed her eyes. "I thought having an only child was the way to do it, you know? Shower her with happiness. But they still get ruined, no matter your watchfulness, your worry, your singular devotion. Ruin. It's just what comes. People see beauty, and they have to destroy it." Her blouse was light pink, and tears splattered darkly. She could have been shot twice in the chest. She wiped her eyes and collected herself. "I'm so sorry. Don't listen to me. Eat your pizza, Jay. Please." She went to the refrigerator. "They were supposed to be back by now. 'Just a quick ride,' he said." She poured me a glass of milk. "Jay, what are you not telling me?"

I told her about the black Civic and gave her the plate number. I didn't have to tell her the plates were stolen. Detective Barrone would find that out fast enough.

"They said it wouldn't happen again, the police," Mrs. Castro said. "And that godawful Schmidt." She grabbed the phone. She lit a cigarette while she waited for the call to go through. Her hands shook. "He's not picking up. They turn their phones off when they're with each other, because they think they don't spend enough time together. *Now* he wants to spend all this time with her." She was talking to herself. I heard the beep. "Rafael, I need you to bring Nicole home. *Immediately.*" She clicked the phone off and then on. I watched her key in the numbers, Barrone's.

Sylvia came in.

"Hi," I said.

Sylvia nodded Mrs. Castro's way. "Now you got her all upset. When she's upset, she's not happy until she makes *me* upset." She dropped my father's book onto the table. It was a wreck, thumbed and gripped to the point the cover was coming off.

The security company put a car on the Castros' house. Nicole and I hung out in the kitchen. Her parents were having a low-voices fight upstairs. Sylvia was stabbing a bunch of yarn into something that resembled a sweater in the living room, with a direct line of sight to me. She nailed me with eyes that said if I so much as tried to hold Nicole's hand, she was going to run a knitting needle through the back of my head. Nicole was eyeing me too. "Are you hacking me?"

"No. No, I'm not, and I won't."

"Promise."

"Promise."

Her mother was really yelling now. "I want to go up there," Nicole said. "I want to make them just shut up and look at each other and remember what it was like back when I was little, when they were young, and they were always holding hands. I used to swing from the bridge. You know, the bridge their hands made?"

Her father came downstairs, heavy footsteps. "Nicole, time to change that bandage."

"Dad—"

"Now, sweetheart. Your mother's waiting for you." He eyed me with a frown. "I'll drive you home."

"Thanks, but I have my skateboard."

"That wasn't a question." He was about three inches shorter than I was, weighed less too, but I had no doubt he could tune me up. His eyes were just scary. Blue like Nicole's, but cold.

The interior of Mr. Castro's BMW was immaculate. He drove right at the speed limit. "I know your father," he said. "Rather, I met him. But you knew that."

"Yessir."

"My wife was never great at keeping secrets. Bit of a hothead, your father, if you don't mind my saying. How is it for you, living with a critic?"

"Terrific," I said.

"You smoke?" Maybe it wasn't a question. "I smell it on you."

"I think that was Mrs. Castro."

"She was smoking in the house? Just what Nicole needs, cancer in the air." We'd come to a light. "Look, we're both men here. We know that when women are vulnerable, *some* men will try to take advantage. Now, I know you're not one of those types of fellows."

"No, I'm not."

"That's fine. Good. Because I think my little girl has gone through quite enough these past few weeks, ey?"

The light had turned green. The guy behind us honked, but Mr. Castro stayed put. He kept giving me those mean eyes, sharp green now in the reflection of the traffic light.

"Mr. Castro? I'm not out to hurt your daughter. I'm simply trying to be her friend."

He nodded and drove. "She likes you a lot. She doesn't know you, but she thinks she does. And isn't it always that way, for all of us? But you can't, son. Right?"

"Can't what?"

"Ever really know anybody. Not even yourself. Do you agree? Don't be afraid to disagree with me."

"I'd like to think that's not true."

"Indeed. We all want to think that way. But the sooner you confront reality, the sooner you'll be able to move on. *Forward*. We must keep moving forward."

I wanted to get out of that car so bad. "I'm over there, next right onto Valedale. I can get out at the corner."

He kept driving, right into the lot.

"I can get out here, sir, or just by the mailbox there would be great."

He drove me all the way up to the lobby. The takeout containers were still there, but the rats had licked them clean. Mr. Castro frowned. "Is he home?"

"My father? Why?"

"Not that I think anybody would be foolish enough to try anything with you, but I promised Nicole and her mother I wouldn't leave you alone."

"He'll be home soon." Okay, so in this case soon meant two days, but I would have said anything to get out of that car.

He gave me a hard nod and wink. "Thank you."

"Sir?"

"For the information about that car. For being alert enough to get the license plate. That was well done."

"No problem." I tried the door but it was locked with the child-proof safety.

"You were looking out for my daughter. You have my gratitude." He shook my hand. I thought he was going to break it. "You need a haircut."

"Yessir, I'll get right on that."

"Do." He pulled his hand away quickly and the automatic locks clunked up. I got out, and the BMW zipped out of the lot. On my way in, I picked up the takeout trash and chucked it into the Dumpster.

The Castros had private security, but in my building we didn't even have security cameras. That woman in the Civic knew where I lived. Now I was the one peeking around corners. I went through the apartment room by room, closet by closet, wondering just what I would do if I found somebody in there. I plugged in my phone for a recharge, and two texts from Angela popped up. The first told me what I already knew, that the license plates on the black Civic backtracked to a red RAV4. The second let me scratch Chrissie Vratos from my suspect list. Angela was able to confirm that Chrissie was at her dentist's when Nicole was hit. She'd filed a note from her mother with the attendance office, requesting that Chrissie be allowed to leave school early that day for a root canal, but records at the dentist's office showed Chrissie had come in to get her teeth whitened. All of my female suspects had been crossed off the list, except one: Nicole. I was desperate for any information that would rule her out as somebody somehow involved in the attack.

On the kitchen counter the clunky old landline message

machine blinked. I hit PLAY, expecting to hear my father's voice and an apology for being bombed when he called in the night before. The caller was Detective Jessica Barrone: *"This is a message for Steven Nazzaro. Steve, I've left word for you twice now. I'd appreciate a call back."*

After my ride with Mr. Castro, I had to face the possibility that my father was somehow involved in this thing—inadvertently, not as the acid thrower, of course, but maybe as an unwitting causal agent. Whatever had gone down between Mr. Castro and him must have been pretty bad to keep Mr. Castro mad so many years later.

I wormed into my father's email. He'd gotten a warning from E-ZPass about approaching a tollbooth too quickly, seventy miles south of Brandywine, down I-95, at an exit called Marathon. I didn't know anything about the place, except that it wasn't near Philadelphia, where he was supposed to be. I clicked up some history on the area, heavily industrial, at least until the economy tanked. Now it was a wasteland of abandoned factories. He'd gotten off the highway at 21:36 last night, and then back on at 23:19. What was he doing down in no-man's-land for an hour and forty-three minutes?

I burned through New Jersey Traffic's firewall, backdoored my way into the E-ZPass database and scrolled through his E-ZPass statements. Two months earlier, he'd done the same thing on his way to a show in DC, exiting the highway at Marathon. That time he was MIA for a little less than two hours.

Girlfriend? He'd dated exactly two women after my mother died, maybe five or six dates total, and he'd never tried to hide them from me.

This was not the big break in information I was hoping for.

My bedroom doorknob twisted. The lock was broken, but I'd wedged a chair under the handle. I grabbed my baseball bat.

THIRTY-SEVEN

"Let me in. Jay, open *up*." My father.

I slapped down my laptop screen and cleared the chair from the door. "I thought you weren't due back till this weekend?"

"Your assistant principal called."

"Dad, seriously, Kerns totally started it."

"We'll get to that later. Why were you blocking the door?"

I told him about the black Civic.

He rolled his eyes. "People are down there hanging out all the time, smoking drugs, fooling around, whatever else. They *sleep* in their cars."

"In their *trucks,* after they've been driving all night."

"You're being paranoid. The woman came to pick up her husband at the train station, crashed for half an hour until his train arrived, woke up late and sped out of the lot. *There.* Nobody's after you, Jay. Relax." He took off his tie and headed for the kitchen. "I picked up a pizza. C'mon, we need to talk."

I couldn't tell him that the Civic's plates were bad. He'd know I was hacking. If he knew that, he'd figure out that I was hacking him too. So much for asking him about Marathon.

"He squirted me with—"

"*Water*, Jay."

"How was I supposed to know that?"

"You're lucky his hand isn't broken. It was a sprain, his mother said. The thumb. Still, it'll be two weeks before he can get back."

"Two weeks from school for a sprained thumb?"

"From *wrestling*. You know, his ticket to Harvard or wherever."

"You're always telling me to stick up for myself. What was I supposed to do?"

"You definitely didn't need to choke him."

"He—"

"*Hey*. I can't afford to get sued, okay? Neither can you. If we have to hire a lawyer, we're out on the street. C'mon, man. Use your head." He poked my temple with his index finger as he got up to get himself a Diet Coke.

"Did you get that message from that detective?"

"Gimme a break, Jay. '*That* detective'? You mean the one you had coffee with?"

I should have known Pete would cave. In my experience, when adults give you their word about something, half the time they'll break it, invoking the old standby clause: I know what I said, but I had to do what was best for you.

My father settled in his chair, rubbed his eyes, eyed me. "The Castro girl. Stay away from her. You're in enough trouble with this suspension crap. And stay the hell away from Barrone too. She's a pain in the ass. I helped her kid on a paper once—"

"She told me."

"Did she tell you the daughter was sending me these book-length emails, calling me three and four times a day at the office?"

"What was it, Dad? Your beef with Mr. Castro."

"Now how the hell did you find about that?"

"Mrs. Castro."

He frowned. "He insulted an artist I happened to think was a hell of a talent."

I shrugged. "So he didn't like his stuff. Free country."

"*Her* stuff. The artist was his wife. He killed her dream the night of her debut."

"What, he like started slashing her paintings?"

"Pretty much. He and I are standing in front of the same painting. I'm smiling, he's frowning. I tell him I think the work is remarkable, and he says, 'a remarkable burden.' He goes on to explain that he's footing the bill for all these 'castles in the air,' as he calls them, gesturing to the paintings. Says he can't even get his wife out of the studio long enough to take her to dinner. She's obsessed, he says. What she really needs to be doing is getting down to the business of having kids and 'being happy,' as he put it. I argue that it's all worth it, the time apart, putting the family thing on hold, because she's great. And Castro's exact words were, 'She's not great. She's very good, and that's not good enough.' Anyway, Elaine had gone to get her husband a Perrier or whatever the hell he was drinking, but she'd come back in time to hear most of what he said. She's standing right there as Castro says, 'The difference between a Pablo Picasso and an Elaine Castro is that Picasso *needed* to paint, and filling Elaine's head with ideas that she has the same need just isn't fair to her. It can only lead to crushing disappointment, and I don't want to have to see my wife suffer like that.' Then he notices Elaine. She's putting up a brave fight, smiling, but she can't hold back the tears and excuses herself. Castro hurries after her, apologizing. It's a scene, you know? A sad one. The damage is done, party over. People are leaving the gallery. I'm getting my coat, and here's Castro again, giving me this sarcastic thank you, like this was all my fault. I had toasted Elaine earlier with something to the effect that she was one of the best I'd ever seen. I was young, but I had a guest column in the *Times* back then, and I guess what I said carried some weight—not a ton, mind you, just the tiniest bit maybe, but I guess it was enough to get Elaine Castro believing in herself a little anyway, which is all I was trying to do. Give her some support, you know? I told Castro he was an asshole, and I left. Actually, I might have said a bit more. Maybe a lot more. The gallery was still half full, mostly his banking buddies, I imagine, lots of Brooks Brothers suits. I embarrassed him in front of his friends, and I meant to. I embarrassed myself too, apparently. I was a little—"

"Drunk?"

"I kept an eye out for Elaine, but she never exhibited again, not publicly. I ran into the husband a few years ago at a gas pump, of all places. He said she was still painting, but strictly as a hobby." My father folded himself another slice of pizza, shaking his head. "Guy's a bona fide prick. He killed her. He killed his . . ." He let the pizza fall to his plate, sat back in his chair, looked up at the ceiling and let out a long breath. "Shit," he said. He glared at me.

"What'd *I* do?" I said.

"Do we have any Tylenol?"

"It's expired."

"You double the recommended dose, it still works."

I got him the Tylenol and then Mrs. Castro's copy of his book. "Could you sign this for her?"

He studied the paint splattered over the book. Mrs. Castro had flagged a page with a Post-it. My father flipped to it. He smiled sadly. "She picked my favorite. Not that I don't mention that fact in the book at least five times."

I was looking at the picture upside down. She'd tagged a Picasso and written on the Post-it: "his best." It was the only one I knew, *Guernica,* his most famous one.

"Should we give her a fresher copy?"

"After it's taken her so many years to get this one like this?"

"Hey," I said. "How come you never painted?"

"I'd have to send you on a Heineken run before we got into that conversation. I know about your fake ID, by the way."

"Seriously, Dad. Why didn't you pick up the brush?"

"I did. I painted for years."

"And?"

"I burned them."

"Why?"

"Fear."

"That the critics would kill you?"

He shook his head. "I couldn't figure it out. What the great ones knew. Inokuma. Picasso. I mean I knew it on an intellectual level. But not in my heart."

"Knew what?"

"What comes after beauty."

"Have no idea what you're talking about."

"Not sure I do either." He flipped the book to the title page, inscribed it and, yawning, headed for bed. I checked the inscription: "To You Who Know What Comes After Beauty."

THIRTY-EIGHT

A little after noon the next day, Friday, I met up with Angela at the *Clarion*.

"And why should I do this for you?" Pete said.

"Because you owe me," I said.

"For telling your father you were about to get yourself tossed into jail?"

"You set me up with Detective Barrone in the first place."

"For educational purposes. I figured you were looking to do a school report about detective work. How was I supposed to know you were involving yourself in an open police case, not to mention falling in love with the target of an acid thrower."

"I'm not falling in love with—"

"Right. Somebody mentions the girl's name, and you get this look in your eyes. Watch: Nicole. See? You're toast." He turned to Angela. "Am I right?"

Angela cracked her gum. "Bread crumbs."

"Pete, I need this favor. Think of my mother."

"Don't do that, kid. Don't try to make me feel sorry for you."

"I'm not. I don't mean it like that, and I don't want your pity. I mean that she would have done what I'm trying to do."

"And what's that?"

"Sticking up for somebody who's having a hard time sticking up for herself."

Pete shook his head and picked up the phone.

Angela, Cherry and I met at Cherry's Starbucks a little before three p.m., when Cherry relieved the person behind the counter. I was back there too, setting up Angela's phone camera inside the pastry case. Angela was sipping a latte and surfing on what appeared to be a brand-new, just-released special-edition MacBook Pro with a seventeen-inch screen that would have retailed for $3900 if its guts weren't absolute garbage I had pieced together for around $40. The nice shiny case itself was from BJ's. The forklift king actually showed up for work the previous weekend and had sailed the blades through a stack of Apple boxes. They were tested, found to be broken beyond repair, written up as damaged freight and tossed, and then I went Dumpster diving.

Starbucks was, per usual at this hour, empty, until Puglisi showed up around 3:45, just as Pete's friend in the *Clarion*'s feature department, aka the gossip room, suggested he should. By now I was hiding out in the parking lot, in Cherry's yellow Honda. I watched Puglisi hurry into the shop. He'd gotten a tip Nicole Castro was meeting her new beau there at about four p.m. If Puglisi got there a little early and put himself near the front door, Nicole and her man would be sitting ducks. Puglisi could get a perfectly clear shot, front-page worthy.

Puglisi barked a coffee order at Cherry and situated himself in the corner, setting up his lens. Four o'clock came and went, and neither Nicole nor the beau or whoever he was showed up. Ten after four came and went. At about twenty after four Puglisi's phone rang. He answered angrily and then hung up even more angrily, having been told that the tip turned out to be bad information. Just as he was about to pack up his stuff, Angela, seated two stools down the window counter from Puglisi, yawned and stretched and said, "Can you watch my laptop for a couple of minutes while I go to the bathroom? Thanks." And off she went.

Puglisi sized up the situation. The bathroom door was closing behind Angela. Behind the counter Cherry was cleaning the espresso machine, her back to Puglisi. He shrugged, tucked the laptop under his arm and headed out to his car. He stopped when he noticed a thick glass Coke bottle on the hood of his Honda. It had been placed there as a paperweight to keep the smiley face Angela had drawn from flying away in the considerable wind. The smiley face also had hands, and both of them were flipping off Puglisi. He turned around to find me walking toward him. I was holding out Angela's phone, playing the video of Puglisi's robbery. He took a swing at the phone, but I saw it coming and held it high over his head. Being much taller than the dude, I had no problem keeping the phone away from him. "Besides," I said, "she got you too."

Cherry was out with us now, looking at her phone camera screen. "So weird. From *this* angle, it looks like you're stealing a four-thousand-dollar computer."

"I believe that's grand larceny," I said.

"It's entrapment," Puglisi said.

"Wanna gamble on a six-year minimum sentence?" I said.

Puglisi smirked and looked around the parking lot. "I'm guessing Nicole isn't coming?"

"I'm happy to relay any message you have for her. Maybe a final good-bye?"

"Okay, champ, I'm off her tail. Be about a day before the *Enquirer* has a new team on her." He got into his car. "Happy now?"

I reached through the window and casually took back the laptop. "I need you to do one more thing for me."

Twenty minutes later, the picture I got of the black Civic swerving out of the parking lot in front of my building the previous night was up on the tabloid sites with the headline BREAK IN BURNED BEAUTY CASE IMMINENT, RECLUSE ON THE RUN.

I'd tried to leak the picture myself, but no media organization would take my anonymous submission seriously. Only the likes of Shane Puglisi and his Scorpion Imageworks had the credibility to get such a shot picked up. He actually sold the picture for five grand, over the phone, from right there in the Starbucks parking lot.

Basically I was trying to buy us some time. The Recluse would see the story. She wouldn't be able move around so easily, not with that picture in hot circulation. She would have no choice but to lie low. At the same time, I knew that if she'd been crazy enough to follow Nicole and me to my building, she wouldn't be backing off for good. We'd get an extra couple of days to do some digging before the *Recluse on the Run* storyline faded from the front page and the psycho couldn't fight the itch to burn again. Maybe that would be enough time to hack the breakthrough piece of information that would help us find her before she found another chance to hit Nicole. I'd given up on the idea that Detective Barrone was capable of stopping the Recluse. If she was stoppable, then Angela, Cherry, and I were going to have to stop her.

Angela and I took the bus west. She fell asleep, her face on the window. Her left hand was closed tightly but her right was open. Her fingernails were chewed bloody. A razor wire tattoo circled her wrist. She caught me looking at it. "Cool, right?" she said.

"Cool," I said.

We got to the Route 22 stop, and from there I walked her home. We stopped at this bodega a block from her house. "I heard you have rock-solid fake ID. Any chance I can get you to man up and buy me some beer?"

"How about a Snapple Green Tea?"

"I believe you've already had the pleasure of seeing me hurl all over the street?"

I was suspended, but she'd cut that day. "Thanks for taking off from school for this," I said.

"Oh, it was a sacrifice. If you were really thankful, you'd get me the Budweiser."

"I feel bad saying this, but as your friend, I have to."

"We're not friends, but go ahead."

"Can I help you get yourself to a rehab program?"

"Many have tried, all have failed, but I'll tell you what. Help me get that fifty-thousand-dollar reward, and I'll check myself into a luxury spa to dry out. Maybe in South America. Maybe I'll never come back. Yeah, that sounds good. Hey, I'm wondering what it would be like to suck your tongue really, really hard."

"Not gonna happen."

"Saving yourself for Nicole?"

Nicole or not, it wasn't going down, not with all that lip metal. "Thought you weren't into me like that anyway."

"Spaceman, that was like two days ago. The way I feel today, anybody's fair game. When you're hungry, meat's meat."

"I'm truly flattered."

She headed into the bodega and I went home.

THIRTY-NINE

From Nicole's journal:

Friday, 29 October—
Nye: "We're in this together, Nicole."
"Really, Dr. Nye, we're not. I feel like I don't have enough skin on my face. That the skin that *is* there isn't mine. That even if it is, it should be on my hip, not my cheek. Is that how you feel?"

Later, I pull up the pictures from my Facebook, the Before, the comments, so many of them, all wishing me a speedy recovery. *Recovery?*

Ctrl + click gets you the Mac Word dictionary and "Recovery, n., 1. the return to normal health . . . 2. The return to a normal state . . . 3. The regaining of something lost or taken away." The definition neglects to mention the maps, the ones that delineate the return trip to normal or the site of the sunken treasure.

A touch to my shoulder. Mom. "Honey, take a nap." She tucks me in and strokes my hair. When I wake, she's asleep next to me. Her eyelids are puffy. They will be puffier soon. Tomorrow, going away with Dad to lake house for weekend. Don't really want to go. Yesterday, Jay rested his head on mine.

FORTY

The Recluse was quiet all that weekend. I pulled half a shift at BJ's but mostly I faked like I was fighting a cold and slept during the day. When my father went to bed, my laptops came out. Angela and I had split the list of female students at the Hollows. Basically, we were on Facebook all the time, looking for Nicole-hate, not finding any. Late Sunday night/early Monday morning Angela buzzed me with a red alert text, a link somebody had posted to the fan page set up by Nicole's well-wishers.

The page was crowded with thousands of comments and videos of Nicole, her pageant appearances, student council speeches, tennis matches, mash-up tributes cut to saccharin music. Angela found one video particularly interesting, a YouTube clip posted Friday night. It played through Mr. Sabbatini's AP chem page. The post was untitled, but the poster was cryforhelp669, an amateur's attempt at anonymity: 669 spelled out NOW on a phone keypad. Angela had backtracked the ID to Marisol Wood, the sophomore who confided to Nicole at the tennis club that her parents were splitting up.

Sabbatini, like a lot of teachers at the Hollows, recorded

his lectures. He was in front of about two hundred kids in stadium-style seats. This was how they did the lab preps, the AP and regular-track students lumped together before they broke up into smaller groups for the actual experiments. I had placed out of chem during home school. Now I was wishing I hadn't. I would have been in that lecture hall.

Sabbatini: "The question was, 'Why does battery acid burn your finger and not the inside of the battery case, which is largely polyvinylchloride?' Nobody? Fabulous. You're all destined to succeed brilliantly. People, what is the pH of water? One hand up. *The* hand. Yes, well then, of course Ms. *Castro* would know. Go ahead."

Nicole: "Seven?"

Sabbatini: "Question or statement? And at what temperature? Care to gamble five points on the midterm?"

Nicole: "Seven at seventy-seven degrees Fahrenheit."

Sabbatini sighed, "Correct." Then, to the class: "What compound makes up most of the human body?"

"Bone," some dude yelled.

That got a lot of muttered "Oh my god," and "Idiot."

Sabbatini: "Genius. Genius." He slapped his hand on his desk with each word: "What, is, the, body, made of? Go ahead, Ms. Castro."

Nicole: "Water. About sixty percent of the body's weight."

Sabbatini: "So then why does one's finger burn when one, if one is *stupid* enough, changes his car battery without proper protective gear on his hands?"

Nicole: "The pH scale goes from zero to fourteen. Liquids

closer to zero are strongly acidic. Liquids closer to fourteen are bases. Water, the liquid in our skin, is effectively neutral. The battery acid has a really low pH, less than one—"

"Point eight, in fact, Ms. Castro," Sabbatini barked.

Nicole: "Point eight. Thank you, Dr. Sabbatini. When you combine two liquids, they try to even out their acidity. The farther apart they are in pH, the more heat is given off in the balancing reaction. The result is that it melts. Your skin just fries."

Sabbatini bent over his SmartDraw pad and sketched out a molecular structure that described the chemical reaction Nicole had just verbalized. The projected diagram was stunningly spiderweb-like, but I'd already ruled out Sabbatini, along with Dr. Schmidt. They had conspired to do no more than get that chem teacher's guide to Nicole.

Sabbatini believed a lot of questions went unasked because students were afraid of looking dumb in front of their peers. He kept a question box outside his office door. If you didn't understand something in class, just drop an anonymous note into the box anytime afterward, and Sabbatini would get to it at the beginning of the next class.

Who had asked the question about the battery acid? The camera's POV was from the back of the lecture hall. I could see little more than the backs of the students' heads.

I had Angela on my screen in an IM box. I typed: Do we really think this is Marisol Wood or Marisol framed? Let's put Chrissie Vratos back on the list.

Aye-aye, Captain.

Cryforhelp669. It was almost as if she wanted to be caught. My phone had started vibrating while Angela and I were IM-ing. I checked the text:

from Arachnomorph@unknowable_origin.net:

> Hello Jameson and Angela,
> The itsy-bitsy spider
> climbed up the waterspout.
> Down came the rain,
> and washed the spider out.
> Up came the sun,
> and dried up all the rain.
> The itsy-bitsy spider
> crawled up the spout again.
> I have six eyes. They're all on you.

Angela IM-ed: Did you just get that?

I typed back: Full-court press on Vratos.

All we had to do was connect her to that black Honda Civic, and she was done.

I looked out my window to the fire escape. Manhattan was deep in the distance. The midtown skyscrapers were black fangs. The sun had just cleared the horizon. The heat rising from the oil burner chimneys across the highway distorted and magnified it. It swelled like a tumor jacked up on steroids, burning through a haze so white it glared. The clock said 7:31 a.m. I'd been awake sixty-four of the last seventy-two hours.

My father peeked into my room. "You want a ride?"

"I'm suspended, remember?"

"Can you go food shopping, then?" He shook his head and left for work.

I checked his room for anything that might give me a hint of what he was doing while he was AWOL those two times in Marathon, New Jersey. I didn't know what I was looking for. I didn't find anything out of the ordinary.

Nicole called. She wanted to hang out but wasn't allowed out of the house.

This old lady was having a hard time getting onto the bus. I helped her. She said, "Thank you, miss," told me I had lovely hair and my, wasn't I quite tall for a girl.

The security guard was parked in front of Nicole's house. Mrs. Castro met me at the door. "Nicole's in the shower. I was worried about you." She took me back to her studio and showed me her paintings. Abstract art isn't exactly my thing, but as far as it went, I thought she was awesome. You kind of had to stare at it for a while, though, to figure out what she was painting; looked like a doe in autumn woods. I wasn't sure I was right about that until she said, "They come right up to the back door at sunset. Did you get your father to sign my book?"

"I forgot to bring it," I said.

Nicole came in. "You look horrible," she said.

"Thank you," I said. She looked a little pale herself.

"You do look a little peaked, Jay," Mrs. Castro said. She had fixed us some tea and handed me a cup. She closed the door behind her to leave Nicole and me alone.

The tea tasted great, then suddenly bitter, metallic. "Peru-gina or Hershey's?" I said. "On your sleeve." Nicole had a dot of dried chocolate stain on her sweatshirt. A squiggle of pink lightning arced across the studio, and that's the last thing I remember.

She was brushing my hair back when I woke. I was on the studio couch. I sat up fast.

"Did I—"

"Relax. You just dropped into a daze, it seemed."

I brushed my hand over my crotch. I was wet. I looked down. The one day I had to wear non-dark jeans. They were dark now all right, just in one spot. I grabbed my backpack and board and made for the front door. Nicole begged me to stay. "At least until you're not bumping into walls, Jay. Please? You're practically staggering."

Her mother came at me with a folded wet towel. I slipped past her, out the side door, into the Castros' yard. Sylvia blocked Nicole, yelling at her in Spanish that she wasn't allowed to leave the house.

I was too dizzy to ride my board, and it had started driz-zling again. I half jogged, half stumbled into the nature pre-serve that bordered Nicole's house. The path was a shortcut to the road, where I could catch the bus.

I made my way through the preserve and walked along the side of the highway. I stopped to catch my breath. The day was gray, but there was a glare to the sky, bright enough that I could see the stain in my pants wasn't really in my crotch but on my thigh, and it was too dark to be urine, more the color of blood. I couldn't figure out how I'd cut myself or where. A car revved up to me. As I looked over my shoulder, the car blinded me, flashing its brights. It swung in front of me, cutting me off. It was the black Civic. No, the Saab, Nicole's. She leaned over the shotgun seat and pushed open the door, and that's when I realized the stain in my pants wasn't blood. "It was the tea," I said.

"What?" she said.

"I must have spilled the tea on myself when I faded out."

"Jay, get into the car."

The road was one muddy puddle after another. Trucks whipped up gray spray. I was cold and beat. I sank into the shotgun seat. "I'm sorry."

"So am I. I'm not supposed to be driving. My mother made me take a Xanax just before you showed up."

She drove fast into the empty rest area, the rain darkening the sky. The brakes whimpered as she stopped short to park. She turned to face me.

"No more chocolate stain," I said. "Wait, you changed your hoodie." This one was pink too, but baggier. I touched her sleeve where the stain had been. She winced and drew back her arm. "Was that blood before, on your sleeve?" I said.

"Cat scratched up my arm."

"You have a cat?"

"The neighbor's. She's always in the yard. I was cuddling her, and all of a sudden she flipped out."

A person who has serious allergies cuddles a cat? Nicole

Castro was lying to me. She leaned across the seat and rested her head on my chest. I put my arms around her. The rain fell hard on the roof. "Tell me what happened to her," she said. "Your mom."

"Some time," I said.

"Okay," she said.

I don't know how long we were like that, just holding each other. Not long enough. Somebody tapped on the side window. The security guard. He drove Nicole home in the security company SUV. A second guard drove me home in Nicole's Saab.

FORTY-ONE

From Nicole's journal:

> Monday, 1 November—
> I think he might know.

FORTY-TWO

At four that afternoon, Cherry called with a promise of hot news. "Tell me in person," I said. I had re-upped my anonymity settings, but I couldn't be absolutely certain the Recluse wasn't watching me. Cherry showed up at my apartment with Starbucks scones. "So my father's cop friend didn't get an ID on the woman."

"And this is hot information because?"

"He got a lead on the car owner." She clicked a picture onto her Droid screen: a shot of the Civic's rear bumper. "A traffic camera picked up the car."

"Okay?" I said. "We already had the plate number."

"Right," she said, "but we didn't have this." She zoomed in on the plate. "The plate itself is bad, yes, but not the plate rack, the kind the dealer gives you to advertise the dealership." Cherry tweaked the picture, magnifying the plate rack: Vardy Dealership.

I nodded. She left the scones on the counter and hurried for the door.

"What's the rush?" I said.

"Work." Cherry DiBenneditto was a very cool girl.

A little after 4:00 Tuesday morning, I cracked the Vardy database. The company had resold four hundred and sixteen 1990s model Civics in the last fifteen years, and none of those went to anybody named Vratos or Wood. By now I'd hacked the class list for Sabbatini's chem lab. None of the last names matched.

I created a map that covered Brandywine and the Hollows outskirts, and I checked the addresses of the Civic owners with Google Earth Street View, one by one. It took hours. Around 11:45 Tuesday night, about three-quarters of the way down the Vardy list, I found what I was looking for, a dumpy little house not far from my apartment building, in lower Valedale, still in the Brandywine school district but definitely low rent. The black Civic was in the driveway. The stolen plates had been swapped out for the ones registered to the address, but I recognized the car by the gash that ran across the driver's-side doors. The Civic owner's name was Roberta Lyles. I tapped up her Facebook page.

Bobbie Lyles listed herself as divorced. She was probably in her early thirties but the lines around her eyes made her look a lot older. She had long blond hair, but she couldn't have been the woman I saw in the Civic hauling out of my parking lot. That woman was thin, and Bobbie was not. Still, she looked familiar. Those eyes . . . I tapped up Chrissie Vratos's page. At a stretch, she and Bobbie could have been distant cousins. Maybe they were friends, and Chrissie had simply borrowed the car? Took me about half an hour to go through Chrissie's posts and albums, and I didn't find anything that connected her to Lyles. Bobbie's page took half a minute to scan. She had nothing up there except a handful of pictures, all of crocheted objects. She was using Facebook primarily to promote her home business, handcrafted scarves, sweaters, blankets made to order. She had six friends, and none of them linked her to Chrissie. I tried to connect Bobbie and Marisol Wood and came up empty there too. I tried to link her to the suspects I had already eliminated from my list, Mr. Sager, Kerns, Dave, Schmidt, Sabbatini. I crossed my fingers when I tried to link her to my father and sighed relief when I couldn't. I couldn't link her to Marathon, New Jersey, either. I had to dig deeper into that and find out what my father was hiding down there, but not yet. I had one more name I needed to cross-reference with Bobbie Lyles. I hesitated. I forced myself to do it.

She didn't connect to Nicole either.

I checked to see if the black Civic had been stolen recently. It hadn't, or Bobbie Lyles hadn't reported it as such. I ran her address into the cable service provider database. The house was wired for basic television, Vonage, and Internet service. The only machine IDs that came up were for a fax machine, an older model TV and a very old desktop PC, the kind Bobbie Lyles might use for her little startup business, to post her wares on eBay. She listed her employer as Dunkin' Donuts.

The low-tech computer, low-rent cable, low-wage job: perfect cover—too perfect. That black Civic was in her driveway. She was involved in this thing somehow.

I pulled a long-standing string I had into BinarTREE,

one of the major manufacturers of cell phone towers. They owned the northeast with nine of every ten towers flaunting their brand. The towers were equipped with sensors that pinpointed wireless data flow. Obviously media companies would pay dearly to know which homes were gobbling up lots of gigabytes, and then push their products there.

Why was Bobbie Lyles importing ridiculous amounts of data into her home, into her back bedroom, specifically; way more data than that crappy desktop dinosaur PC with its half a gigabyte of RAM could handle? I'd found her. I'd found the Recluse. She had a very powerful computer in that back room, the kind I had, homemade, no machine ID, untraceable, the kind you never dock to an Ethernet cable, to keep yourself invisible. The only way I was going to be able to suck the information from Bobbie Lyles's hard drive was to dock to it with an external drive. My phone beeped midnight. Knock on my door.

"Yup?"

My father leaned in, yawning. His gut hung over the waistband of his pajamas. "Saw your light on under the door."

"And?"

"Did you vote today?"

"Dad? I'm sixteen."

He eyed the laptops. "What the hell are you working on that you need two computers going?"

"Project."

"Fascinating description." He rubbed his eyes. "This is what you do all the time. Bird with the broken wing syndrome. Of all the girls out there, you have to fall in love with this one?"

"I'm not in *love*—"

"Look, I'm traveling a lot the next couple of weeks. It can't be helped. It's the heart of the fall season, you know? I'm thinking I want to take you with me."

"Yeah, thanks, *no*."

"Jay, if you keep messing around with Barrone's case and you get pinched, I can't help you. After Pete, I have no connections to PD. You screw up, you're on your own."

I was thinking the same about him. Traveling a lot? Would he be making any stops in Marathon?

I called Angela to tell her where I was in the hunt, but she was out at a club and in no mood to talk. "Call me tomorrow and we'll divvy up assignments," she said. But by tomorrow it would all be over, one way or another.

FORTY-THREE

By nine a.m., my father was off to a gallery for a private show-ing. I tucked my hair into a blue ball cap and studied myself in the mirror: blue work Dickies and this blue button-down I wore like once a year, Christmas at my aunt's, but it could pass for a work shirt. I holstered a Game Boy control. From far away, it might pass for an electric meter reader.

By 9:15 I was at Roberta Lyles's house. It looked differ-ent in real life. Bigger, creepier. The black Civic was gone. I knocked on the front door. No answer. Same way after ring-ing the bell. This was just a double check. I already knew she was at her Dunkin' Donut shift. I'd hacked her schedule from the local franchise's Google calendar the night before. If she had any kids, they were at school or in daycare. I went to the side of the run-down house and pretended to get a reading from the electric meter. I slipped a pin blade into the base-ment door lock and broke it with a twist.

The basement wasn't quite finished, bathroom project abandoned years ago, toilet bowl off its sewage site, half inch of dust coating it.

Upstairs: curb junk furniture. Really old TV. Coffee can by the window, overflowing menthol butts. Cheap arts and crafts everywhere, dusty God's eyes, faded cobwebs of yarn. Cigarette burn in the filthy, track-worn carpet. Cracked window patched with secondhand USPS packing tape. Kitchen was clean, but the shelving sagged like a triple-decker smile. A bead kit on the table. Never-to-be-finished necklaces. Cheap-framed sketches, ranging from really good to great, all pencil, mostly people, lots of self-portraits, snippets of her trying to grin her way through the everyday. Two bedrooms. Big one had big clothes draped about, big pair of underwear hung over the back of an exercise bike to dry. Potted plant, dead, on the bike seat. Small bedroom: mattress on the floor. Sketches all over the walls, taped up. Studying them, I felt the room turn very cold, and very suddenly.

The faces. I recognized them. These were BHHS students. My classmates. Me, on the floor, in the gymnasium. The pep rally. No puddle, though. Is that Angela, kneeling at my side? She's kissing my forehead. Yet more sketches on a card table that passed for a desk. Angela and a big dude, his face shadowed but vaguely familiar. Maybe Rick Kerns? They're getting it on. I was dialing Angela to tell her she was a target when I realized I was in Angela's bedroom. That she had drawn all these pictures.

The night before I could have sworn I knew Bobbie Lyles from somewhere. Now the resemblance was absolutely clear. She was either Angela's much older sister or her young mother. The address Angela had given me, the one on the other side of Valedale, really was her father's crib, but she lived here. She had me in her sights from day one, Nicole's first Schmidt session. Angela had come into Schmidt's that day as a walk-in. She knew Nicole was coming into school, and she wanted to see the damage she'd caused up close. She caught the way I was falling for Nicole, even that first day, and decided she had to team up with me to keep an eye on me.

My face burned. My hands ached from balling them so tightly. I felt stupid, of course. Profoundly so. But even more than that I felt guilt. In sharing information with Angela, I not only hadn't helped Nicole; I'd put her directly in harm's way.

I studied the dark walls covered with darker sketches. I had befriended the acid thrower, had actually begun to feel sorry for her. I was so stunned I couldn't remember the sequence of events that had led me to this point. What was I doing in this sociopath's bedroom, in her mind, rummaging through her dreams, her nightmares?

Her desk. The power adapter was there but no laptop. A portrait had fallen off the desk into a basket of dirty laundry. It was half photo, half sketch. It was Nicole. The photo was ripped from her Facebook. I recognized it, a close-up of Nicole at the family lake house. She's combing her hair in front of a mirror. Angela completely blocked out the left side of Nicole's face with glossy red pen. She'd noted it in the corner with what appeared to be a matrix of some sort:

GB

AM

I was trying to figure out what it meant, when hinges squeaked. The front screen door. I slipped into the basement stairwell. Somebody behind me said, "Very, very bad, Jay." Girl's voice.

I ran, but she kicked my foot from behind. She smashed my head face-first into musty green mini-golf carpet. I felt her knee in my back and something smooth, cold and heavy behind my ear. Metal, the nose of a pistol. She hissed, "You should have stuck with virtual breaking and entering." Her gum. The flavor, strawberry. No, cherry.

FORTY-FOUR

"How about a piece of that cherry gum, then?" I said to Detective Barrone. I'd asked her to take off the handcuffs. My shoulders ached from keeping my hands behind my back. The precinct interrogation room looked more like file storage, browning manila folders everywhere, lots of unsolved cases. "What about my three phone calls?"

"What three phone calls?" She peeled me a piece of gum.

"That's how they do it on *The Shield*."

"You get the calls after you've been arrested."

"If I'm not under arrest, why am I wearing bracelets?"

"Because for your own protection I needed to take you in for questioning."

"What exactly are you protecting me from?"

She put the gum into my mouth. "You, Jay."

"I demand my rights."

"These are your rights: You're mine for twenty-four hours before I have to arrest or release you. We had that house under surveillance with remote cameras from the buildings across the street. We have you on video. Burglary is a felony. It can get you locked up for fifteen years."

She had to be bluffing. This was my first offense. I was

more worried about the hacking. I'd tapped government agencies. Search warrant in hand, the cops were sure to be on their way to my apartment, my laptops.

"Jay, I want to help you. And I will. But you have to help me." She clicked open the handcuffs.

I felt a bit better now that I could see my hands. "I want to help you too, Detective. I do. But can you at least call my dad? I don't want him to freak out when he comes home and I'm not there. He'll take your call this time, I promise. He has an emergency cell number."

She pulled her phone. "What's the number?"

I gave it to her. She dialed and cracked me a can of Pepsi as she waited for my father or his voicemail to pick up. Neither would happen. The phone would ring indefinitely. She'd just dialed my kill code, the one that told my computers to fry themselves and all traces of my hacking. "What made you go to that house?" she said.

Barrone's partner leaned in. "Jess?"

Barrone went out into the hall. I wondered if Nicole knew I'd been arrested or if she'd tried to call me. They'd taken my phone. After a minute, Barrone was back. "Your friend Angela tried to run when she saw the police parked out in front of the high school. They caught her on a bus bound for Newark." Barrone kicked the door shut and eyed me. "Last chance: Tell me how you figured out Angela Sammick threw acid at Nicole Castro, or I'll slap you with obstruction of justice on top of the burglary. I'll petition the DA to go full out on you in court, no concurrent sentencing. You could do twenty-five to life."

"Didn't I just help you catch the perp?"

"Are you serious? I had that house staked out for weeks, and then you go busting in there? You could have tipped her off that we were onto her. She makes it to that airport? Forget it. *Gone.*"

"One question—"

"No. No questions from you now. Now you give answers."

"If you had Angela pegged as a suspect for weeks, why did you wait so long to arrest her?"

Barrone glared at me. "You have fifteen seconds to make up your mind: Tell me every single thing that took you to Angela Sammick's house this morning, or you will cook. And Jay? That pretty hair of yours? They're gonna love you in jail." She checked her wristwatch.

I eyed the wall clock. It had maybe twenty years' worth of dust on the rim, but the second hand ticked out just fine: 5 seconds to go, 4, 3 . . . I would tell her everything, almost. No way I was bringing Cherry into this. "The black Civic. I had to run down the tag number—"

"Jay, do not say a *word.*" My father rolled into the room and dropped his giant hands on my shoulders, shielding me or getting ready to strangle me.

"I'm disappointed you never found the time to return my calls, Steve," Barrone said. "That the only way we could talk is under these ridiculous circumstances."

"I'm not talking to you now, either. Is he under arrest?"

"Not yet."

"Then arrest him."

FORTY-FIVE

The holding cell was cold, and I had to share it with this kid who kept crying and another who was picking on the crier. I told the idiot to chill or I'd hammer him, and he chilled. My experience is that people often confuse tall with tough.

The next morning, Thursday, my court-appointed lawyer pled not guilty for me. My father was there to post bail. He'd had to hock one of his paintings. We were driving a while when I said, "Dad? Marathon. Those two trips—"

He grabbed my jacket collar, his eyes wet, face red. He spit as he yelled. "You're spying on *me?* I'm scrambling like an idiot to raise bail yesterday, last night, all these *years.* For *you.* You know what, Jay?" He let go of my collar with a shove and hit the gas. "It's none of your goddamn business what I was doing in Marathon." He turned up the stereo, annoyingly repetitive baroque organ. A few minutes later we were home. He pulled up to the lobby entrance. "Get out," he said.

"Where you going?"

"*Food* shopping." He sped out of the lot.

Nicole had called. I called her back. A half hour later her Saab was pulling up to my lobby. I hopped in. "I'm furious with you," she said. "You could've been killed." She kissed my cheek.

"Let's go visit Emma," I said.

"I was by this morning. She's feeling sick today."

Nicole wanted to walk around. We went to Jersey City. We parked by the waterfront shops and hiked to Liberty State Park. It was packed. The weather was crazy for November 4, low seventies, dry, breezy, no clouds. At one point Nicole just stopped and drew in a deep breath. "Nice," she said. "I keep forgetting to do that. Let's go into Manhattan."

"I can't leave the state." I lifted the cuff of my jeans to show her the tracking bracelet.

She took my hand, led me to a bench and rested her head on my shoulder. "The detective said she'll be tested today. At the lockdown hospital. A prolonged psychiatric evaluation. If they declare her sane, she goes to juvenile detention. According to the detective, she'll likely cop a plea."

"Do you hate her?" I said.

"I want to."

"You should."

"You don't have to tell me how to feel, Jay." She leaned forward and looked out onto the water. "I do, okay? I hate her." She did a double take to something on her right. "Oh god, let's get out of here."

Some kid in a leftover Halloween mask was flying a skeleton kite intentionally low, buzzing us. The mask was Phantom of the Opera. The half face mask.

—

We went back to her house. Sylvia was in Newark with her family for her day off, and Mrs. Castro was with Emma. We shot some one-on-one hoop out in the driveway, under a flickering garage light. "You throw some sharp elbows there," I said, rubbing my ribs.

"You have me by like ten inches and seventy pounds, and you're crying about my D?" She stole the ball, quick-stepped over the paint line to check it and drove for the hoop. I grabbed her at her waist, lifted her so she could slam-dunk the eight-foot rim.

A woman called out to us from the mansion across the street. "Nicole? Is that *you* making all that racket?"

"Sorry, Mrs. Wooly."

Another one from the svelte-granny-in-the-canoe section of the L.L.Bean catalog. "That ball bouncing is awfully loud, isn't it? We don't do that here." She was talking to me.

"Sorry," I said.

"As indeed you should be. It's almost dinnertime. Can't we eat in peace?"

"I apologize," I said.

"Don't," Nicole said. She took my hand and led me into the house.

We were up in her room, at her desk, ostensibly to cram for her home school chem test. "Do you think you'll come back now?" I said. "To the Hollows?"

"Maybe eventually, I guess. I don't know, maybe not."

"I forget, you know? When I'm with you. About the seizure. The pep rally."

"Me too. About the attack, I mean." She looked away and combed her hair over the bandage on her cheek. "Until I remember."

I held her hand. "Six years ago. I was ten. My folks and I were at the *Clarion* for the annual holiday party. My father promised he would stay dry and be designated driver, but 'just one' turned in 'just one more' and so on. He asked my mother to drive. She'd had a few herself. She liked to have a good time, my mom. To laugh, you know? This guy Pete, my uncle sort of, said he'd drive us home, just give him a minute to get his coat. He got hung up talking to his boss, and after a couple of minutes my father was like, I'm exhausted, I have to get home, let's go. My mom voted we wait for Pete, but Dad was on his way to the car."

"Oh Jay."

"My father says the car hit black ice, but my mother was looking at me, in the rearview, right before the crash. Her eyes weren't on the road. Whatever happened, she swerved to avoid an oncoming truck, and the car spun out into a light pole, head on. The airbags deployed, and my Dad was okay except for some minor neck trauma and a broken collarbone, but Mom hadn't been wearing her seat belt. I didn't do too well in the backseat. The doctor defined it as 'serious head trauma.' The swelling in my brain went away a couple of weeks later, and then they came on fast. The seizures."

"He's trying, though, right?" she said. "Now, I mean. Trying to stay sober. He's there for you as much as he can be. He didn't abandon you. He created a situation, and he's owning up to it." We were facing each other. She turned to hide her left cheek.

I put my fingers to her chin and gently turned her face to mine. "I won't run away. You don't have to hide from me."

"I do, though. You don't want to see it. Trust me. I'll be right back." She went into the bathroom. The door closed softly, the lock clicked.

I flipped the textbook to a page she'd flagged, the chemical diagram for hydrochloric acid.

FORTY-SIX

Nicole didn't come "right back." She was in the bathroom for a while. She was pale when she came out. She said she was feeling under the weather. I checked the window: perfect sunset, balmy breeze. "I'll let you get some rest," I said.

"Stay."

"I have to go to work anyway."

She walked me to the door. We hugged, and when I broke to leave, she held on a little longer before she let me go.

I was on one of our archaic computers, checking to see if BJ's online had an item we had sold out of in the store, a forty-dollar piece of junk chiminea. The customer I was trying to help was practically leaning his head on my shoulder, trying to see the computer screen. His breath reeked of the onion rings we try to get you to buy when you walk in, because of course everybody needs to have his mouth stuffed with fried junk food while shopping for staircase bunk beds with a merlot finish.

I was about to log out when the sidebar ad changed from one that tried to sucker you into thinking that only a 99-inch television was acceptable when watching *X-Factor* to one about weed killer. A cartoon spider climbed a daisy. The spider was a happy little guy. He lay back on the flower, put four of his arms behind his head and winked.

Why didn't Barrone seem at all happy after Angela Sammick's arrest?

"Jay." Dave Bendix gripped my hand and clapped my shoulder. "Thank you, man. For everything you did for Nicole."

"How'd you know I work here?"

"Nic told me. I told her I had to talk to you. Look, I want you to know it's okay. You and Nic, I mean."

"Dave, again, we're just friends. Seriously, nothing's going on."

"Maybe not on your end. I heard it in her voice." He teared up. "I want her to be happy. You're a good dude. I just wanted you to know that we're still cool, okay? You have a tissue?" I gave him my coffee napkin. He blew his nose. "What gets into somebody's head that they ruin somebody like that? Did you get any sense from Detective Barrone why Angela did it?"

And that's when I knew Dave Bendix was hiding something big. "No," I said. "It's a mystery."

Ten minutes before we closed, I picked up the cheapest laptop BJ's offered, came to a hundred and eighty bucks cash with my employee discount. The police had seized my computers, but fortunately not until two hours after the kill call, according to our building super, who had to let them into the apartment.

I rode my bike home, two blocks past my building to this house that had been foreclosed on and abandoned. In the basement was a bucket of filthy rags. Beneath those were a bunch of computer parts and one totally sexy bandwidth thief I'd picked up at swap meets, all untraceable. I mixed and matched them into the crappy laptop shell, and in half an hour the machine was built. I was invisible again.

The next day, Friday, the story went wide under the title GOTH GIRL BURNED BEAUTY. The detectives found Angela's laptop in her backpack. She'd done it all, the chem lab video post, the emails to Mrs. Marks, to me. I was particularly grateful to her for the one with the strobe lights. I was betting that at her size, she wasn't having a good time in jail. No bail for Angela Sammick, obviously. The more I thought about her, the madder I got, and not just at her. I was disgusted with myself for having let her dupe me. Not wishing serious pain on her was a challenge.

Nicole invited me over for lunch, but I was going to have to pass. Her father was spending the day at the house. I admired him in some vague way, but in the end he had to land on my jerk list. I just didn't want to be around the guy, his intensity, those eyes that cut right through you and made you feel like you were hiding something, even if you weren't. I had some digging to do anyway.

I had hit Dave's Facebook page at least twenty times in the past couple of weeks. I'd scanned everything he'd posted, and I'd never found anything out of place. Yet I went at it again, reviewing every picture, clip and comment for anything I might have missed. Nothing. I shifted over to what wasn't there anymore. You might think you deleted that goofy picture you slapped onto your wall when you were huffing Magic Markers, but the moment you clicked it up there, it was and is there forever and for the taking by anybody with kindergarten-level hacking skills. Once you post, you're toast.

Sure enough, Dave had deleted a video from his gallery. He'd pulled it from his wrestling videos folder the day after the attack. It was a recording of one of his matches from the previous spring. In the video, he finishes crushing his opponent with a savage pin job. Nicole, watching from the first row of the bleachers, jumps up clapping and screams, "*Woohoo.*" She leans out from the bleachers toward the home team wrestlers' bench. Dave is sitting now, and Nicole whispers something into his ear. He turns to her, glares, and then turns back to watch the next match. Nicole leans back into the bleachers. The whole exchange lasts less than two seconds.

I replayed the video again and again. Sure, every couple has arguments, but Dave was treating Nicole coldly. They'd only been going out for a couple of months at that time. No way Dave would disrespect her like that. I zoomed in. The girl whispering into Dave's ear wasn't Nicole. She was a dyed chestnut Angela Sammick.

My quandary: Do I tell Nicole that Dave was cheating on her? No, she has enough sadness in her life.

Dave had held back information from the police, the kind that could have led them to Angela a lot sooner. That's obstruction of justice, the same charge I was facing. If I'd seen this video, so had Detective Barrone. Did Dave know she was onto him? And why hadn't Barrone arrested Dave?

FORTY-SEVEN

"Perhaps it fascinates you," Schmidt said.

I was still suspended, but as part of my bail agreement I was required to honor my obligation to meet with her once a week.

"You mean *she*, don't you, Doctor?"

"I was referring to her disfigurement."

"I don't care about it, okay? It's so not important. What, you're afraid that once I see it, I won't want to hang out with her anymore, right? That once the mystery of what's underneath those bandages is over, the fascination will have worn off for me. Or that maybe it'll disgust me? The lack of symmetry? Is that what you're thinking?"

"No, Jay, *I* wasn't thinking any of those things at all. I wasn't even aware you hadn't seen the burn yet. I was merely suggesting the act fascinates you. That it may well be impossible for a person like you to understand how someone could willfully do such a thing to another human being."

"A person like me?"

"Yes." She leaned forward, tapped a note into her computer. "I'll have to write a letter to the DA about you, of course."

"Going to tell him I'm a nut job, right? Thanks a bunch, Doctor."

"I'm going to tell him you're a great kid."

I was actually touched, but not so much that I was above setting my magic phone onto her desk and ripping off her BlackBerry's new password.

Later that Friday afternoon and into the night, I raided Schmidt's patient files for Angela Sammick's case folder. Angela had made no mention of Dave Bendix, but she had body image issues that Schmidt rated severe. She noted that Angela had a plastic surgery wish list on perfectbeauty.com. I torched through the firewall, maybe five seconds. Angela had uploaded pictures of herself. Using the site's graphics tools, she reconstructed her body, but most of her wish list focused on her face, new nose, chin, cheekbones.

I went out onto the fire escape with a cup of what I thought was instant cocoa until I sipped it. It was one of those no-frills brands, and the label had said chocolate mint, but it tasted more like boiled Scope. The fresh air felt great for all of ten seconds before it became too cold for somebody wearing a tee and boxers. The stars didn't so much twinkle through the pines as sever them.

I sat on the living room floor, pressing my back against the radiator grate. Across the room, the wall looked weird. Until two days ago, my father's paintings had covered it entirely, gifts from friends and artists. But now there was a box of blank wall where the painting hocked for my bail money had been, I couldn't remember which. The art had become ordinary, the way you rarely look out a window to take in the view after a month or so of living in a place.

Nicole called. "My dad just left," she said. She sounded really groggy. "I can't drive. Come over. Please?"

The security company SUV was back out in front of the Castro house. The door opened. Sylvia was teary. She led me to the kitchen, where Mrs. Castro was crying. "A hit job," she said. "The detective thinks it's possible the Sammick girl was paid to do it."

I'd been contemplating the same idea on the ride over. That new Angela on perfectbeauty.com didn't come cheap, $135,000. Now I understood why Detective Barrone hadn't seemed too happy when Angela was caught. She was holding back on the arrest in the hope Angela would make contact with the person who hired her to do the hit on Nicole. Could Dave Bendix have promised to pay for all that plastic surgery in exchange for Angela's burning Nicole? Why, though? How could burning Nicole help Dave? It couldn't. Being connected in any way to the attack almost guaranteed he wouldn't get into Harvard.

"Your father's book," Mrs. Castro said. "Did you remember to bring it?"

I hadn't. "How's Nicole about all this?"

"Actually, she seems to be hanging pretty tough about the Sammick situation. We just got the call. Emma died this morning."

Her bedroom was cold and dark, but sweat glistened on her forehead. The only light came from a miserable crescent moon being dunked into brown clouds. She was lying on top of the covers. Her pajama bottoms stuck to her legs. She wore a thick hoodie. The front was rolled up to cool her sweaty stomach. The window was open. I went to close it. "Leave it," she said. "Please." Her hair was messy, straggly over the bandage on her cheek. She put out her hand for me to hold it. "Prozac," she said.

I looked to her night table for a prescription bottle and found none. "Where is it?"

She shook her head. "The shrink made me take it. Or made Mom make me."

"I thought Schmidt was a psychologist." You needed to be a psychiatrist to prescribe Prozac. My father was on it after my mother was killed.

"The other shrink," Nicole said. "I can't get out of bed now, but I don't want to be asleep. I took her with me to the national Girl Scouts conference speech last spring. The pageant directors, you know? They set up these events. This was one of my first speeches after the coronation. All those mothers looking up at me, their daughters looking up to me. I was trembling. Emma calmed me down. She introduced me, not a twitch of nervousness I could see. She spoke so well, a little adult. She was amazing. 'You are so going to rock this,' she whispered into my ear as I took the podium. 'No way you can't. I'm your good luck charm.' She was, too. She was my good luck angel. People say it all the time: The world was a better place with her in it. You dismiss it as a cliché, but the problem is it's true. It also means that the world is a worse place without her in it." She put her hand to my cheek. She pulled me to her so that I was spooning her. She smelled of strawberry shampoo and antiseptic. We watched the moonlight go weak on the walls with the thickening clouds. After a few minutes she started to breathe more slowly and then snore, very lightly. Then she sneezed and fell into a sneezing fit. She went to the bathroom.

The neighbor's cat was at the window, staring in. When I went to close the window, the cat jumped away. Nicole watched from the bathroom, blowing her nose.

FORTY-EIGHT

The next day, Saturday, I called Nicole's cell, and she didn't pick up. I tried the house phone and got the machine. When I got home from work Saturday night, I hadn't heard back from her. Sunday afternoon, I got her mom on the house phone. "She's sick with a terrible flu, Jay. She's been sleeping all weekend."

I hadn't slept all weekend. I had been trying to figure out what my father was doing in Marathon. I couldn't get it out of my head, what he told me that night when I asked him what he'd done with all his attempts at painting. "I burned them," he'd said.

I met Cherry at Sbarro for a slice. "Here's the thing about boys," she said. "You're all idiots. This isn't PMS bitchy she's going through, okay? She lost a sister."

"Technically, they weren't sisters."

"Technically, you're brainless. This is exactly what I'm talking about. You need to give her space, Jay. Tell me you didn't text her."

"A couple of times. Okay, four."

"You're worse than a girl. Give her a few days. How are you doing, though? About Emma, I mean. Are you okay?"

"Me? Fine. I mean, yes it sucks, but you know. It's not like I knew her. Collectively I spent maybe a couple of hours with her. Seriously, I'm cool."

"You're so not cool, you poor boy." She pulled me into a hug. I was exhausted, and I sort of cried into her hair. "Crying can be sexy when it's done in a rugged albeit sensitive dude way," she said. "Can I bite your earlobe? Just a nibble? No?"

My suspension ended the next morning, Monday. I was eating by myself, under the B-wing stairs. A bunch of dudes from wrestling rolled up on me. Rick Kerns was suspended for another week, but this other heavyweight was happy to fill in for him as pack leader. He nodded. "Spaceman. Heard you and Dave are cool about Nicole."

"Nothing's going on," I said.

"Whatever," he said. "Hey, that was ballsy. What you did for her, I mean. Jay, seriously, man, come to practice sometime. We need dudes like you on the team." He nodded again as he headed off.

"Later, Jay," somebody else said as they left.

After school I headed down to the Hoboken waterfront to meet my father and his friend from the old days. She was a lawyer. She couldn't take the case because she wasn't licensed to practice in New Jersey, but she knew we were broke and was happy to give us free advice. Her name was Camilla, and she chain-smoked. "I think your best bet is to try to get the Lyles woman to drop the burglary charge," she said. "That might get the judge in the mind-set to reduce the obstruction charge or maybe even throw it out."

"How do we get her to drop the charge?" my father said.

"Steve, not to tell stories in front of Jay, but do you remember that time you had a couple too many from the frat house keg and ditched me to hang with that pretty little blond thing? What did you do the next day?"

"I apologized."

"On bended *knee* you apologized. And you were sincere. We worked it out." She nodded to me. "Offer her compassion, Jay. She just lost a daughter." Her phone beeped. "Fellas, I have to get a man out of jail. See you around."

The air was cold, but the sun was warm. "Steakhouse or salad bar?" my dad said.

He didn't need to be gnawing on rib fat. "Afraid it'll have to be rabbit food."

He slapped my knee. "Maybe I ought to go with you to see the Lyles woman."

"Thanks, but it'll be better if I go solo. You know, so it doesn't look like I'm going because my old man forced me to."

"You ever gonna cut that hair?"

"When I start stepping on it."

"That'll be an interesting look." He sighed as he pushed himself up from the bench. "Salad, huh? *Bleh.*"

"Dad, seriously, it's cool if you have a girlfriend in Marathon."

"Jay, seriously, back off. There's nothing going on down there. Let's go, we're getting steaks."

After school the next day, Tuesday afternoon, I headed for Mrs. Lyles's house. I bought flowers but realized they would make me look like a kiss-ass, and I gave them away. I wasn't into my second rap on the door when it opened. Her eyes were puffy slits rimmed with washed-out mascara. She smoked a cigarette. "I'm just on my way out," she said.

"Ma'am, my name is Jay Nazzaro."

"What do you want?" Her eyes widened. "Oh, wait, you're him. You're the . . ." She slammed the door.

I nodded to nobody but myself. I was at the curb when I heard "Wait."

I headed back up to the porch and waited at the threshold. "You see me holding the door for you, don't you?" she said.

The house was more of a wreck than the last time I'd . . . been there. We went to the kitchen. "Sit." She laid out coffee mugs. "That night at the party a couple years ago. Angela told me you stood up for her." She poured old coffee. "The detective told me your name, but I couldn't place it until just now, when I saw your face." She pulled a faux leather bound album from a stack on the table and flipped to a sketched portrait of me. Angela must have drawn it from memory, because I couldn't remember posing for a picture like this. She nailed me, my eyes, my trying not to look scared. I hated her a little more for getting inside me like that.

"She told me the whole story," Mrs. Lyles said. "Or at least the story that was told to her. She herself remembered just tatters of it. I told her she should go out with you, but she said she wasn't good enough." Her eyes went to her wristwatch. "I have to visit my daughter now. I'm afraid. I'd like to know if you would come with me."

FORTY-NINE

The last place I should have been with a tracking bracelet on my ankle was a juvenile detention center, but I had to get Bobbie Lyles to drop the burglary charge. I was stunned when the guard let me in. "Perfectly legal and more common than you would think," she said. "Parolees visiting prisoners, you know?"

Angela was considered too dangerous to others and herself for a non-secure, face-to-face meeting. A guard escorted her to the chair behind the Plexiglas partition. She was a mess with a black eye and a split lip. Her mother gagged and hurried out for the bathroom. Angela eyed me. "So sweet of you to visit, Jameson." She was definitely medicated, spacey eyes. All the face jewelry was gone, of course. The pinhole by her lip was infected. She was pale. "The other girls aren't really feeling me," she said.

"Especially when you're around anything liquid, right?" Her jumper was an oddly cheerful color, bright teal. "Why'd you follow us to my apartment house that day?" I said. "What, you just couldn't resist?"

"I was bombed."

"Driving drunk. Nice. Lucky you weren't killed."

She laughed. I'd never seen her laugh before. "Yeah, lucky me."

The room was freezing, but Angela's sleeves were rolled up. Her arms were a mess, lots of scars, cigarette burns. One of them was elaborate, a pentangle. She caught me looking at it. "Pretty, right?"

"The test run?" I said, referring to that very first email she sent Mrs. Marks.

She turned her forearm out so we both could see the burn better. "I think it looks righteous. Should have seen when I did it, the tiny little bubbles. I swear, I was salivating. Like it was juicy, you know what I mean?"

"No, I don't, Angela. So that thing about Nicole giving you her jeans. You made it up."

"No, it was true."

"Then how could you burn her after she was so nice to you?"

"*Because* she was so nice to me." She picked at the pentangle scar. "You don't think it looks cool?"

"Why are you protecting him?"

She rolled down her sleeves. "Have no idea what you're talking about."

"Angela, did you ever ask yourself, Why me?"

"Are you kidding? Since I'm like three years old."

"No, I mean why this nutcase picked you to do the job. He must have known you hated Nicole, right? The only dude that comes to mind there is Dave Bendix. I know about you two, okay? I have video."

"No you don't, Spaceman. You have Dave Bendix at a wrestling match I happened to be at. You have me cheering him on, like the three hundred other people in that gym. You have shit. Look, my lawyer tells me that in like a week the shrinks will have gotten together and deemed me nuts, and I'll be whisked to a psych center for four years. I'll be drawing pictures and watching movies all day and getting all these great meds. After that, three years probation, self check-in parole. I'm not saying anything about anybody else who may or may not have been involved."

"But Dave can't touch you now. It's done. You're not going to get any more time added to your sentence for turning him in."

She smiled and shook her head. "You just don't get it. You don't get *any* of this. You're perfectly incapable of understanding."

"You don't want to see the dude who put you up to this fry?"

"I would love to see him fry—are you kidding? But it wasn't Dave. Trust me."

"Trust you? Are *you* kidding? Then who did it? Who paid you to burn Nicole?"

"I. Don't. *Know.* Like I told Barrone. I wish I knew. She offered to get the DA to halve my sentence if I could ID the contract issuer. Why are you winking at me?"

"I'm not. My eye twitches when I haven't slept in three days. How could you not know who made you burn her?"

"I got a letter, maybe three months ago, no return address. Letter says, basically, 'Nicole Castro needs to burn.' Letter says how it might happen, maybe somebody should throw battery acid into her face. If I do the job, I get a hundred grand, enough to get the hell out of here, maybe go to France, where people are cool and leave you alone, start a new life, go to art school or some shit, you know? Of course I'm like, this is too good to be true. There was a combo code and an address to this storage place off I-95. I go there, small locker, only things in it are a pair of Priority Mail envelopes, again no return address of course, but lots of hundred dollar bills with a note that says half now, half after. And what do you know, all of a sudden I have fifty k in my backpack."

"Why two Priority envelopes? He couldn't fit the money in one?"

"You don't have to go to the post office window if a package is under thirteen ounces, which both were. Fifty k weighs a little over a pound—I checked. Cut the stack in half, you have two roughly nine ounce packages, just drop them into any old mailbox."

"You believed him, that he would pay you the second half?"

She leaned in. "Dude, are you serious? I would have done it for *five* thousand. And anyway, he paid me the balance."

"You're kidding."

"Unbelievable, right? A psycho with morals. Barrone seized it all anyway, the bitch." She leaned back. "Not doing the job wasn't an option. He had my address. Anybody nuts enough to advance me fifty k to burn Nicole is nuts enough to drop a bullet into the back of my skull if I tried to beat him out of the money. I'm the victim here too, Jay. I had no choice."

"Except maybe to go to the police?"

"You're funny. I tried to get info on him, in case he tried to get away with not paying the second fifty k, but I couldn't turn up anything. I hacked the storage place's files. Dude ordered the locker rental by mail, like sent a hundred-dollar cash down payment with an actual paper form. Who does such things anymore, I ask you. Registered as Joe Smith of Hopper Lane someplace in Florida. That checked out to be an unoccupied HUD-owned foreclosure."

"You tapped HUD?"

"Please, it was easier than planting Trojans in Canadian discount drug spam. You know, Spaceman, you just might have the chops to run this dude down." She waved me closer to the glass and whispered. "The money? It was actually a hundred k for the down payment. I left fifty of it where Barrone could find it, but I have the rest tucked away. You track this nut down, get me his name, let me be the one to break the news to Barrone, and I'll take care of you. I swear."

"First, you're lying. You don't have any money." Her eyes had ticked right when she mentioned it. "Second, the idea of helping you halve your sentence and getting you back out and at large on the street two years earlier? Not terribly appealing." I got up to go.

"It was a business transaction, Jay. If I didn't do it, somebody else would've. It was unstoppable. Take comfort in that."

"But it wasn't somebody else, Angela. It was you. For the rest of your life, you'll be the girl who burned Nicole Castro."

"Dude, you are hilarious. So that's her problem, then. And you really think people will remember any of this? It's old

250

news already, now that there isn't going to be a trial. Then again, Nicole'll probably remember it, right? But even you, Jay. Year from now, you'll be moon-eyed over some other fantasy queen, and Nicole Castro will just fade from your heart. I'm saying cheer up, champ. Time heals all wounds, excluding burns. Hey Jay, how much are you hating on me right now, scale of one to ten?"

I turned back to take her in one last time. She showed just the slightest hint of a smile as she waited for my answer. She would be out in four years, maybe less. With therapy, counseling, meds, she'd recover, get a job, marry, have children. Her kids would never know what she had done. And then there was Nicole: How would she get through the next sixty or seventy years with half a face? "Angela, to be perfectly honest, you're too much of a mess to hate. I feel sorry for you."

Her half smile turned into a nasty little pout. Her lips quivered. She winced as she wiped her split lip. "Look at me. Look what they did to my *face*." She glared at me now. "That bitch deserved it." She pounded her fists into the Plexiglas. "I hate you, Jay. Seriously. You and Nicole." She slammed her head into the Plexiglas, and then slammed it again. The guards were on her and pulling her away from the glass.

A horrible thought came to me only just then. "The storage place," I said.

"I hate you, Nazzaro!"

"Was it in Marathon?"

"I *hate* you." She sobbed as they dragged her around the corner and out of sight.

FIFTY

Angela Sammick was right. I needed a lot more than that wrestling match video to connect her to Dave. Somewhere she had to have something big on him. Why else wouldn't he have come forward and told Detective Barrone about Angela?

The cops had her laptop, and she wouldn't have kept anything incriminating on that drive anyway. She undoubtedly had it stored in the cloud somewhere. I could hack her password, but without a username, I had no chance of finding it. The best I could do was go back to those BinarTREE phone tower logs. I kept picking up on a data string that Angela repeatedly imported from a cutters' chat room. I spent the rest of that Tuesday night throwing darts into the void, setting up my laptop to shoot endless combinations of usernames and passwords into iCloud and the thousands of other digital storage warehouses. I was firing scattershot. Finding Angela Sammick's data was hopeless. I was feeling pretty down. Nicole still hadn't called me back.

Wednesday morning, my father woke me, shaking my foot. He was on the phone. He tapped out a one-hand piano tune on the wall, and then he punched the air in silent triumph.

"Mrs. Lyles, I cannot thank you enough. You've literally saved the boy's life. Your compassion will inspire him to be a better man. He truly is sorry." They talked for another minute, my father clicked off the phone, and we high-fived. Now all I had to do was get Detective Barrone to drop the obstruction of justice charge.

"You don't seem so happy," my father said.

I smiled, but I had a hard time maintaining eye contact with him. Steve Nazzaro was hiding something down in Marathon.

"Dude, chill, she'll call," Cherry said. This was Wednesday afternoon the tenth of November, though it felt like September. The weather was sixty degrees and sunny. We were hanging out in a skate park at the edge of the Meadowlands. "So if the detective gets the obstruction of justice charge to stick, where's that leave you?"

I was showing her how to coast a curb rail. "For starters, forget about college with a felony on my record."

"I thought you didn't want to go anyway. Oh, I get it, we want to follow Nicole to school now." Cherry landed hard on the recycled rubber. "I refuse to keep bruising my ass. I'll do anything but this. Your call."

I studied the highway. The I-95 traffic was moving fast. "Let's go for a ride."

Cherry's duct-taped Civic chugged south down I-95 to the Marathon exit. "What are we looking for, by the way?" Cherry said.

"Something bad."

"Gee, I hope we find it. Loving the specificity too."

"Watch the—"

"I see it."

The car practically bottomed out in a pothole that was more of a crevasse. "Then why did you drive through it?"

"I like scaring you."

The service road cut through industrial wasteland and dead-ended at a strip mall. I didn't see anything that looked like a storage/mail receiving facility. I pointed out one of the shops. "That one showed up on my father's AmEx statement as food/bev."

"The Saloon?" Cherry said.

"Actually the Salon. Wonder where the second *o* went."

"Oprah took it."

"What do you think it means?"

"I'm gonna go with a saloon is an establishment that serves alcoholic beverages. Guessing. You're thinking it's not a saloon, though. You're thinking it's more of a salon. Why would they put a whorehouse in the middle of a godforsaken industrial wasteland where the only customers you're going to get are—"

"Truckers?"

"Oh."

Inside was crushed velvet, tassel-trimmed tables, dusty chandeliers. "Doesn't it feel like we're in that historical museum they have out in Vegas?" Cherry said.

"I haven't been there."

"I haven't either. I just watch a lot of TV."

A cocktail waitress played piano, Debussy, "Clair de Lune." The dude behind the bar said, "Help you?" He was chipping ice with a mini-harpoon.

"We work for Steve," I said. "At the newspaper?"

The dude squinted. He was the son of Captain Ahab and Captain Hook. I nudged Cherry to get her to stop staring at the man's eye patch. She hid behind me.

"He wanted us to pick up the jacket," I said. "Blue blazer, size fifty-two tall? Said he left it here a week or so ago?"

"What was the last name again?"

"Would he have told you his real last name?" I said.

"Why wouldn't he?"

"Well, I mean, you know."

The captain frowned. "My friend, this isn't *that* kind of saloon."

"Told you," Cherry said.

"Steve Nazzaro," I said.

"As in rhymes with Sbarro?"

"Ex*act*ly."

"Oh, you mean *Steve*. Steve's a sweetheart. So shy, you know?"

"That's what we call him at the office," Cherry said. "Shy Steve."

"Yeah," Ahab said. "He gets really nervous before he plays."

"Plays?"

"The piano. We have these open mic nights, poetry, music, whatever you want. It's a safe environment to experiment with new material or just to get yourself up in front of people. The truck drivers are a good audience, you know? They don't expect Rachmaninoff, and they'll clap sincerely for 'Chopsticks' too. Steve's pretty good, though. He did just fine the other night. Seemed to be a lot more comfortable in front of the crowd. He's in the newspaper business? I thought that business went out of business." He gave us two sodas with cherries. We got hamburgers and left a big tip.

"Tell Steve I said sorry about the jacket," that nice old pirate said.

Back in the car, Cherry patted my knee. "This must be very traumatizing for you. It's not every day one finds out his father is actually a pretty nice guy."

An hour and a half later, we were back in Brandywine. My boss had called to beg me to come in for a few hours to help stock the major shipment of Christmas crap that had landed that afternoon. I said yes because Jimmy did me a lot of favors with scheduling, and I was too out of my mind to hack anyway. I had no idea where to start looking for the person who contracted Angela to hit Nicole.

Cherry was going to drop me off at BJ's, but when we stopped in at Starbucks to pick up her check, the girl working behind the counter was looking really sick, and Cherry covered for her. BJ's was just a mile up the road, and I wanted to walk. I was hoping the fresh air would wake me up. I was about fifty feet from the warehouse entrance when a black

BMW SUV pulled alongside me. The tinted window rolled down. "Heya Jay," Dave Bendix said.

"Dave, I kind of feel like you're following me."

"I went into BJ's, and they said you were on your way. Jay, man, I really screwed up. You're the only person I can talk to about this. Nicole's in trouble, and I need you to help me help her. We'll grab a quick slice, five minutes of your time, max. It's a life or death thing."

I had this idea that if I nudged him just right, gently, I could get him to turn himself in; that maybe he *wanted* to turn himself in but just needed emotional support to get himself to go to the precinct. He was looking for a little compassion. I was ready to give it to him. He'd messed up, hooking up with Angela. They both had. He'd tried to cover his mistake. It was blowing up in his face now. He was coming clean and ready to accept the consequences. I respected that.

The shotgun seat was loaded with wrestling crap, a net bag filled with pads. Dave started to swing it into the back, but it was too big to squeeze over the seat back.

"I'll get in the back," I said.

"I'm really scared, Jay," Dave said. "Word is you're like this phenomenal hacker. Can you find out something for me?"

"Depends."

"There's this lie going around about me, and I want to know who's spreading it. You heard it, right? That I was doubling on Nicole with Angela Sammick?"

I nodded, immediately regretting my yes. The theory that

Dave and Angela were hooking up hadn't gone public yet.

"That's what I thought," Dave said. His eyes flicked to the rearview. By the time I turned around to check the cargo spot, the arm was around my neck, and the chokehold was tightening.

Rick Kerns jerked me backward. My neck was pinned to the edge of the seat back. The BMW sped up and made a quick left toward the highway. I dug at Rick's arm, but I couldn't break the hold. I was fading out. It's not the choke to the windpipe that takes you down. It's cutting off the carotid arteries, the ones that feed oxygen to your brain. Rick was threatening me, Dave too. I kept hearing "if you ever" but that's all I remember. When you can't breathe, listening carefully to what people are saying isn't exactly a priority.

Looking back, I can only assume they weren't going to kill me. Dave had gone into BJ's and asked where I was. He's going to make me disappear an hour later? No. Then again, how could they just leave it at a threat? They actually thought I would keep my mouth shut about Dave and Angela? What could they have threatened? The only thing they could have said to make me keep quiet was that they would kill Nicole if I opened my mouth. Then again, that probably would've had me running to Detective Barrone. I really don't know what they were going to do with me that night, and I never found out. But at that moment, my neck creaking, my lungs burning, I was sure they were going to kill me, and I panicked. With images of that childhood car crash blinding me, I drove my feet into and through the back of the driver's seat.

My kick threw Bendix into the steering wheel. The horn sounded briefly as the BMW spun. I hugged the seat back as Kerns was thrown over the seat, into the windshield. The glass webbed around his skull. The car flipped over the guardrail and slid upside down into the gully. I don't remember anything after that, until the ambulance lights. Somebody said, "Relax, buddy." So I did. My eyes itched.

Dave had the airbag and made out okay. I was belted in and had the side bag and seatback. Kerns suffered a concussion and shattered a shoulder and both of his arms.

FIFTY-ONE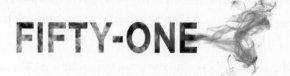

In the hospital that Wednesday night, or maybe it was into Thursday morning already, I was enjoying the painkillers too much to open my eyes, but I heard Detective Barrone just fine. "He admits to having sex with Angela but denies he put her up to burning Nicole. He insists his father would have disowned him if he found out he was in any way responsible for the acid attack, not to mention withholding information about the perpetrator. Apparently no Bendix has ever not been admitted to Harvard."

"Those calls," my father said. "What'd you want to talk with me about anyway?"

"I wanted your expertise. I'd interviewed Angela Sammick's art teacher, and she'd shown me some of Angela's work. Some of the pictures looked vaguely familiar, as if she'd copied some paintings that an art historian would be able to identify at a glance. I was looking for you to save me some time."

"And why are you here now?" my father said.

"To check in on your son. I'm glad he's all right."

"So you're dropping the obstruction of justice charge?"

"No."

Later, I woke hungry. My father was still there, dozing in a chair at my bedside. I pretended to be asleep, enjoying the fact that we could be in the same room and relatively peaceful, even if it was a hospital room. The doctor came in. I watched through slit eyes as he showed my father the latest MRI on his iPad. "He'll be fine," the doctor said. "I'm releasing him tomorrow. But I just wanted to make you aware that your son has significant scar tissue buildup in his frontal lobe."

"I am aware of that, Doctor," my father said.

"This is not from what happened last night," the doctor said.

"I know."

"This is from an older injury—"

"I *get* it, okay? I get it." He got up and went to the window and ran his hands through his hair, pulling it.

The next morning, Thursday, I felt a soft hand on my cheek. I opened my eyes. Nicole looked beat up, but she was trying to smile. "I'm sorry," she said.

"I thought you weren't supposed to leave the house."

"I snuck out."

"Can you sneak me out?" I took the saline IV out myself, got dressed, and we just walked out, no problem. We stopped in the hospital cafeteria to pick up my father. He'd gone down to grab coffee, but now he wasn't there. I tried his cell, no pickup. I texted him to let him know I would meet him at home.

We went to the diner. Nicole seemed oddly relaxed—not happy, but calm. The real Recluse was still out there, and Nicole didn't seem to care. I was beginning to think Schmidt was right. The guy who paid to have Nicole burned had gotten what he'd wanted, and he'd gotten away with it.

Nicole picked up on my anger. "It doesn't help," she said. "Believe me, if it did, I'd have no problem hating them day and night, Angela and whoever put her up to this."

"And Dave?"

She looked down at her burger. She'd only had a bite. She pushed her plate away.

FIFTY-TWO

We went back to Nicole's. She wanted to hang. All I'd wanted to do was get her back home safe, and now I had to get home myself, back to my computer. "I have to check in with my dad," I said. Nicole seemed sleepy anyway.

Mrs. Castro drove me home. She had this meditation track playing, the word *om* hummed over and over. It was making me drowsy.

"Jay, I want you to know how grateful I am for all you've done for Nicole."

"I didn't do anything, ma'am."

"You got yourself arrested for her. Mr. Castro insists that you let him hire a lawyer for you."

"My father'll never go for it."

"You have to let the police do their job, Jay. I see it. Your anger. You have to let this go. We all have to move on."

"Okay," I said. "I will."

She frowned and mussed my hair. "You're horrible."

My father wanted to go to the Palisades. He went there sometimes to smoke a cigar. "Pete says there's a regatta going on.

We could watch the boats, catch some fresh air, the sunset, grab dinner after?"

"Gotta sleep," I said. "You go, though. Hang with Pete."

He hadn't gotten any decent sleep the night before either, at the hospital. He hit the couch and clicked to a hoops game he'd DVR-ed. He was snoring in five minutes. He was lying on his side, and his gut was hanging out of his undershirt. I wondered if he'd live to fifty.

I kept my bedroom door open with one eye on my father. I had some bullshit history assignment on my laptop screen in case he walked in on me. I followed the BinarTREE maps tracking Angela's data flow into a chat room called Cutter's Way. Angela had been using the site heavily. And then there it was again. She'd been calling herself GBAM. It was just such sad stuff. I kept looking at a string Angela was into the night before she was arrested:

GBAM: Blood?

Blood Princess: Howdy GBAM. You stay dry last night?

GBAM: Epic fail. I was going to be good, but at 3am, after my mother was asleep, I couldn't hold off anymore.

bOYS cUT tOO: Carved the letters WOL into myself. I feel real when I see them.

Up Not Sideways: WOL?

bOYS cUT tOO: Waste of life. Why can't I stop?

GBAM: Oh bct. I want you to love you. I want to help you stop. I want to help me. But how? It feels too good, burning blue.

Reading that last line in the string, I can't say I forgave

Angela Sammick, but I hated her a little less. That was the best I could do.

I didn't have time to try to figure out what GBAM meant, but I figured if it was her username for Cutter's Way, maybe she'd used it as the access name for her online storage vault. I took a shot at the major cloud vaults:

Username: GBAM

A password request came up on UniversalStorageTime. com. Maybe twenty minutes later I jumped the password wall. I started clicking wildly, opening multiple files at the same time.

An audio file, DBphonegrabOct21.aiff, from the same day I met Nicole in Schmidt's office:

DAVE: You knew what you were getting into.

ANGELA: You were with me for three months before her, though.

(Eagles screeched in the background. There was a preserve at Ramapo.)

DAVE: I was up front with you from the beginning. I told you this had to be under the radar.

ANGELA: Under the radar. Right. You let me suck your dick no problem, but you're embarrassed to be seen in public with me.

DAVE: Do you know what my father would do if—

ANGELA: Yeah, I know exactly what he'd do. He'd tell you I was a low-class whore, way beneath a Bendix's station. Then, if you had any balls, you'd tell him to go to hell.

DAVE: Look, I'm sorry, okay? You want me to screw up

my life? That'll make you happy? It was a mistake, Angela.

ANGELA: A mistake? You have got to be kidding me.

DAVE: Why can't you just be cool about this?

ANGELA: You're part of it now, Dave.

DAVE: Part of what?

ANGELA: You waited too long. You had your chance to come clean when Barrone interviewed you the day of the attack.

DAVE: I didn't know you were the one who did it until now.

ANGELA (laughing): Liar.

DAVE: I didn't see you.

ANGELA: You didn't *want* to see me.

DAVE: My head was down. I was drinking water—

ANGELA: You were looking right at me, Dave. We locked eyes. You know we did. And then that night, in the precinct, you panicked. You knew your father would kill you if he found out about us. You get implicated in burning Nicole? The story plays everywhere, with your name out there, as the one who jilted the sideline slut who burned the beauty queen? You held back. You had all that time after the interview too. If you'd come forward within twenty-four hours of the attack, you would have been okay. Maybe even forty-eight, with a generous DA. But we're six weeks later now, dude. Six weeks you're holding back info that could've nabbed the Recluse. You go forward now, you are *screwed.* You're an accessory now. An accomplice. You obstructed justice. You'll get as much time as I will for burning Nicole—if you turn me in. And even if you don't do time, good luck getting into the Big H with a felony tacked to the bottom of your application. Maybe that's what your essay could be about: How I learned about obstruction of justice by obstructing it. You good at keeping secrets, Dave? You better be, because this is one you're going to have to keep for the rest of your life.

DAVE: You really think you can play me like this?

ANGELA: This isn't playing. This is a promise: I'll *throw* you to them.

DAVE: You have no proof I so much as held as your hand. And as for the attack? Yeah, I saw you burn her, you sick bitch. But you can't prove that either.

ANGELA: I'm recording this, Dave.

DAVE: Are you serious? Turn it off, Angela.

ANGELA: If you don't take your hand out of my pocket, I'll stab it!

DAVE: Turn it off!

ANGELA: I'm relaying it real time to my cloud account anyway!

Untitled.aiff, from the day Angela was arrested:

ANGELA: I'm being followed.

DAVE: Shit.

ANGELA: I'm not going to make it. The plane doesn't leave for another half hour.

DAVE: Are you recording this?

ANGELA: No, I swear.

DAVE: Just keep quiet. Do the sentence. It'll probably be like three years max. After, I'll move you up to Cambridge. Stick to the plan, Angela, and we'll be able to be together. We'll wait a few years and then we'll—

ANGELA: I have to nuke this phone. They're like a couple hundred yards away. I love you. . . . Say it *back*, Dave.

DAVE: I love you.

ANGELA: So convincing. You have three years to make yourself mean that. You better be there when I get out.

Barrone had told my father that Dave was under house arrest. The DA initially threatened an attempted murder charge for what went down in the SUV with Kerns and me, but Dave's lawyers were too good to let that stick. They were negotiating final terms for a plea to assault. Dave probably wouldn't do more than eighteen months home confinement with probation after. Same with Rick Kerns. But Harvard wasn't about to let either one of them trash its rep, and Kerns would never wrestle again, not with that shattered shoulder. Angela would pay the biggest price: No way Dave would be there for her when she got out. Not that I thought he'd have been there anyway.

I clicked BurningBlue.doc, desperate for anything that would point to the person who hired Angela to do the hit. It began with a journal entry: *What day is it? What night? I'm burning, burning, burning blue. —NC, 10/28*

That was when I knew for sure. Just to be even more certain, I wormed a line into GBAM's profile on Cutter's Way. The registration tracked back not to Angela's email but to Nicole's.

The supposed cat scratch on her arm. The long-sleeved hoodies. Nicole really was mutilating herself after all. Could Chrissie Vratos have been right? Did Nicole hire Angela to burn her? Whether she in effect burned herself or not, Nicole Castro was definitely cutting. She needed help. Her therapists needed to know. Did they?

I scanned BurningBlue.doc. Angela had compiled a series of Nicole's journal entries with lines highlighted here and there. If you could, would you read the diary of the person you were in love with? Or do you love them enough to trust them?

I couldn't find anything in the document that suggested anybody but Nicole and her Cutter's Way friends knew about her cutting. Angela had hacked audio files too, of Nicole's sessions with Dr. Julian Nye. I had to listen to them. I had to.

Nicole and Nye Oct19.aiff:

NYE: I'd like to offer you as a case study at my next Princeton lecture.

NICOLE: "Offer me"? No thanks, really.

NYE: You're doing remarkably well, considering the circumstances. My students would have many questions for you. You could help them a great deal—help them help others.

NICOLE: You're saying you want me live? As in you want me to be online with them?

NYE: I want you to come to the lecture.

NICOLE: Are you insane?

NYE: I don't think so. You would be in shadow. They

would know who you are, of course, but they wouldn't see your face, if that would make you feel more comfortable."

NICOLE: Comfortable? Seriously, Julian? I can't be up in front of people, even in shadow. Let me have that much at least.

NYE: Have what?

NICOLE: The dark. Total dark.

Nothing. They didn't know—Nye, Schmidt, Mrs. Castro. I had to get Nicole help. Before I did that, I had to confront her about it. She would never forgive me if I went behind her back and ratted her out to her mother. She might never forgive anyway. She'd wonder for all of two seconds how I'd found out about the cutting, and then she'd think I was hacking her. I'd promised her I never would. Technically I wasn't. Technically I was merely checking out Angela's hack. Technically Nicole wouldn't give a damn how I'd gotten the information. Either way, I was invading her privacy. She would never speak to me again. But I had to out her, even if that meant losing her.

I called her, inviting myself over for dinner. *"Mom's making dumplings,"* she said. She sounded better. Actually, she sounded good, maybe even great. I'd spent a lot of time with her the last three weeks, and this was the happiest I'd ever heard her. She sounded playful. *"Get on over here, boy."* I could only think she was on a new prescription, and that made me even sadder. I grabbed my backpack and board and tapped my father's foot.

"Uh?" he said, his eyes still closed.

"Heading over to Nicole's for dinner."

No response.

"Dad?"

He snored. I taped a note to the TV. I was about to go when the blank spot on the living room wall caught my eye. The place where the painting used to hang, the one my father hocked for my bail. My memory of it sharpened. It was almost the exact picture I found when I broke into Angela's house, the half-photo/half-sketch of Nicole sitting in front of a mirror, half her face covered with red ink. The one Angela had noted with sparkly glow pen in the corner of the sketch with that GBAM matrix or chat room name or whatever it was.

My father had a lot of artist's prints, limited edition copies approved and signed by the artist of the masterwork they emulated. Which meant the original was likely hanging in a museum someplace. I had seen the original painting, the inspiration for my father's print and Angela's sketch, and I was pretty sure I'd seen it recently—very recently—but I couldn't remember where. Somehow that painting connected Angela, Nicole and my father.

FIFTY-THREE

Sylvia got the door. She was in her pajamas.

"Hi," I said.

"Mr. Castro's here," she said. "I'm just kidding."

"Why do you hate me?"

"I don't. I just don't like you. Go. They're in the kitchen."

The kitchen smelled great. Mrs. Castro had the dumplings going. She was massaging Nicole's shoulders. They were in their pajamas too. "It's a pajama party," Mrs. Castro said.

"I'm betting he sees that, Mom."

"Go downstairs and get him some of your father's PJs from storage."

"Nah, I'm okay," I said.

"He doesn't want to wear Daddy's clothes, Mom. Daddy terrifies him."

"He terrifies everybody," Mrs. Castro said. "Go. No pajamas, no dumplings."

Nicole took my hand and led me downstairs. The basement was immaculate, and that made it creepier for some reason. Lots of storage racks. Nicole led me to the back. She sat on a wicker chest and patted the spot next to her for me to sit. I had the feeling she was going to kiss me. If she did, I wouldn't be able to say what I had to say. So I just said it. "I know about it. The chat room."

"The chat room?" Her eyes ticked right.

"Cutter's Way."

"What are you talking about?"

"Don't do this, Nicole. Please don't."

"Do what, Jay? What exactly am I doing?"

"We need to get you help. We're going to. I promise."

"You *promise?* Really? Oh, that makes me feel so much better. He *promises.* You know what you promised, Jay? You promised you would never *hack* me."

"I had to."

"No, you really didn't. Nobody asked you to. Nobody wanted you to, either." She pulled up her sleeves to reveal the bandages. "This is mine, okay? This is the one thing I can own. Just me. This has nothing to do with you."

"It has everything to do with me. You're my friend."

"Then honor our friendship. Honor your word. Please don't tell my mom. *Please.*"

"I'm not judging you, okay?"

"Judge me or don't, it doesn't matter. Shit, you *broke* it. How do I trust you after this? I can't. God, I feel your fingers under my skin. You know what? Go."

"The username," I said. "GBAM."

"Get out of my house. Now."

"Just tell me how you came up with the chat handle, and I'll leave."

"It's an acronym for a painting, my mother's favorite, my destiny." She pushed past me, upstairs.

I followed. "The Picasso? *Guernica*?" I stopped cold in the main vestibule where I'd left my backpack. I heard the bathroom door shut, the one just ahead of the kitchen. I fished in my backpack for the book I'd had my father sign for Mrs. Castro. The one I had been dragging around with me for how many days now, forever forgetting to give it to her. I flipped to the page Mrs. Castro had flagged "his best." But she hadn't been referring to Picasso's *Guernica*. She'd meant the picture on the opposing page, another Picasso, a vision of a woman standing in front of a mirror. This was the original, the basis for the artist's print that used to be on my living room wall. I checked the caption and the title: *Girl Before a Mirror.*

GBAM.

Mrs. Castro's favorite painting.

The inspiration for the sketch I'd found in Angela's bedroom. The one where Nicole reaches out to her reflection, exactly as the girl does in Picasso's original. In the mirror, half of her face is perfect beauty, and the other half is horrific, rearranged, red.

My eyes ticked to the corner of the vestibule, the wall space next to the grandfather clock, above the umbrella stand. There it was again, the same image, locked in a small frame. I hadn't given it but a half a glance the other day when I dropped Nicole's umbrella into the stand, a black-and-white sketch copy of *Girl Before a Mirror.* I studied the sketch, the artist's initials: E.C.

274

Elaine Castro and Angela Sammick were in love with the same work of art. Obsessed by it.

I had taken my anti-seizure meds that day, and they generally softened things, but at that moment I felt as if an intense and rough-edged heat was trying to squeeze between the hemispheres of my brain. I had to slump into the chair next to the grandfather clock to take it in. How the two women had come together was a mystery, but this much was definite: Mrs. Castro had hired Angela to burn Nicole. Angela had come up with the Arachnomorph ID that inspired the news sites to the spider-themed nickname, but Elaine Castro was the real Recluse.

It made no sense and perfect sense. Nicole told me that her mother wanted her to find the good in the burn, the fact that Nicole and Mrs. Castro could spend more time together now that Nicole didn't have to run off to this match or that meeting, off to college, marriage, a life away from her mother, one that would leave Mrs. Castro even more isolated than she was after her husband left. Burned, Nicole would never leave her, would need her mother forever, would give the woman purpose. Elaine Castro had no one and nothing else. Her dreams of living life as an artist had been ripped from her that night of her debut when the doubt stared her in the face: Was she truly meant to paint? She *wanted* to, yes, but maybe she didn't have that thing that makes it all worthwhile, whether you hit it big like Picasso or not: the *need* to.

I needed to get Nicole. Book in hand I rounded the corner to the bathroom off the kitchen. I tried the knob, locked. "Nicole, we have to get you out of here. Now."

The bathroom door swung open. Mrs. Castro was drying her hands on a bright blue towel. She looked as I'd never seen her before, ugly somehow, her brows arched. She eyed the book in my hand, my fingers tucked into it at the page she'd flagged. "What's wrong, Jay?" she said.

"I thought you were Nicole."

"I gathered that. What's the rush?"

"What do you mean?"

"You said, 'We have to get you out of here.'"

"My father texted he got us tickets to the St. John's game. It's at the Garden, courtside. We have to get out of here now if we want to make the opening jump—"

"No, Jay, you said, 'We have to get *you* out of here.' Meaning Nicole."

Nicole's sobbing echoed from down the hallway.

I was terrified. Not of Mrs. Castro. At that moment she seemed smaller to me. Shrinking. I was terrified of myself. Of what I might do to this trembling, cornered thief in front of me. I felt *she* was a guest in *my* home, an uninvited guest who'd charmed her way into my heart and then pocketed my treasure, my trust, while my eyes were turned. I glared at Elaine Castro. "How could you?" I said.

"Ex*cuse* me?"

"Why?"

Her eyes reddened. "Let's just sit down for a second and

talk about this. We, I have no idea what's going on here, except that you're upset. You need to calm down."

I pushed past her, nearly knocking her over when she tried to block me.

"Jay, wait," she begged.

I strode through the kitchen, into the studio. Nicole was on the couch with Sylvia, crying on Sylvia's shoulder. Sylvia held her, rubbing her back. A tabloid magazine played quietly through the TV. Sylvia glared at me. Over her shoulder, in the backyard, a pair of deer looked in on us. They scattered into the dusk. Sylvia's eyes widened on something behind me. "No, Elaine," Sylvia said.

Nicole looked up and followed Sylvia's eyes. "Mom?" she said.

I turned around slowly. Mrs. Castro was standing right in front of me, holding the pot of dumplings. The oil smoked. "You've ruined it," she said to me. "You ruined *us.* I warned you, Jay. I warned you to let the police do their job."

"Mom, what are you talking about?" Nicole said.

"Nicole?" Mrs. Castro said. "My baby, I'm so sorry."

I tried to grab the pot from her, but she was too quick. She poured the oil onto herself.

FIFTY-FOUR

Five weeks later, Thursday, December 16, Nicole, her father, and I were in a joint therapy session in Dr. Schmidt's office. Nicole had just come back from a month's stay at an in-treatment center for teens coping with self-injury impulses. The particular program she was in required her to stay off the phone and offline, but she was encouraged to write, and we'd exchanged a dozen or so letters. But now we sat facing each other, staring at each other as Mr. Castro said, "I can't do that. How do you not see that it's my fault?"

"What does holding on to your fault, Elaine's fault, anybody's fault do for Nicole?" Schmidt said.

"But you don't just let it go, Doctor. It won't. It can't. It's its own thing, and it lives in you until it dies, if it ever does decide to die. If you try to cut it out too soon, you risk all this collateral damage."

"Like what?" Schmidt said.

Mr. Castro closed his eyes tightly and dug his fingertips into his temples. He still wore his wedding ring. "Nicole, I can't do this, honey. I'm sorry." He stood up.

"Dad?" Nicole said.

"I can't work it out like this, in here. I don't know if I'll ever be able to stop hating her or Dave or that monster of a girl or me most of all, but any sense of forgiveness I can discover in myself has to come on its own. Not with people watching for it. Waiting for it. I'm not even sure it's in me to find. Look, I'll be waiting in the car. Doctor, I'm sorry." He left quickly.

"I didn't get to say it," Nicole said. "I waited too long. I should have said it in the beginning of the session, when you asked me the first time, but now after hearing what he just said, I don't think I'll ever be able to tell him. To get it out."

"Tell Jay," Schmidt said. "He's here for you. Go ahead, Nicole. You can do it."

Nicole took my hands in hers. "Jay, I need you to know why I do it. Why I cut, I mean. I do it to control the pain my way. Without meds. To feel. To see my imperfection spill out of me. It started after the attack. Shortly after. I wanted to draw the heat in my face downward. I couldn't bear to look at myself in the mirror in the beginning. I had no idea what the burn looked like. I needed to see it, but at the same time I couldn't look. So I put it where I could look at it. Where I could control it in every aspect, how it appeared in my skin, how long it lasted. I could start the fire, and I could put it out at will. Remember in biology, that picture of the circulatory system? The blood pumping away from the heart is bright red. The arteries squeeze it through you fiercely, almost uncontrollably. Then there's the other blood, the blood that goes to the heart, the softer flow, the blood that's blue. It's not really. Really it's just a very dark red, but in the right kind of light, the soft light, the night-light with the sapphire shade, you can convince yourself that it's the same color as the blood in the picture, that cool blue." She rolled up her sleeves. The bandages were gone. The scar lines were parallel, all roughly the same length. "We've started to talk about it, Dr. Schmidt and I. About her. My mother. I hope at some point I'll find the courage to contact her, maybe even to see her. I know I'll have to do that, to hear it directly from her mouth, to know why. Jay, I haven't cut in thirty-one days."

"You are amazing," I said.

"I can't say I'll never do it again. Not yet. Maybe I'll never be able to say it."

"You'll always be amazing."

Nicole was supposed to exercise a lot. Cutting unleashes endorphins in the bloodstream, but so does running. We took up jogging. We were at Palisades Park one beautiful winter day during Christmas break. Not that Nicole had come back to school. We took a breather underneath the George Washington Bridge, at the river's edge. We hiked the trap rock and found a bench-like slab with a great view of northern Manhattan across the water. A double-flash of bright light hit us. We turned into it with our hands up in front of our faces to block the camera, but the flash had come from the sunlight's reflecting off the window of a turning Coast Guard speedboat. "How bad was it while I was gone?" Nicole said. "The media attention?"

"Bad." Actually, it was insane. Everywhere I went those first few days after Mrs. Castro was identified as the person behind the attack, I had at least two reporters tailing me. The stalking died down after a couple of weeks of my not saying anything. What could I say? I didn't have any answers for them or any answers period.

"Detective Barrone called this morning," Nicole said. "She wants to talk. Not Barrone, my mother. Talk with me, I mean. She's cooperating, answering all Barrone's questions, except one."

"Why she did it?"

"She says she'll only answer that to my face. All the stuff you told me about my dad and yours, that night at her debut, then needing to keep me around after the divorce, not being able to let me go. It makes sense on an intellectual level, but I won't really understand why she did it until I hear her say the words. Until I see her eyes as she tells me. But how can I be in the same room with her? How can I be near her ever again? I swear, when my father told me the doctor said she would probably die from the infection? I was just so relieved. You know? Like I'd been spared my own death sentence or worse, my own life sentence. If she was gone, I'd never have to face her again. I could put away all the pictures and . . . Oh my god. Oh my god!" She buried her face in balled hands and rocked back and forth. "My mother had me *burned*, Jay. My own mother. My mom. I miss my mom."

She got a job working at the stables, teaching the young kids to ride. She was starting to look at colleges with programs in early childhood education. One night her friend from the stables called and asked her if she wanted to see a horse foal.

When we got there, the barn was dark except for a double stall in the corner. The horse was lying on her side and getting ready to deliver. This dog, a boxer mix, I think, sat at Nicole's side and leaned into her. He kept sticking his nose into her elbow and flipping up her arm and wouldn't stop until she stroked him.

"No allergies?" I whispered.

"Not that bad, actually," she said. "The doctor said at some point I might outgrow them."

We stayed like this for some time, crouching in the stall on upturned crates, just waiting for the colt to be born. The stable master held the mother's head and stroked her neck. Everyone was quiet and smiling. When the colt was born, everybody laughed.

Her father had put the Brandywine Heights house on the market. He was renting a town house in a luxury condo complex down by the Hudson River, just south of the George Washington Bridge, where Nicole and I ran and hiked. The first floor was Mr. Castro's office. He'd left his company and was working for himself now, to be around for Nicole. Upstairs was homey, lots of sun and space. Nicole's room was on the water-view side. We were hanging out on her bed, playing dominoes. Sylvia came in. "Feet on the floor," she said. She grabbed my ponytail. "If only I had a pair of scissors. One clip, and you would be handsome. Now go downstairs. Let Nicoletta get ready."

Nicole had been asked to give a speech at the annual Girl Scouts conference in Manhattan.

That night, we were at a midtown hotel. After dinner, Nicole was introduced. She looked stunning, her hair back, her smile wide, except I could see her lips were quivering. The bandage had become smaller, but it still covered all signs of injury. "I'm grateful to you for this opportunity to tell you how much you girls inspire me," was how she started. "You're leaders, and we're all depending on you to lead with kindness. What's our motto?"

"Be prepared," half the girls yelled.

Nicole nodded. "Prepared in mind, prepared in body, right? We train our minds to be ready when we need to act to make a situation a bit better. We train our hearts to be strong, to have the courage to give of ourselves to help somebody who—"

"Mommy, what's wrong with her face?" a Brownie in the front row said.

Nicole kept going. ". . . train our hearts to help those who might need . . . help." She brushed her hair with her fingers and covered her face with it. "I'm . . ." She hurried away from the podium.

I caught up with her backstage. She was hyperventilating in the corner, facing the bathroom door. "Somebody's in there," she said. "The people, they're still looking at me, Jay, but they can't see me," she said. "They can't see past it."

She rapped on the door. "Please, I have to get in there."

I held her hand and led her to the street. Mr. Castro went for the car, and we got her home. I slept over at her house that night, on the short couch in her bedroom. When I woke up, she was curled into me. The next day we got her in to see Schmidt for an emergency session.

Her second surgery didn't go as well as planned, and a third had to be pushed back to the spring. She relapsed with the cutting, but this time she reached out to me about it. She continued with her therapy, but only with Dr. Schmidt and on a private basis, never in the school office. She continued with private tutors, but not in-home. She went to a center in Englewood for one-on-one sessions. She poured herself into her studies. In February, she took the SATs and nailed them.

In early March I met Detective Barrone at the coffee shop. She'd petitioned the DA to drop the obstruction charge. She was putting together her final report on the Recluse case for a study Princeton was doing on near-filicide as it relates to child abuse by proxy syndrome. She wanted to see if I had anything to add, but I was there looking for answers.

You see it in the papers, parents doing horrible physical harm to their kids out of jealousy or spite or for attention—any number of reasons. You say, "Wow, that's crazy," and then you click to the TV schedule for something light. You dismiss it as someone else's hell and get back to your life. You have to, or you lose your mind. I couldn't do that here. Every time

I was with Nicole, the bandage reminded of the mystery of it. I still didn't know the extent of the burn. Sylvia was the only one Nicole would allow to see it.

Mrs. Castro was recovering at a lockdown hospital. She'd corroborated Angela's story about the letter and the money. It started at a huge end-of-the-school-year party the Castros had at their house the previous June, when half the school was over. Angela came drunk. She and Dave had been hooking up for a while by then. Apparently, seeing Nicole and Dave together was too much for her. Mrs. Castro caught Angela following Nicole and Dave from a distance as they held hands. Angela was glassy-eyed, forlorn. Later Mrs. Castro found Angela inside, alone, crying in the painting studio. She was going through Mrs. Castro's wallet. She pulled the cash and stuffed it into her pocket. She was about to slip out the side door when something caught her eye: my dad's book. Mrs. Castro had left it out on her desk, opened to her favorite painting, *Girl Before a Mirror.*

After Detective Barrone informed Angela that Mrs. Castro was the mysterious patron who had commissioned the attack, Angela testified that *Girl Before a Mirror* just blew her away. Right there in Mrs. Castro's painting studio, she grabbed a pencil and a piece of drawing paper and sketched it. Mrs. Castro came in, surprising Angela. Angela apologized and started to leave, but Mrs. Castro begged her to keep drawing. She asked Angela if she could keep the sketch and had Angela sign it.

Mrs. Castro had been plotting the attack for several

months before the party, shortly after her husband left. But now that she found Angela, she had her acid thrower. The girl was poor, jealous of Nicole and extremely vulnerable—one could see that in the remarkable art she exhibited via her Facebook gallery. Angela had an unrelenting thirst to absorb the beauty around her and desperately tried to make it her own. In other words, she easily could be swayed.

This was the only association the two women had, and Angela truly must have been ignorant of the fact that her mysterious benefactor was also her victim's mother.

Mrs. Castro had continued to be extremely cooperative, down to the smallest details. The bounced checks were a result of too much money juggling. She was pulling a thousand dollars here and there from a lot of different accounts to keep the transactions small and avoid suspicion as she put together the money to pay off Angela. She still refused to answer Detective Barrone's last question: Why? "Let me see Nicole, and I'll tell her," Mrs. Castro pleaded. "Let me see my daughter one last time, face-to-face."

FIFTY-FIVE

On a cold clear Saturday in late March, I was at the driving range behind the mall with my father. We'd made a deal: If he lost fifty pounds, I'd cut my hair. I no longer looked like a Visigoth.

After hitting through a couple of buckets of range balls, Dad dropped me at Starbucks. Cherry got me a job there, though that day I wasn't scheduled to work. Nicole was picking me up, and I wanted her to meet Cherry. They hugged when they met and talked as if they'd known each other for a long time and discovered they actually did. They'd both been in the same ballet class when they were five years old. They agreed quitting was the right call, because, per Nicole, "The shoes were murder on your pedicure," and, per Cherry, "Picking leotard wedgies out of your butt crack in front of the boy dancers was a total drag."

My new iPhone beeped one o'clock, which is when visiting hours started.

"Time to go?" Nicole said.

"Only if you want to," I said.

Nicole pushed her sunglasses closer to her face and nodded.

287

She was quiet on the drive through the Meadowlands. The psychiatric center was a lockdown facility. It had been built on the site of a pre–Civil War prison called Snake Hill. A guard escorted us to a large room with a strangely high ceiling, maybe twenty feet. The paint peeled in patches from an old water leak. At the far end of the room, a few patients clustered around a TV and *Jeopardy!*

Mrs. Castro sat serenely in a chair by the barred window. She wasn't restrained, not physically. Her pinned pupils betrayed heavy medication. The only evidence I saw of the oil splash was a wide burn scar under her chin. Her turtleneck collar and long sleeves covered the rest. Smiling, she appeared to recognize Nicole, but she didn't seem to see me. She moved stiffly and in slow motion, as if she were underwater, motioning for Nicole to sit. As she spoke, she didn't look at us but out the window at the bright blue day.

"I was losing you," she said. "To your father, soon to college, then surely a husband. Burning you was the only way to keep you. You needed me, desperately. The only time I didn't feel alone was when I was with you. Every moment you were out of the house, the sense of separation was increasing. It hurt more deeply than being cut off. I felt I was being cut out. The broken-down heart after the transplant: Where does it go? Even at the hospital with Emma, the children: I knew they were leaving me. But you would stay. I would care for you in a way that you couldn't care for yourself. My beauty was my curse. In school, my teachers would offer false compliments as they looked not at or into but through my paintings. They would stand behind me, peeking over my shoulder, pretending to look at my work when really they were gawking at my breasts. Your father, too. I was a prop on a Christmas card. But you, my darling. You knew me. You loved me. You saw my art. You were my art. I had made you, and you were perfection. And to keep you, I was willing to destroy you. Nicole?"

Nicole needed a second to find her voice. "Yes?"

"I'm so afraid to be alone, darling. I'm looking out there and seeing just absolutely *nothing*." Her eyes clicked from the window's picture of the beautiful day to Nicole. Mrs. Castro's face was perfectly peaceful, but a tear dropped from her chin. She held out her arms for a hug.

Nicole hesitated, and then she hugged her mother.

"My sweetheart. My Nicole, I'm sorry. I stole it from you to save you from letting them objectify you."

Nicole broke from the hug and rushed out.

"Stole what?" I said to her mother.

"Her beauty."

"You didn't come close to touching it." I hurried after Nicole.

We drove deep into the Meadowlands to a nature preserve and hiked to the river's edge. We sat facing each other on a backless bench, straddling it. We locked hands and watched the cattails duck and weave against the cold clear afternoon sky. We were all alone.

"The hug," I said. "Does that mean you're in forgiveness territory?"

"I don't know. Maybe I'm on my way there. Maybe it was good-bye. Except, it's too late for good-bye. She's already gone. She doesn't feel the same. Like her spirit evaporated, and the only way I can know her now is in my memories of her. Like when we were with Emma this one time. We took her to the beach. We were in the water, waist high. Mom was holding Emma. The waves were crazy that day. Each time one came in, Emma scream-laughed and Mom said, 'I got you. Relax, Emma, I promise. Ready? Now hold your breath.' The wave rolled over us, and we pushed up through it and floated out of the back of the wave. And Mom said, 'See? Nothing bad happened. I kept my promise. I had you the whole time. We were flying, right? We were flying.' That was my mother." She took off her sunglasses and looked out past the cattails, to the psychiatric hospital in the near distance. It rose red and solitary from the swampland. "I want to go back, Jay. To school, I mean. I'm ready, I think. Yeah, I'm ready." She turned so I couldn't see the wounded side of her face. She peeled away the tape, balled up the bandage and tucked it into her pocket. Her hair hid the burn. She was breathing quickly, heavily. She turned to me. She brushed back her hair with her fingers.

I studied her naked face. I took it in, every bit of it. I held her hands and put them to my face, and then I put my hands to her face as I leaned in and kissed her. I kissed her cheeks, her eyes, her mouth. In time, we stopped trembling, and the cold was gone from us and the day and my world and maybe hers too, if only for a while. I tasted the sun in her lips, a

warmth as gentle as it was strong. I'd always thought of surrender as a giving up. It wasn't. To surrender deeply, truly,
was to give in to an idea that hadn't occurred to me until this
kiss: that your admiration for somebody could be as great as
your adoration of her. It moved me, her trust in me, her faith
in herself, her belief in us.

I didn't feel sorry for Nicole Castro. I felt hope for her.
She wasn't a victim or a snob, a pageant queen or an athlete, a scholar or a saint or any of the other things I'd labeled
her over the past few months. She was Nicole, and she was
beautiful.

Burning Blue ACKNOWLEDGEMENTS AND A NOTE:

Thank you . . .

Kirby, Ian, Alicia and everyone at WME. My Penguin/Dial/Speak family, especially Regina, Jasmin, and Steve, Lauri and Kathy, Dani for the cover, Scottie, Marie, Erin and Emily, Courtney and Anna, the amazingly awesome Jess S, Donne, Kim, and Draga, Mary, Colleen, Eileen and Dana. Sheila and Heather, you are rock stars. Most of all, thank you, Kate. You are the most amazing editor and friend—love ya a ton.

My Griffin-Morimoto family for the enthusiasm, especially Kath and Mom, for assigning themselves the title "Manager" and having fun with it. Eileen and Trev. My niece Sarah, for being an awesome early reader. For their encouragement, Scott Smith, Coe Booth, Barry Lyga, T-Rock Maldonado and David Levithan. My Text friends Penny, Michael and Steph. Anne, Jessica, Regan, Karlan and literacyforincarcerated teens.org. Mica, Jo, Kris and behindthebook.org. My cousin Sheila for her twenty-plus years of providing compassionate psychological counseling, often pro bono, to traumatized young adults, and for giving me a chunk of her scant free time to help me glean a bit of an understanding about self-injury impulses. Lastly (and firstly) thank you to my best friend, my wife, Risa.

The NYPD Citizen's Police Academy, particularly Sgt. Shelley Greene and PO Adolph Kiah. My friends at the Central Park Medical Unit, an all-volunteer ambulance corps 150 members strong. Please check us out (and feel free to donate!) at cpmu.com. Some background on *Burning Blue*: A few years ago my ambulance was called to aid a man who had been attacked on a subway platform. The victim, blinded and showing signs of moderate chemical burns, did not know the assailant. Someone simply tapped his shoulder, he turned, and the assailant sprayed his eyes with Mace. Even after the victim hit the ground, covering his eyes, the attacker continued to fire Mace into his mouth and ears. In the subsequent treatment and transport to the hospital, the randomness of the attack induced in the victim confusion, despair, and self-blame that still sadden me.

In another subway incident, I was called to aid a man who had suffered a seizure on the train, halting the express line during evening rush. The man was facedown on the subway car floor, in post-seizure recovery. Several frustrated passengers cursed my shabbily dressed patient and called for him to be dragged from the car to get the train moving again, but a witness told me the man hit his head as he fell. I couldn't move him without taking precautions to protect his spine with immobilization devices. One onlooker was laughing at the patient, who was snoring loudly in a puddle of his own urine. The laughter reminded me of a time I was in the park, walking my dogs, and one of them, a big old boxer who suffered from epilepsy, collapsed in a seizure. This one guy was snickering, recording the seizure with his phone. Somebody else asked him why he was laughing, and he said something along the lines of, "I don't know. Maybe I'm scared."

Finally, while at college I was friendly with a guy whose name I'll withhold out of respect for his family, but he was stellar, Ivy League basketball's Rookie of the Year, an activist as popular off the court as he was on it. "B" was the nicest person you could hope to meet. Great smile, soft-spoken—a very humble guy. This was back in the late 1980s. A few years ago, I was stunned to learn that after his separation from his wife B had killed his daughter and son and then himself. Writing this story was, in part, a way for me to try to understand how a man who was so creative in the way he brought people together with his leadership could sink into a hopelessness so deep he destroyed his own children. I can't say I'm any closer to understanding what happened with B, but I'm reminded that isolation breeds despair. If you see a friend or family member cutting herself off, reach out to your teachers, parents, friends and guidance counselors and help her get the help she needs. Peace from NYC this Feb 14, 2012.